LANGBOURNE'S

Loyalty

ALAN P. LANDAU

Langbourne's Loyalty (2018)
©2018 Alan P Landau

NATIONAL
LIBRARY
OF AUSTRALIA

A catalogue record for this
book is available from the
National Library of Australia

ISBN: 978-0-6482493-0-6 (Paperback)
ISBN: 978-0-6482493-1-3 (Ebook)
ISBN: 978-0-6482493-3-7 (Audio Book)

Contact details for the author can be found at
www.landaubooks.com

Cover design : Scarlett Rugers, The Book Design House, Australia
First Edit : Cindy Kramer, South Africa
Final Edit : Mike Kantey, Watercourse Plettenberg Bay

First published 2018

For Robert Landau,
With thanks.

BOOKS IN THE LANGBOURNE SERIES :

(In sequential order.)

Langbourne

Langbourne's Rebellion

Langbourne's Empire

Langbourne's Evolution

Langbourne's Loyalty

Langbourne's Legacy

Also by Alan Landau:
To Brave Men

By Brenda Kate
Of Sand and Stars

CHAPTER ONE
Southampton – 1900

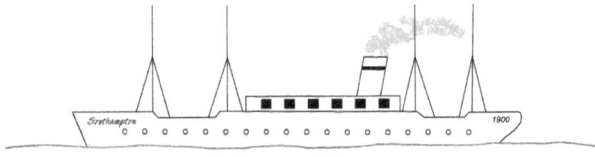

Despite the dullness of the morning, David was smiling broadly at the bow of the steamer as it glided gently into Southampton harbour. After all, he was soon to look upon the face of his beautiful fiancée, whom he had not seen in almost two months. Firstly, though, he needed to proceed to London to make a formal call on his older brother, Morris. It was essential to brief him on the news from Africa about their business interests in Bulawayo and Johannesburg. After these two necessary reunions, he would then be able to see his family in Ireland, the first time in almost ten years.

The journey on board the *Dunottar Castle* had been enjoyable; a far cry from the voyage on the sailing ship that he had endured on his way to southern Africa in 1891. That ship, constructed of wood, had been much smaller and had lacked the luxuries of this new-fangled steamship with its several decks, a restaurant, and a bar. On the earlier journey to the south, the many stops along the western edge of Africa had been a welcome break from the monotony of the sea voyage which David and Morris had taken, but even so, those three months at sea had remained something of a test. The Dunottar Castle and its modern steam engines, on the other hand, had made the same journey in a mere seventeen days.

As the ship slipped gently into the harbour, David caught the urban scents drifting along with the headwind that seemed to welcome him onto solid land. He could vaguely smell manure from the horses that plied the cobbled streets of the port, as well as the dull, unpleasant odour of human sewage, leaking from the buckets that were carried by men in heavily oiled leather coats. By far the most potent smell of this entry point to modern civilisation, however, was that of burning coal; its tattle-tale, blue-grey smoke escaping incessantly from a myriad of chimney stacks that littered the rooftops.

Holding a rail with one hand and with a slight frown creasing his brow, David reflected on the early stages of the trip and his brief visit to Port Elizabeth, where he had arranged for the transportation of Morris' purchases that had been held up as a result of the outbreak of the Second Anglo-Boer War.

David had left Bulawayo by train and had stopped in the war-ravaged town of Mafeking where he and his brother Louis had been detained for several months during the siege conducted by the Boer forces. He had then continued on his southbound journey, passing through the diamond town of Kimberley. During the brief stop there he had taken a look around the town that had protected many famous men, including Cecil John Rhodes, during its own siege. The settlement was not as severely damaged as Mafeking had been, but the unmistakable signs of a raging battle had remained.

Sometime later, David had arrived at a nondescript railway junction called 'De Aar', from where he had caught a train bound southeast for Port Elizabeth, via the picturesque village of Graaff-Reinet. Arriving in his old stomping ground of Port Elizabeth had seemed like a breath of fresh air for David. He had been so filled with exhilaration and a sense of well-being, that he had hardly been able to contain his excitement as he had strode off briskly in the direction of the Grand Hotel.

Nothing had changed.

The hotel was just the same as it had been when he left a few years before; mounted animal trophies still adorned the walls of the reception area, and even old Mrs Bunting had still remained behind the reception desk, happy to see him again and flirt as she had always done.

"I'm engaged to be married," David had told her excitedly. "I'm on my way to England for the occasion."

"I can't say I am pleased to hear that, David," she teased in her raspy voice, "but I wish you and your future wife the very best of everything. You deserve it, young man."

David had then greeted the staff he knew and had taken the time to ask Shadrek, now the head waiter, about his health, his wife, and his children, as was the African custom. After checking into his room, David had gone directly to see his good friend Jack Shiel at the Standard Bank. He always found it pleasant to spend time with the courtly man and had enjoyed the rekindling of their friendship. They had joked and laughed while David had filled him in on all the news about his side of the family and the dreadful time they had experienced while besieged in Mafeking.

"Now," David had told him proudly, "I am engaged to be married. If you were in England, Jack, I would ask you to be my best man."

Jack had been both delighted and honoured. He had known David almost since the day he and Morris had arrived in southern Africa in 1891. "Tell me about her! Who is the lucky lady?" he had inquired.

"I am the lucky one, Jack. She is the most beautiful girl I have ever laid eyes upon. She is sweeter than honey and has the kindest heart you could ever wish for, and we love each other dearly. Oh, how I wish you could come to England with me to meet her."

"So do I," Jack laughed, "but you will have to bring her to Port Elizabeth to meet me after she has been anointed 'Mrs Langbourne'. That's an order, you hear?"

"I will, Jack, you can be sure of that," David had smiled, before changing the subject abruptly. "Thanks for your involvement in getting Morris' purchases to Sonja Du Plessis. We are very grateful for your help."

Then Jack had become quite earnest for the first time. "David," he said, "do you have any idea as to how much stuff was on those ships? Your brother is completely mad, I tell you. Simply because her own house had become so entirely filled up with his purchases, Mrs Du Plessis had to rent a room from her neighbour. Even her bedroom was packed to the ceiling."

David had looked at Jack in horror and disbelief for a moment before a nervous laugh escaped him. "Are you being serious?"

Jack chuckled, "It's alright, though. I believe that after the initial indignation of being manoeuvred out of her home by Morris – who hadn't even been in the country at that time – she has settled next door and appreciates the rental Morris is paying her. She also is enjoying the company of her neighbour, a lovely lady. They have a lot in common, and I see them out in the evenings a fair amount; bingo nights, Sunday fairs, that sort of thing."

"Well, that's a relief. I'm off to see Sonja as soon as we are done here."

"Good show. It's the house next door, just to the right of her place."

"Perfect, thanks. Now, I need some cash. I must arrange to withdraw some money for Nguni and Daluxolo to buy livestock - I'll explain later. I must also arrange to transfer Morris' shipments to the railway station."

"You have much to do, then, so I won't keep you. Let's get the finance matters sorted out, and then perhaps dinner at the Grand at six o'clock? I'll bring my wife."

"You got married?" David almost shouted. "Who is the lucky lady for you?"

"Right there," Jack beamed, pointing over David's shoulder.

He spun in his seat and saw a beautiful, slender lady enter the banking hall.

"You married Margaret?" David shot back at Jack.

"Yip," his smile was contagious. "We just fell in love."

David had then proceeded to pump Jack's hand vigorously and, having congratulated him equally profusely, had taken his leave.

His reunion with Sonja Du Plessis had been yet another enjoyable occasion, with many a tongue-in-cheek sarcastic joke about Morris and his ability to turn her entire residential house into a commercial warehouse. When David and Sonja had visited next door to check on exactly how much of Morris' purchases had been stored there, he had been relieved to find that the front door opened outwards because he would not have been able to open it otherwise. Since he had not much option, David had chosen merely to laugh at the sight.

It had taken a week to document and move the stock to the station, and then to load it all onto a rail-freight carriage. David had negotiated and settled all the accounts and contracts until, finally, early on a Tuesday morning, he had watched the train chug westwards out of the station on its way north. He had then sent a coded telegram, using their 'black rhino' code (among other agreed codenames) to Louis, with a waybill and carriage numbers. A second, coded telegram had been sent to Morris in London, letting him know that the goods had left Port Elizabeth and that he would be leaving for Cape Town in three days, the time he felt might be required to clean Sonja's home and bring it back to a habitable standard again. Everything had seemed to be going according to plan.

On the morning of his departure, David had received a telegram from Louis to say that the goods had arrived and that Louis had been busy splitting the consignments into merchandise for both the Rhodesian and the South African markets. Langbourne Coetzee in Johannesburg was about to become fully operational.

Confident that all was under control, David had bid his friends a fond farewell, had checked out of the Grand Hotel, and had boarded a train for Cape Town. The journey would take him back past Graaff-Reinet to join the main north-south line once again at De Aar, where he would disembark and head south. Because he had been so anxious to get to Cape Town the journey had seemed painfully slow and monotonous. What had held his attention, though, had been the many British Army camps that had been dotted all along the railway line, and the numerous soldiers within them.

Now, after seventeen days at sea, he was gliding effortlessly into Southampton harbour. Carrying only one tote bag in his hand for luggage, and proudly wearing his signature Derby hat, David caught a steam train to London as soon as he had disembarked. He consistently consulted a scribbled note in his pocket that gave him rudimentary directions to Flat 12, Finsbury Pavement, in London, the new home of Morris Langbourne.

After boarding two different trains, one travelling underground for some considerable distance, David found himself looking down Finsbury Pavement, a reasonably significant roadway with multi-storied buildings on both sides. A gentleman wearing a top hat and a very glum expression stood halfway up a ladder that leant against a street lamp, and carefully lit the wick. Then, having climbed down the ladder, he appeared to be in no hurry whatsoever. He reminded David at once of a particular undertaker he had seen earlier, drawn as a caricature in a newspaper.

A rush of adrenalin and excitement gave David butterflies in his stomach. Here he was in a thoroughly modern metropolis, with horses and carts bustling about the streets, the streets themselves adorned with regal street lamps, about to meet his brother in his new home, and then – on top of everything else – his fiancée, Hanna. They would be married very soon and, after that, the prospect of taking her to Ireland to meet his family was all just too exciting for words!

As the encroaching dusk brought a small measure of tranquillity, David once again pulled the scrap of paper from his jacket pocket. Shaking it open with one hand, he re-read the address under the light of the street lamp. He knew it off by heart by this time but just wanted reassurance that he was correct.

"Excuse me, sir," David politely asked the lamp-lighter as he passed him on the way to the next lamp post, "I wonder if you would help me, please?"

Although the man halted in his occupation and made it clear that the unwarranted interruption did not amuse him, he said nothing.

"I'm looking for Flat 12, Finsbury Pavement. You wouldn't happen to know where it might be, would you?"

The man slowly reached over his ladder with his free hand and took the note from David's grasp. He read it silently, then looked up and down the street with disdain.

"Who gave you this address?" the man asked icily.

"My brother, Morris Langbourne," David answered, hoping the name might help, but suddenly beginning to feel somewhat nervous of the man.

"Well, 'e's a right, bleedin' Charlie, innie?" the undertaker grumbled.

"I beg your pardon?"

"Wozzer street number? Wozzer building's name, 'ay? Most ovva bleedin' buildings on 'is street 'ave bleedin' twelve flats in 'em, don' ay?"

"Oh…" David suddenly realised his dilemma.

"Good luck, my son. You're gonna need it," the morbid man mumbled and handed the piece of paper back to David. He then moved on without looking back.

"Just grand," David muttered to himself as he stared at the address on the piece of paper, an address that he had copied down precisely as the telegram instructed. As smart as his brother was, and as much as he respected Morris' sharp wits, he knew that sometimes Morris could be just a little careless. The loss of their wagons in the Rhodesian bush came to mind.

With evening setting in and corner shops beginning to close their doors,

David quickly walked into the nearest of them in the hopes of finding someone a little more helpful than the undertaker, or lamplighter, or whatever that man was. He discovered that he had walked into a florist's store, and the strong scent of a garden in bloom caught his nostrils.

David greeted the shopkeeper as cheerfully as he could.

"Good evening to you, ma'am," he said. "I'm afraid I have run into a slight dilemma and find myself somewhat lost."

"Good heavens," the middle-aged lady smiled and put a bunch of sad-looking flowers on the counter. "We can't have that now, can we?"

David's hopes picked up. "I have just arrived from southern Africa, where my brother had telegraphed me his home address. Sadly, he only gave me a partial address." David passed her the offending note.

"Oh dear," the florist said, shaking her head resignedly when she looked at the address written down and clucked her tongue in despair. "Well, you have the right street, I must agree, but short of knocking on every door of every building with a number 12 on it, you may not find him."

"I was afraid of that," David agreed, inwardly down-hearted but managing to hold his pleasant smile, regardless. "Perhaps you have seen him? A short man, about my age? Dresses in a suit most days."

"There are a few young men that call in to buy their intendeds flowers from time to time, but I have no idea which street they live on."

"Morris wouldn't spend money on flowers," David grumbled, and then instantly regretted saying that. "I buy my fiancée flowers often, though," he chirped happily, "and I am hopefully meeting up with her tomorrow. I dare say I'll need to call in tomorrow and buy the biggest bunch of flowers you have."

The florist acknowledged David's slip of the tongue with a smile. "Sadly, I can't help you with your address dilemma, young man, but I look forward to helping you out with the flowers."

David sighed and resignedly looked out the window onto the street. He thought he would ask the friendly florist where he might find some lodgings in the area. He felt that if he were to stand on the street in the morning, he might spot Morris heading to the warehouse, eventually.

Just then, as if by Divine intervention, he saw Morris walk past the window with a determined stride, and a glare that depicted a foul mood. He was wearing a black, woollen overcoat that reached down to his knees and a black Bowler hat. The matching black hatband was of lustrous silk, making Morris look quite dapper and debonaire, and much older than his years.

"There he is!" David exclaimed, quickly reaching for his tote bag and retrieving the note from the lady. "I'll be back tomorrow to buy a large bunch of flowers. Thank you, thank you."

"I did nothing," the florist smiled as she watched David back away towards the doorway giving a quick wave of thanks and a grateful half bow before he vanished from sight.

In a flash, David caught up with Morris and kept in stride with him, holding a distance of about two yards behind. Then, barely containing his excitement, he gave a gentle click with his tongue, a signal that he and his brothers used so that they could communicate in the shop without the customers' knowledge.

Morris' reaction was immediate. He stopped and turned so quickly that David almost walked slap-bang into him.

"David!" Morris exclaimed with such enthusiasm that they were stared at by other pedestrians in the vicinity.

"Hello, Brother. I see you. As you can tell, I made it."

They clasped hands in the way of the traditional amaXhosa when greeting a friend. For a moment, Morris was at a loss for words. "I didn't expect you for another two or three weeks. Welcome!" Morris took David by the elbow and led him along the pavement. He very quickly slipped into his usual way of asking several questions before the first question could be answered. "Come, this way, I'll show you where I live. Let's get you settled in. How was the journey? Well? Good to see you. Our brothers, how are they?"

"The address you gave me was not exactly explicit, Morris," David replied, somewhat relieved he had a place to sleep that night. "I'm fortunate to have found you."

"Nonsense!" Morris fobbed off David's objections. "If you can find Nkosazana in 1,000 square miles of Rhodesian bush you can find me in London. Anyhow, you're here now, aren't you? Look at that tan on your face! I'd forgotten how much sun we see in southern Africa. Since everyone here is pale with rosy cheeks, you will certainly stand out!"

Then Morris abruptly changed the subject. "Tell me, how're Louis and Harry?"

"They are well," David replied hesitantly, a little confused by his brother's response, "but as you know, I haven't seen them in over a month. I was sorting out the consignments in Port Elizabeth for about two weeks, and then ..."

"In here," Morris interrupted, turning sharply to the left and ushering David through the large, wooden double-door of a drab, multi-storey building.

David took in the nondescript foyer. "Is this where you have made a home?" he asked. He had not expected this at all.

"Yes. I hope your carry-all is not heavy, you have four flights of stairs to climb."

"I would have thought you would have saved money by combining a warehouse with your living arrangements," David said, as he looked at the interior of the stairway. A dark grey paint was peeling away in protest at the acidic mortar behind it.

"I did try that," Morris confessed as they reached the first level, "but it was awful. It can get frightfully cold in London, and I was most uncomfortable. Anyhow, this place came up for rent and, through a wonderful gentleman I met, whom you will meet shortly, I got this place very cheaply."

"It looks cheap," David grumbled as they rounded the stairs to the next level. There was no lighting in the stairwells, and, as it was getting dark, David wasn't impressed at all. He could even feel a chill emanating from the dungeon-style walls.

"Cheap it is, Brother," Morris chirped happily. "But wait until you see what I have done to the interior of the flat. I hear you are engaged to get married? Congratulations! Who is the lucky lady? Where did you meet her? What's her name?"

"Yes," David smiled, instantly forgetting about the cold, damp and miserable building he was trudging up, their footfalls echoing menacingly around them. "Hanna Rubinstein, an adorable lady. She came into the shop on Fife one day, and I met her there." He deliberately avoided telling Morris that Hanna's mother had cunningly brought her daughter into the store to specifically introduce her to him, for which he had been secretly grateful ever since.

"Rubinstein?" Morris mulled as they rounded the next flight of stairs. "A good Jewish name. Don't know them. I don't recall a Rubinstein on the

Zionist committee I briefly chaired."

"Mr Rubinstein is a manager with Rhodesia Railways. He travels up to Salisbury quite a bit. Hanna is lovely; I will make my way to where the family is staying tomorrow."

"No, tomorrow won't do," Morris immediately took control of his younger brother's plans. "Tomorrow I have a luncheon at the London Chamber of Commerce. I'm a member there now. You must come as my guest."

"But ..." David tried to object.

"Your timing is impeccable, David. These luncheons are a magnificent opportunity to rub shoulders with influential gentlemen in society. Important people. You can't miss this. Hanna can wait another day. Where is she staying?"

David rummaged in his jacket pocket for the note with the address scribbled on it as they rounded the last flight of stairs. "The Langham Hotel ..."

"Oh yes, I know it. Very nice hotel. I had a meeting there last month. Fully electrified! They have electric lighting all over the hotel. Indeed, very nice - good choice. You can walk there in about an hour, or you could catch a train or two, but that will cost you a few pennies."

"I can walk there?" David's spirits lifted suddenly. "Maybe I can go there after the luncheon?"

"Yes, perhaps you can." Morris stopped at a door with the brass numerals depicting that they were at Flat 12.

"Ahh..." David smiled at the numbers, "the elusive Flat 12 on Finsbury Pavement."

Morris missed the sarcasm as he fumbled for a key in his pocket. "Before we go to the luncheon, we need to fit you out with a quality suit. You can't go to the Chamber of Commerce dressed like that." He nodded with a scowl at David's grey business suit.

"What's wrong with it?" David sounded offended; it was his best.

Ignoring David's response completely, Morris rattled the key in the lock and opened the door. "Now, come in," he commanded.

David's first view of the interior of Morris' flat was a dark hallway with a small table pushed against one wall. He could vaguely see a rack of hooks attached to the corridor above it. Morris hung his Bowler hat on one of the hooks and told David to hang his Derby on a vacant one, which he did. A flare of a match illuminated the hallway. David noticed a coat-stand with a jacket hanging from it and watched as Morris lit a candle. A vase of white flowers was standing elegantly on the table. Morris removed his overcoat and jacket, hanging them on the coat-stand, and again, told David to follow suit. As he instinctively closed the door behind him, David felt a sudden comfortable and welcoming warmth in the flat

Lighting a second candle, Morris carefully took it through to the lounge, which was to the left of the hallway, and David watched him light other candles in various candelabra. The interior of the dwelling began to expose its glory and grandeur as the candles took to their flames.

David stood in awe as he watched the room come to life, as if he had stepped into an Aladdin's Cave of treasures. Statuettes stood to attention on small side tables, while plush leather furniture invited him to sit comfortably upon elegant scatter-cushions. A dining suite made of rich, dark wood boasted yet another silver candelabrum for eight candles.

Attractive landscape oil paintings graced the walls, while flower arrangements stood in intricate vases, adding yet more visual warmth and homeliness to the room. Against a broad set of windowpanes was a grand office desk with leather inlay, upon which stood some fine, leather-bound books of account; a ledger, a journal, and others that clearly demarcated the area as his brother's office.

What immediately caught David's attention, however, were the walls themselves. Painted upon them from floor to ceiling were faint, but intricate patterns that repeated themselves throughout, not only making the walls attractive to the eye but enveloping the room in a warm welcome he had not expected. He had never seen wallpaper before.

"This is..." David had to search for the words as he was overwhelmed by what had unfolded in front of him. "I can't believe what I am looking at."

"Nice, isn't it?"

"It's incredible!" David marvelled. "And here we all thought you would be sleeping in blankets on the floor of a warehouse."

"I was, but not anymore. Come, let me show you to your room." Morris took a candle and, protecting the flame with a cupped hand, walked past David. "This is the kitchen. It has an exceptional oven, an AGA, which I keep alight all day long. It keeps the flat warm. This is my bedroom, and yours is across the corridor over there," Morris indicated as he lit candles during the walk-through.

"We have running water here," Morris continued. "Over there is a lavatory with a bath. Before you use the bath, you need to boil some water on the AGA. You'll find some pots in the cupboards next to it. Don't try and have a cold bath in this country; you'll freeze. It's not like southern Africa."

"Well I'll be, Morris," said David in awe. He was genuinely amazed by what his brother had achieved.

While putting on some fresh vegetables to boil, Morris warmed up some leftover beef stew that he had enjoyed the previous night. The two brothers then proceeded to sit together at the dining table under the silver candelabrum to exchange their news. Since most of the news was business related, Morris was particularly interested in how David had sorted and shipped all the stock out of Sonja Du Plessis' home and onto the trains.

Satisfied that David had done a sterling job, the conversation turned to more personal matters. David asked after their father, and Morris related how his visit to Ireland had gone. He talked about how he had met Yoni Goldberg, the influential businessman, who had given him the breaks he had needed, including his introduction to the Chamber of Commerce.

Morris paused to wipe his lips with a serviette.

"It was through Mr Goldberg," he said, "that the stock which arrived in Cape Town and East London was diverted to Port Elizabeth. He is a brilliant man, and extremely successful in business. Because he's in the shipping insurance business himself, by the way, he knows a lot of people from all around the world, as well as what's happening internationally." Having finished his meal, Morris politely placed his knife and fork together on his empty dinner plate.

David leant back in his seat as he cast his eyes over the flat. "I would say Mr Goldberg has had a huge influence on you, Morris," he grinned. "You were not the sort of person to be as lavish as this before you left southern Africa."

"Oh, this was all done on the cheap, believe me," Morris airily replied. "Rose Bertha has something of an eye for decor, and she also has a way with second-hand dealers. All this stuff here is second-hand merchandise that she purchased at discounted prices. Even the rental on this flat is very cheap, thanks to Mr Goldberg."

"Who is Rose Bertha?" David asked curiously.

"Oh, I forgot to mention her. Like you, I'm engaged to Rose to be married."

David was amazed. "I cannot believe you forgot to mention such an important detail to me! Well, I'll be...! Nevertheless, I am sure that proper congratulations might be in order, I suppose. Well done. When do I get to meet the lovely lady, I wonder?"

"Oh, in good time you will," Morris said casually. "She and her family live quite close by. She was introduced to me by Mr and Mrs Goldberg. Rose Bertha's family members are close friends of theirs.

"So, when is the wedding?" David asked, finding this new revelation almost humorous.

"In the fullness of time; no plans yet. And yours?"

"As soon as possible. I can't wait," David enthused. "Hanna's mother is making all the arrangements, so I am sure I will find out the finer details when I see them. I'd like you to be my best man, if you would be so kind."

"By all means, I'd be delighted, of course," Morris beamed, sitting bolt upright. "This calls for a celebration. I have a special bottle of French brandy I bought when I was in Paris. A toast!" Morris stood up to retrieve a couple of small goblets and a bottle of liquor from a sideboard.

"Paris, France?" David exclaimed. He was beginning to wonder what other surprises his brother had in store for him. "You went to Paris?"

"Yes, indeed," Morris replied nonchalantly as he poured two small tots of brandy into the delicate, Waterford crystal glasses. "Mr Friedlander, Rose Bertha's father, took me there for ten days. Delightful place. My favourite city. Have you made any plans for your honeymoon?"

"No...," David said cautiously.

"You must go there," Morris insisted, as he passed David a tumbler of brandy. "Absolutely lovely city. I have made some interesting connections and contacts there. I even made a friend called Paul Follot, about my age. He designs jewellery and wallpaper. Why, you could even insert a bit of business into your honeymoon."

"Wallpaper? I saw the labels on some of the boxes in Port Elizabeth. What's that?"

"This," Morris pointed at the wall nearest him. "Printed designs on heavy paper that is glued to walls. A splendid invention. Paul designed this pattern, and his father, Monsieur Follot, duly manufactured the paper.

They have a wallpaper factory in Paris. Look how stately a room becomes with such designs on the walls."

David followed his brother to stand close to one of the walls, where he gently ran his hand over the texture of the paper.

"This will sell well in Rhodesia, and in the other southern African territories. Well done, brother." David was now secretly convinced that he was in for many more surprises over the next few days.

"Let's adjourn to the lounge, and you can tell me what happened to you and Louis in Mafeking."

David let out a deep sigh and shook his head slowly. "War is a terrible thing, Morris. Terrible."

The brothers took their brandy balloons to the lounge, where David related the story of his and Louis' experiences in Mafeking, without interruption. Since Morris had received little information about his two younger brothers' brush with death, or their exposure to so much of wartime death and destruction, he was horrified by what he heard. The cruelty of war to both man and animal was abhorrent to him. When David got to the point where they were eating ground and dried insects, and where beef had been replaced with horseflesh, Morris winced. David related how Colonel Baden-Powell had held off the Boer commandos with limited men by employing brilliant games of deception and bluff, and how the colonel had helped him and Louis escape the siege one night.

David told Morris how their loyal assistant and friend, Nguni, had come to find them, how he had stolen into Mafeking and then had led them, barefoot and camouflaged in mud, out of the besieged town; how they had stolen horses and rifles, and how a small Boer commando had hunted them. On the subject of Mafeking, David told Morris that Julian Weil had fallen out of favour with the military, having made huge profits on the scarcity of food.

Morris shook his head in dismay. "I can understand people making a profit out of a war," he grimaced, "but withholding food in the interests of financial gain is simply not right."

"Yet Mr and Mrs Weil were good to Louis and me, Morris," David replied. "They gave us board and lodging and were very hospitable, so I was quite disappointed to hear that he would resort to this type of shenanigan."

"Yes, me too," Morris sighed. "I do like the man, but perhaps the stresses of war have turned him. Mind you, he was also taking advantage of us, you may recall."

Being rather late, the young men called it a night and Morris duly blew out the orchestra of candles.

"Right you are, then," said Morris, as he bid his brother good night, "tomorrow I will take you to the storeroom, get you fitted for a decent suit, take you to lunch, and then you are free to walk on over to the Langham."

"Sounds like an acceptable plan, brother. Sleep tight, because I know I will."

Morris yawned and slapped David on the shoulder. "Good to have you here, my dearest brother."

CHAPTER TWO

London - 1900

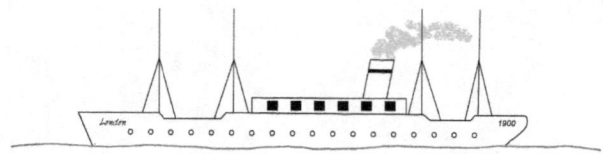

After a standing breakfast by the AGA – consisting of toast and marmalade, washed down with a cup of hot tea – Morris and David bustled out of the building and made their way to the warehouse. Although the building was somewhat decrepit and in serious need of attention, it served its purpose quite adequately. It was a quarter filled with an assortment of boxes and crates; new purchases that Morris had begun to acquire before the stock that had been sent to Africa had even reached its destination.

David immediately walked up to a stack of three rough wooden crates that lay atop each other. Each was about the size of a large door, and about 18 inches thick.

"What on earth are these?" David demanded, slapping one of the crates with an open hand, then immediately regretting the action as he picked up a splinter. "There were two of them in Port Elizabeth, and I had to employ 14 strong men to lift each one. Even then they struggled under the

16

weight."

Morris laughed. "Yes, I probably should have warned you. They are strong-room doors, made of iron, and filled with concrete. The local banks use them."

"I had to buy ropes and levers and hire a special cart just to move them to the rail yard."

Morris laughed again. "I suppose we should send Giraffe and Badger a telegram and warn them, too." As was becoming quite natural for them all, Morris used the code names of their two younger brothers.

David shook his head as he picked at his splinter. "Too late for that," he grumbled. "Next time, ask your supplier to send them directly to the shipyard. I'm certainly not going to be lifting these when you choose to send them off."

"I've already arranged that." Morris winked, then gesticulated widely around him. "This is where I began. I had a mattress on the floor at the back, but as you can tell, this place is frigid and isolated. Also, I needed a presentable place to have meetings with suppliers." David realised that Morris was trying to justify his new, rather lavish lifestyle.

"Us three brothers have bought land in Bulawayo that was going cheap," David said. "We will each build a house to live in. Sleeping on the warehouse floor has become a bit tedious, but sadly, we will never live as luxuriously as you."

"I was going to suggest you find suitable lodgings now that we are making money."

It was David's turn to wink. "Especially now that I will soon be married."

Morris chuckled. "Yes, indeed. We can't have your Hanna sleeping on a warehouse floor, now can we?"

He showed David around the warehouse, and the crate he had modified to form a receiving office. The boys then locked up and walked to a gentleman's outfitters that Morris had suggested; a company highly recommended by Yoni Goldberg, and which Morris frequented.

David was quickly dressed in a fine, navy-blue, morning coat with brass buttons and a wide lapel. He chose a quality tie to match and a pure white shirt with a stiff collar. Morris tried to convince him to buy a Bowler hat, but David declined, arguing that he preferred the Derby style. Nevertheless, David was persuaded to buy a black Derby hat to go with his new formal outfit. To top it all off, he purchased – at considerable expense – a pure wool, jet-black morning coat, which (like the one belonging to Morris) fell past his knees. A black umbrella finished his outfit off nicely. No longer did he look like a smart young man from southern Africa, but a high-class Londoner. Looking in the full-length mirror, both David and Morris beamed boyishly.

Being close to midday, they strode off in the direction of the London Chamber of Commerce. For David, this was a most notable experience. Had it not been for Morris by his side, he would have felt very awkward around the gentry, some arriving in long tails and top hats. Most of the men were much older than him and spoke with very refined accents. Having become used to a far less formal way of life, David found the entire episode a rather strange affair.

When Yoni Goldberg arrived, his manicured, thick beard made quite a statement, while his piercing blue eyes, having fallen on David without wavering, helped the younger brother feel a lot more relaxed. Yoni questioned David closely about his voyage over on the Dunottar Castle and asked all sorts of interesting questions about it, such as the ports of call, the docking procedures and of other vessels that had passed on the journey north, all of which David found strangely insightful and unusual. Yoni then turned the conversation to David's involvement in the Boer War and was so enamoured by the ensuing discussion that he almost monopolised David's company, placing him in a seat beside him when lunch was served.

Morris, meanwhile, having become distracted by an imposing bank executive, and, suspecting that his new-found connection might prove useful in business someday, left Yoni and David to their own devices. Every now and again, however, Morris would steal a glance in David's direction, and smile when he noticed how his brother had attracted the attention of all who sat at his table and was thoroughly engrossed in his relating the latest news of southern Africa.

When lunch was finally over, David felt quite exhilarated, and – if that had not been enough – even more excited about the prospect of now finding his way to Hanna.

"Morris," David whispered hoarsely into his brother's ear as they exited the Chamber building, "I need directions to the Langham Hotel."

"It's easy," Morris replied calmly, "I'll draw you a map in a minute."

Having turned a few corners, Morris promptly pulled out a notepad and drew a rough sketch that would lead David to his destination. With some hurried descriptions of various landmarks along the way, the brothers parted company, and David took off determinedly.

"I'll leave the door unlocked," Morris called after David as an afterthought. "Take your time getting back."

Looking briefly over his shoulder, David threw a mock salute of thanks before picking up his pace.

Since the map that Morris had drawn was accurate enough to be followed without much difficulty, David entered the foyer of the cavernous and impressive Langham Hotel about an hour later.

Morris had been right. The reception area was illuminated with electric light-bulbs, giving it an outstanding, even regal, atmosphere. The doorman, concierge, and reception staff were all dressed in very formal attire, and David once again felt for a moment both overwhelmed and out of place. When the doorman bowed slightly out of respect as he opened the grandiose door, he caught David entirely off guard. With a great profusion of nodding and welcoming smiles, the staff also seemed very friendly, but only when he walked past one of the many mirrors did he suddenly realise that he was looking very dapper in his brand new suit and Derby hat, umbrella neatly folded by his side.

Having freshly gaining a broad and confident smile, therefore, David boldly approached the reception desk and announced that he would like to see anyone in the Rubinstein family. The clerk didn't even refer to a register or check the pigeonhole key compartments behind him, but merely stated blandly that the Rubinstein's were out, and that they might return later that evening.

The look of disappointment on David's face was unmistakable.

"Perhaps, sir, you might be inclined to enjoy a cup of tea in the library while you wait?" the clerk suggested politely.

David smiled and nodded. "I might just do that, thank you kindly, but do be sure, if you please, in telling them that I am here when they return. They are expecting me."

"I shall most certainly do my utmost best, sir," the man replied with such an air of grandeur that David almost let a chuckle slip. He noticed that nothing in the man's entire anatomy moved one tiny iota, only his mouth appeared to move alone when he spoke. "Might I inquire as to the name, sir?"

"Langbourne. David Langbourne."

"I dare say you are in luck, Mr Langbourne," the clerk replied without so much as a twitch.

"Excuse me?" David asked, cocking an eyebrow.

"The Rubinstein's have just returned," he said calmly, casting a brief look over David's shoulder.

David spun around, and there, walking through the main door was his Hanna, her mother and father right behind her.

She wore a pure-white blouse that enhanced her shapely figure, her bright pink skirt billowing copiously down to her ankles. A light blush on her cheeks and a subtle shade of lipstick strove equally with one another to enhance her natural smile.

For his part, David was utterly lost for words. For yet another moment, he could not quite believe that she would soon be his wife, but he quickly fell helplessly in love with her all over again.

Hanna noticed the young man standing at the reception desk, umbrella in hand, looking so dashing, but only afforded him a fleeting glance. Yet, something about the coy smile managed to catch her attention in a manner which commanded a second glance. When she finally realised who it was, she shrieked in delight and ran to him, dropping a shopping bag in the process. Wrapping her arms tightly around him, she proceeded to burst into tears. David promptly returned her embrace and was determined never to let her go again, until that old killjoy Mr Dignity finally got the better of him – or perhaps it was the desk clerk, who happened to clear his throat rather forcefully.

"How good it is to see you, my dear Hanna," David said softly, gently extracting himself from her embrace.

"Oh David, oh David!" was all Hanna could say, dabbing at a tear that escaped her eye.

"I'm right here," David soothed.

"David," said Mrs Rubinstein, interrupting her daughter's renewed intimacy by also firmly wrapping her arms around him. "What took you so long?"

Mr Rubinstein somehow managed to shake David's hand before his wife broke off her hug. "Welcome to you, David," he murmured.

"So good to be here at last," David grinned back at him. "It has been quite a journey."

"Come," Mr Rubinstein insisted, taking control of the situation, much to the relief of the desk clerk, "we have much to discuss. Let's go to the lounge and have some tea, shall we?"

They adjourned to a lounge close by, Hanna locking her arm tightly around David's elbow. David was so happy he thought he might explode, and noticed that Hanna was smiling more than he had ever seen before. He also noticed that his future mother-in-law was dabbing her tears with a delicate handkerchief.

"So, what are the plans?" David asked anxiously as they took their seats in some very plush armchairs. It was one of those times when David did not particularly enjoy the luxury of these high-class chairs, because he couldn't hold Hanna's hand.

"The wedding will be in ten days at a synagogue just two blocks from here," Mr Rubinstein stated. "We were worried that you weren't going to get here on time, and were about to postpone it. There will be about 40 guests from our side, and – please – no more than 40 from your side of the family."

David smiled. "There will be one other guest, my brother Morris, who will also be my best man," then quickly added, as he remembered his meeting with Yoni Goldberg, "Perhaps one or two of my brother's associates.".

"What about your family in Ireland?" Mrs Rubinstein asked.

"No, the logistics don't really allow for it. After the wedding, I would like to travel to Ireland and introduce Hanna to my family. We will have a little celebration there, I am sure. And then, perhaps," David stole a smile at Hanna, "We might go to Paris for our honeymoon."

Hanna squealed in excitement. "Oh yes, please!" she exclaimed. "I have always wanted to go there. Oh David, how romantic!"

"Morris went there a little while back," David replied, "and said it really is a must. He did some business there and said I should call on some of the contacts he made."

"Oh no, you won't!" Hanna interrupted bluntly. "There is no chance you will do any business while we are on honeymoon, and that's final."

David smiled. "Then so be it." He so wanted to reach over and squeeze her hand, to remind himself that finally he had been reunited with her.

While David quickly took in all the finer plans of the wedding ceremony that were explained very excitedly, he occupied himself in making silent plans of his own. Hanna wanted to go to Paris first, before Ireland, but David later convinced the family that Ireland would come first, as he had not seen his family for nearly ten years.

David then stayed on for an early dinner, after which Hanna's parents adjourned to their room to give the young couple some time alone. They promptly took a walk through the dimming streets of London, chatting lovingly between themselves. David insisted that somehow they should all meet for a meal at Morris' new home, and perhaps even meet his new fiancée before they left for Ireland. As one would expect when lovers meet after some absence, the evening soon flashed by, and David very reluctantly led Hanna back to the Langham Hotel, where he bid her good night with a gentlemanly kiss on the back of her hand, under the unblinking gaze of the desk clerk.

The ten days leading up to the wedding were a tight juggle for David, having to split his time between Morris and Hanna's arrangements. David had no idea who was more demanding.

Morris, of course, wanted to make the most of David's brief stay in London. Therefore he insisted on a fair deal of manual work in the warehouse, moving stock around, stacking, un-stacking, and re-packing. Much administrative paperwork was required, too, checking invoices, compiling manifests, coding the cost and retail prices into their black rhino code and receiving stock when a transporter delivered goods, unannounced. Then Morris constantly seemed to schedule a series of incessant meetings at the most awkward times with bank managers, accountants, lawyers, suppliers, and of course, Yoni Goldberg and Mr Lionel Friedlander, the commodity trader and future father-in-law of Morris.

And yet David found that the meeting with Mr Friedlander was the most interesting. Because Mr Friedlander kept a finger on the pulse of world events, owing to his international business interests, he seemed to know a great deal about developments in southern Africa. He also expressed an interest in what David had to say about his close encounter with the Boers in Mafeking, and what the younger brother felt about the Boer War as a whole.

"It was very much at the end of the war when Mafeking was relieved," David said. "Very soon after that Johannesburg and Pretoria were occupied and the Boers went into retreat."

"Yes, they did," Mr Friedlander concurred, "but they didn't surrender altogether, did they?"

"Not exactly," David reflected. "They just went into hiding, retreated, or simply gave up. Many of the Boer commandoes returned to their farms. The war seemed to us to be over, and we all celebrated."

"I see," Mr Friedlander said, pausing thoughtfully. "Indeed, that is how the papers reported it as happening... So, tell me more about this Colonel Baden-Powell, the man who defended Mafeking against thousands of Boers, they say he is a brilliant military strategist, a hero. You knew him personally?"

"Indeed," David smiled, "he used the most ingenious tactics against his enemy. Strategies he would call 'a game of bluff,' to confuse them, then he would go out and give them a hiding, or a 'kick' as he liked to call it. I must admit I found some of his strategies quite... creative and imaginative. Furthermore, he was dedicated. He worked on his plans day and night. They used to call him 'The Wolf' because he never seemed to sleep."

Mr Friedlander leaned back in his seat slightly and rubbed his brow, "Well," he said, "I read a great deal about world events because my business depends on knowledge, such as the presence of droughts, floods, plagues, that sort of thing. And, of course, war commands a big part of my interest.

"You claim that Colonel Baden-Powell is a military genius, and certainly, he may well be, but I believe there are other military men just as brilliant, or even more so than him."

David was immediately curious. "Is that right?" he asked. "Who do you have in mind?"

"A Boer general they call Koos De La Rey. Now that man is not only a brilliant military man, but he demonstrates the bravery of a lion and a passion extraordinaire. I don't think much of their President, Paul Kruger, personally, but De La Rey? Well, if he had been in greater charge of the Boer commandos and the government, I think that war would have gone the other way. In fact, I think that the Boers may have even won the war in very short order. The British only won because of sheer numbers."

"Huh..." David exclaimed and cast an inquisitive look at Morris. "I never thought of it that way."

"That's probably because you only saw the war from the British point of view, and also because you got caught up in it from their side, so it's only natural you take the British view. Personally, I believe the war is not over yet."

"Really?" Morris exclaimed, joining in on the conversation for the first time. "How can that be?"

"Well, think about it. The Boers did not officially surrender. De La Rey once predicted that President Kruger would flee and go into hiding, which is exactly what happened, and then he said he would continue fighting long after Kruger ran away. De La Rey has not been found or captured yet. He is still out there, is he not?"

"Funny you should say that," David's brow creased, "I met a chap on the train from Bulawayo recently. His name is Johan Colenbrander, a fascinating man, and he said the Boers were regrouping and commencing a guerrilla-type war, destroying infrastructure, rail lines and the like. He was on his way to hunt them down."

"There you go!" Mr Friedlander slapped his thigh and smiled. "I was right. The war is not over."

"I wonder if that will affect our business?" Morris looked worried.

"I'm sure it will, Morris." Friedlander was concerned. "Start planning and get your strategic response in place right now for whatever ensues. Smart people can make money out of a conflict. As for me, I will be concentrating my business only in Europe, America and the Far East. It will be more difficult for you in southern Africa."

David looked at his brother. He knew that Morris' mind worked in rapid and exciting ways, and already he could see that his dynamic brain was in a high state of alert. He was obviously planning at that very moment, and – as it always was with Morris – he probably had a strategy in place already.

"Good show!" Morris suddenly stood up to leave. "A good meeting and much food for thought. Thank you, Mr Friedlander, we must be off."

David stood and shook Mr Friedlander's hand. "Good to meet you, sir. I look forward to seeing you again."

"Indeed, a most enjoyable encounter," Friedlander reciprocated with the handshake. "Morris, would you like to join us for dinner tomorrow night? Bring David, too, I'm sure Rose Bertha would like to see you and meet your family."

"Tomorrow night?" Morris thought quickly. "Yes, that would be wonderful, thank you."

"And bring your fiancée, David."

As soon as the two young men stepped onto the pavement, they became engrossed in what had been discussed indoors. Morris was laying out his contingencies, and David was rapidly agreeing or countering what Morris suggested. By the time they had reached Finsbury Pavement, the brothers were a lot calmer, knowing more or less what had to be done to keep their business alive in southern Africa.

It was not going to be easy, but they were both sure that, if the Johannesburg office were to struggle, the Rhodesian branch would continue to thrive. It was agreed that, if the situation became uncomfortable, Louis would have to mothball the Johannesburg warehouse and return to Rhodesia, not just to be useful and productive there, but also for safety's sake. Nevertheless, they agreed that their plans should be designed to be as flexible as possible.

The real issue would be money - hard cash. There was just not enough money in circulation in Rhodesia, and when the end of the Boer War gave promise that cash would begin to flow again, a resurgence of the war would put an end to any hope of that happening. Already the Administrator of Matabeleland, a Mr Hugh Marshall-Hole, had started making temporary money in the form of cards with postage stamps glued and stamped by his office, which depicted the value of the stamp as cash, also to that value. The system worked well - in Rhodesia, but was useless anywhere else in the world.

"We literally need to take our own money back to Rhodesia to use in our day-to-day trading," Morris complained. "After your wedding, take a trunk of cash with you to Bulawayo."

David looked at his brother incredulously. "Excuse me?"

"That will alleviate the problem for a while," Morris replied

"After my wedding, Hanna and I are going to Ireland to see the family," David insisted. "Then we are going to Paris for our honeymoon. I won't be back in southern Africa for many months to come. Put the cash in a carton and ship it over."

"And what am I supposed to write on the manifest? '£10 000 Sterling

Cash'? That box won't get past the back door of the London warehouse."

"Exactly," David declared, "and I'm not cutting my honeymoon short for anyone. I haven't had a holiday since… since… ever! I've been caught up in three wars, who knows how many plagues, nearly killed by hundreds of animals…"

"Of which one was a big bird," Morris drily interrupted.

David looked at Morris in disgust and was about to continue with his tirade when he saw an almost indiscernible smile hook at the corners of his brother's lips. Both brothers immediately began to laugh and kept laughing until they reached the flat. Morris put a kettle on the AGA and prepared a teapot for tea, while they continued their conversations on a much lighter note. Morris assured David that taking money back to Rhodesia was too risky, and in any case, it was probably illegal. He would make other arrangements.

David then changed the subject to more personal matters. "Morris," he asked, "when last did you see Rose Bertha?"

"Oh, about a week ago. Why?"

"I just find it strange that her parents have to invite you around for dinner to see her. Don't you ever take her out for dinner in a classy restaurant, or go on picnics?"

"I have taken her out for dinner on occasion," Morris admitted casually. "It's not something we do all the time. I'm quite occupied with growing the business. In fact, my next move is to concentrate less on suppliers and start finding customers. I actually want to start selling our goods here, in England. I believe…"

"Hold up," David raised his palm in objection; he was not ready to discuss business again. "Don't change the subject. I'm talking about Rose Bertha. Don't you love her?"

"Well of course! We are going to be married," Morris objected.

"When?"

"We haven't even thought of that yet, but there's no hurry."

"Well, I find that hard to understand," David shook his head as he poured a little milk into their teacups, "I can't stay away from Hanna for any length of time. I need to be around her constantly, and I know she feels the same way about me. I find it hard to accept that you and Rose Bertha can go weeks at a time without even seeing each other."

"We are happy with the arrangement. The Goldbergs and the

Friedlanders are very keen for us to get married."

David shook his head gently. He knew he and his brother had very different personalities, and this indeed came through when romance was involved.

"So, are you finally going to introduce me to Rose Bertha?" It didn't escape David's attention that Morris made no effort to arrange for him to meet his fiancée, and it puzzled him that Morris turned down his invitations to join him at the Langham Hotel to meet the Rubinsteins on two separate occasions, albeit for rather genuine reasons.

"Yes, tomorrow evening, and both our respective fiancées will meet too. How fitting!"

"Indeed," David smiled. "Well, I must be off. It seems the suit we bought for the Chamber of Commerce is "not appropriate" for the wedding, so I'm meeting Mr Rubinstein to select something more acceptable."

"Heavens!" Morris whined, "what more do you need for a wedding?"

"Don't complain," David said, pointing a warning finger at Morris as he turned to leave, "your turn is coming. And by the way, once we find an acceptable suit, you will be required to come down for a fitting too – that's what best men do!"

As he closed the door behind him, David chuckled heartily at what might be going through Morris' mind at that moment.

Hanna's excitement during the build-up to the wedding day was contagious, and – although her planning demands seemed far too excessive for what David felt was a simple affair – he went along with the Rubinstein's arrangements, hiding his frustrations, by agreeing and smiling at every opportunity.

After five days of trudging for one hour across town at least twice a day, David still couldn't decide whose attention was more demanding, Hanna's or that of Morris. Nevertheless, he enjoyed the idea of being wanted, and it made him feel needed. He also thoroughly enjoyed arriving at the Langham Hotel, where he enjoyed a loving welcome from his bride-to-be each and every time he saw her.

Finding a dress suit that was agreeable to the ladies was not difficult, and, David thought, he could well use the variety of attire in his business commitments. Although not required with a dress suit, one item that he would not budge on was the Derby hat. He was happy wearing a variety of colours, but no other style would do. It was his signature headwear.

The evening the two families met for dinner at the Friedlander's home was a joyous one. David hired a coach, driven by a man in top hat and tails. It took them from the Langham Hotel to Finsbury Pavement, where they collected Morris, and then took a short drive to the Friedlander's home.

Hanna and Rose Bertha took to each other straight away, chatting incessantly from the moment they met to the moment they left. It pleased David immensely to see them get along so well, and he felt that Hanna was certainly enjoying meeting other young ladies of her age, an aspect that had been somewhat neglected by her parents since her arrival in England. As was usual, the men seemed to congregate on one side of the room, and the ladies on the other. David and Hanna immediately invited the entire family to attend on their wedding day and suggested that Morris and Rose Bertha formally ask Yoni and Ruth Goldberg. These parties would then, effectively, represent the Langbourne family along with Morris.

At the end of a most enjoyable evening, therefore, David and Morris accompanied Hanna back to the Langham Hotel in the coach, and – feeling somewhat satisfied and mellow – asked the driver to return them to Finsbury Pavement, thereby avoiding the necessity of taking the hour-long walk in the darkened streets.

In the days that followed, David noticed how that particular evening seemed to have changed something in Morris, who subsequently became more accepting of David's invitations to meet the Rubinstein's, even asking if he could bring Rose Bertha along with him.

From that day on, a great deal more social interactions occurred among the three families, which caused David some pleasure. It later dawned on him that Morris perhaps had become too accustomed to being on his own, immersing himself in business, and lacking a family life. It further appeared that Morris had equally come to his own realisation and had since softened significantly in his demeanour.

The day of the wedding finally arrived, then, with much excitement. Standing in front of all the invited guests, bearing corsages in their lapels and beaming proudly, David and Morris appeared very dignified.

Hanna, of course, was magnificent; her face glowing with love and affection for the man in her life. Her wedding dress was spectacular and elicited several gasps from the assembled guests as she entered the synagogue. Many a tear was shed, not least of all by David himself, who upon seeing her, gave thanks to his Lord for blessing him with such a lovely woman, and such a life.

After the ceremony, strong bonds were formed by all who attended, and a few humorous and risqué innuendoes were bandied about at dinner, with a particular focus on when the babies might be expected to arrive, much to the embarrassment of the newlyweds. And when the evening was drawing to a jolly close, the happy couple departed in a horse-drawn coach pulled by two beautiful stallions to a destination not far away, a destination that Hanna had kept a tightly guarded secret from everyone, including her husband.

Not surprisingly, their first-born child, a beautiful daughter whom they would name Ettie, would be born exactly nine months later.

CHAPTER THREE

Dublin – 1900

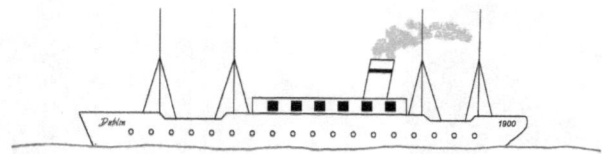

Acting on a recommendation made by Morris, David and Hanna checked into the Fitzwilliam Guest House in the Irish capital of Dublin, unpacked their bags, and freshened up after the long journey from London. After studying a roughly drawn map of where Jacob Langbourne now resided with his family, the newlyweds hailed a buggy and set off for St Kevin's Parade in Wood Quay.

The beauty of a bright and crisp day reflected the sunny mood of the young couple as they sat in the buggy, holding hands and basking in their joy. Alighting at the top of the street, David and Hanna paid and tipped the driver, who acknowledged the gratuity by doffing his hat, before driving off with a flick of the reins.

"I'm nervous," Hanna said shyly, squeezing David's arm.

"I'm nervous too, but also excited," her husband replied, staring at the identical black doors on each side of the street. "I don't know if I will recognise anyone."

"I think it will be your family that doesn't recognise you, to be honest," said Hanna with a smile. "From what I understand, you were but a teen when you left, thin, undernourished and wearing clothes barely one button more than a pile of rags. Now look at you," she smiled again and looked lovingly into his eyes. "You're a successful business owner, filled to the brim with worldly knowledge, and a very handsome man, all strong and muscular."

David chuckled at her last remark but admitted she was right on the other aspects. "Well, I suppose you can say that the last ten years have been quite extraordinary from anyone's point of view."

Hanna changed the subject. "Remind me of those we are about to meet," she asked.

"Well, I have told you about my father," David said, his gaze fixing on the street ahead of him. "He is very emotional; happy one moment and very sad the next, for no apparent reason. We accept that now, but it does prevent him from working, he just never appeared to care for work after my mother died."

"Your mother was Esther, am I right?"

"Yes, a lovely lady. She came from high society and loved us all dearly. She brought us up well, taught us good manners, and how to put our best foot forward. Bloomy, our older sister, took over when Mother died, and she too did a great job. You'll like her," David smiled. "Morris says she has blossomed since she got married to Bernard, whom I haven't met yet. She has had two daughters already, probably a third child by now. Mother's youngest is Sally. Last I saw of her, she was only three years old, and now she will be 13, a young woman. I certainly won't recognise my sister…"

Hanna permitted a cute giggle to escape. "No, indeed, you certainly won't."

"Father sent for Helena, my mother's niece and hence my cousin, whom he asked to live with us to help care for Louis and Harry when my mother was too ill to look after them. After Morris and I left for southern Africa, he married her." David scowled. "Morris seems to have a problem with that."

"Do you?"

"No, not at all. They both make each other happy, and that's all that concerns me. They went on to have more children, according to Morris – four more, I believe – with another on the way when he last saw them.

That child will probably be almost a year old by now. First, there was Rachel Raie, then Erin, whom they call 'Paddy' for some reason, then Ernest and Tillie. I have met none of them."

"This should be rather interesting, then, don't you think?"

"Indeed," David grinned. "Well, shall we?"

"Let's," Hanna smiled, and drew in a deep breath.

Arm-in-arm the young couple walked down the street, counting the black wooden doors as they went. Since no numbers were to be seen on the doors, it seemed as if the Irish were not concerned about such helpful matters at all. If one were lost or looking for someone, they would ask for help from a resident. Again, since nicknames were often used, letters could quite easily be addressed merely to a nickname on a particular road, in a specific suburb or county and the addressee would be found at once.

David and Hanna stopped and stared at the door which they rather hoped might correspond to number fourteen. David straightened his jacket, adjusted his tie, and tweaked the angle of his Derby.

"Go on," Hanna urged, giving his arm a gentle squeeze and releasing him.

David stood on the step in front of the door and knocked three times. A moment later it swung open and revealed none other than his father, sporting a neatly manicured full beard, a mop of jet-black hair, and piercing blue eyes.

Jacob Langbourne looked inquiringly at the suave gentleman standing before him and then took in the beautiful young woman by his side. For the briefest of moments, he did not recognise either of them. When a second glance at David, however, brought all the memories of his second-born son rushing to the surface, Jacob gasped and covered his mouth with his hand. "David? Is that you?" is all he managed to say between his fingers.

David could not help but smile. "Hello, Father. It is indeed I."

The intense emotions evoked by his son's unexpected return were just too overwhelming for the father, and he burst into uncontrollable sobs. Stepping down to the street level, he embraced David in a powerful hug, while David hugged him back with equal fervour.

To his embarrassment, David's own eyes began to well with tears, before he painfully extracted himself from the embrace. Turning to look at Hanna, he saw that she, too, had a flood of tears streaming down her cheeks. "Father," he proclaimed, "I want to introduce you to my wife, Hanna."

"Your wife?" Jacob exclaimed. "You are married, my son? Praise the Lord God Almighty!" Jacob immediately gave Hanna one of his all-enveloping hugs.

"We have married just four days ago, Father," David tried to explain, but the old man was beyond listening.

"I have a daughter? I have a daughter!" Jacob was almost beside himself. "Helena!" he boomed through the open door, "Where are you? Come here at once, come here. David has returned."

After a wild scurry at the front door, Helena emerged into the daylight, looking somewhat flustered. Peering from behind her were several children, all inquisitive about the commotion, anxious to find out what had disturbed their playtime.

"David?" Helena looked at him in shock, "Heavens above, I would never have recognised you. Look at you! Give me a hug," she demanded.

Hanna was thus duly introduced to the family with a great deal of fanfare, and David was just as delighted to be re-introduced to his youngest sister, Sally. David found it difficult to believe that his baby sister – only three years old when he had left – was almost an adult woman in the Jewish tradition, soon to approach her Bat Mitzvah or rite of passage. He could not keep his eyes off her. She had grown into a truly beautiful young woman since he had left for southern Africa.

David did not recognise Helena either, who, when he had left, had been a thin waif of a woman; shy, insecure, and half starved. Now she was rather attractive, a glossy sheen having been woven into her long, raven hair, a glow in her cheeks, and a very shapely body.

Once inside the house, and normality having begun to prevail, David and Hanna were introduced to the new additions of the family, Helena's children: Rachel, Paddy, Ernest, Tillie, and Lillie. Hanna was quick to notice that Helena was with child again, confirmed by Helena gently caressing one side of her stomach with a knowing smile. The two ladies took to each other exceptionally well, and pottered about in the kitchen, chatting and laughing like young girls. It gave David a welcome opportunity to have a quick personal talk with his father. With all the excitement of the reunion, though, nothing much of any substance was discussed, which pleased David. As the ladies were pouring the tea –

which duly released a cacophony of chatter, laughter, and crying infants that reverberated off the lounge walls – Bloomy and her husband Bernard arrived.

Bloomy's reunion with her brother brought yet another cloudburst of tears. Bloomy had also produced another child, whom she called Thida, since Morris had last seen her, and was seemingly pregnant yet again.

"When will you stop having children?" David joked, casting a look at her bulging stomach. "I'm not used to seeing my sister in this way."

"Never!" Bloomy responded with a laugh before skilfully turning the joke on David. "As long as I can have children, I shall. I love children. What about you, my brother? Come along, hurry up,"

David glanced at Hanna, blushing profusely. "We've only been married four days, Bloomy!" he objected.

Dinner under Jacob and Helena's roof that evening was a joyous event, with many a tale being told. David related how he and Morris had landed in Port Elizabeth and had begun their business by making cigarettes by day and selling them by night in the Grand Hotel, which became their unofficial office. The sale of their business to the American Tobacco Corporation one year later had left them flush with cash, and in a position to start a trading company in Matabeleland, to the north of the Transvaal Republic.

David had also told the tale of how the brothers had walked for three months through the African bush to get to KoBulawayo, as it had then been known, and how war had erupted almost as soon as they had arrived. He described how the Matabele King Lobengula had fled from the British South African Company, known as the BSAC, and how the king had burnt his royal village to the ground in retreat, which had then become the site of the new settlement, afterwards simply called "Bulawayo", and how the land conceded to the BSAC by the Crown had then become known as "Rhodesia", named after the wealthy diamond magnate and Cape Colony Premier, Cecil John Rhodes.

In the process of hunting down the fleeing king, however a pursuing party called the "Alan Wilson Patrol", had been attacked by the king's rearguard. All but two men had made it out alive, and the king's whereabouts remained a mystery to that very day.

Still more stories, about the rinderpest plague and how they had lost their wagons in the bush, really caught the family's attention, though. David quickly realised that Morris had not told them about that incident, which – owing to Morris' short temper and his ability to quickly offend people – had nearly made them bankrupt.

At one stage they had possessed barely enough money among the four brothers to buy a meal. While relaying the story, David made light of the matter, glossing over how Morris had sent Daluxolo scampering back to the stranded wagons without ascertaining first where they had been located.

Because of his father's strong religious faith, David refrained from describing the mysterious African customs and beliefs which had ended up having a direct bearing on how he had found Nkosazana, who subsequently had led him to their lost wagons. David was prepared, however, to go into great detail about the recovery exercise; the price increases that had occurred while the wagons were lost; and how they had made a very healthy profit once the wagons had been discovered, and their contents were able to be sold.

Holding his rapt audience enthralled, David briefly talked about the time he and Louis had been caught up in the Siege of Mafeking for almost three months, and it was at this point that Hanna joined in the conversation.

Hanna related how she had been beside herself with worry when David had appeared to have been lost and unreachable, to be followed by worse news after the Boer War had broken out. For three months she had worried herself sick, and – after David and Louis had escaped and returned, he had been malnourished, as thin as a rake, and a total wreck. She had taken more than a month to feed and nurse him back to a reasonably healthy state. David tried to object that he was never that thin or affected by the siege, but Hanna would have none of it, and this further development of the story continued to horrify the family.

News about Louis and Harry, however, was very welcome, and David took time to expound the younger men's fascinating ability in adapting to social and business situations, and how the Langbourne name – thanks to all his brothers – had become one well recognised and respected throughout the community.

"Louis is currently in Johannesburg," David continued, "where we are expanding our operation. We have a silent partner and personal friend there too, in Danie Coetzee, a wonderful gentleman. He helps with the administrative side, leaving Louis to concentrate on growing the business. Morris procured a massive amount of stock from suppliers and agents he has signed up from all over England, Paris and Hong Kong…"

"Hong Kong? Morris has done that since his return?" Jacob interrupted, fascinated by what he was hearing.

"Yes, Morris doesn't waste any time. The friend that you introduced him to – Mr Yoni Goldberg – has been a godsend for Morris, and our company. He is quite taken with Morris and his business acumen. I dare say you had a lot to do with that, Father," said David, nodding and smiling in the older man's direction.

"Well, I did teach you boys well, but then Morris is also unusually smart."

"Oh yes," David was suddenly serious, "I could tell you a few stories about Morris and what he has achieved, and how he has outsmarted the most educated and qualified businessmen. Make no error, Father, Morris is brilliant, without a doubt the smartest man I know – apart from you, that is … " and he laughed.

Jacob laughed, too, though he knew that his eldest son was in a very different league to himself, even if compared to his former days when he was a successful and well-respected businessman in Poland – before they had had to leave their home and country, and before his Esther had passed away.

"Harry is looking after our two shops in Bulawayo," David continued, "and I can tell you he is doing an excellent job; you would be well pleased with him, Father. Harry has some unusual habits of his own; he has a way of communicating with us brothers without talking, his eyes are that expressive, and he has a specific click of the tongue that, in a particular circumstance, speaks volumes to us. Although customers and the general public like him, he does have a way of making them nervous – just enough, though, to keep them on their toes. Harry has a strange sarcasm that many people just don't seem to understand."

David turned to one of his sisters. "Sally," he said, "Harry misses you immensely. You are his favourite, without a doubt."

"Does he?" Sally beamed. "Well, he does write to me about twice a year."

"So, will you be returning to Africa, my son?" Jacob asked, with some trepidation in his voice.

"Yes, Father. We will spend a few days here in Ireland before going to Paris for a month on our honeymoon," he looked at Hanna and smiled, "and then we will return to Bulawayo. It is where I belong now, thanks to our successful business. With Harry in Bulawayo, Louis in Johannesburg, and Morris' intention to re-open our office in East London or Port Elizabeth, I will be expected there. Louis, Harry and I have purchased land in the suburbs of Bulawayo where we will build ourselves houses to live in. It may be that we will have to sell them in the end, if we become too mobile."

At this, Helena posed a question of her own. "Do you know that Morris bought the old farm he worked on before he left?"

David chuckled. "Yes, we did hear about that. He purchased it in a most unorthodox manner, but that's another story. I never thought we would own a farm. Morris is a very unpredictable person. I hear he contracted Elaine, the lady who had also worked there, as the manager. I plan to go out tomorrow with Hanna and have a look around. Morris wants me to report back to him."

"She is doing very well, it seems," Jacob smiled. "We see her about once a month. We like her very much, and she brings us fresh produce from the farm; potatoes, vegetables and eggs usually."

"I have made a good friend of her," Bloomy announced proudly.

David looked thoroughly pleased with the news. "Splendid!" he exclaimed, before standing up. "Well, it is getting late, my dear family, and we must return to the Fitzwilliam."

With copious farewells, punctuated with happy laughter, a thoroughly enjoyable evening came to an end.

As there was a fair amount of rain about the next morning, David hired a fully enclosed coach to take him and his lovely bride to the outskirts of Dublin in order to visit the old farm that had, by a most peculiar set of circumstances entirely orchestrated by Morris, fallen into the ownership of Langbourne Coetzee (London). Using some of his smart tactics and his powers of persuasion, Morris had managed to wrestle the ownership of the farm out of the clutches of a corrupt ex-policeman for the tidy sum of £100 and six bottles of whiskey. Morris had had a great deal of fun setting up the one-sided negotiation with the miserable man and had not thought that he would be able to pull it off. But he had, and he had been very quick to tell David what he had done over dinner in London one evening.

When the coach entered the gates of the farm, David saw Elaine standing by the big barn where the original owner, a Mr O'Connor, had met his untimely end. For a moment he didn't recognise her, because, like Bloomy and Helena, she had been perilously thin and undernourished when he had last seen her. She had filled out well, and farm life seemed to do her proud. On her hips, she carried two infants that looked to be less than one year old, while in a field of potatoes barely one hundred yards away, a man worked hard at the soil.

With David holding her hand firmly to prevent her from tripping, Hanna stepped gracefully to the ground when the coach came to a standstill. Elaine stared intently at David for a short while before she began to smile in recognition of his facial features.

"Good morrow to yer, Mr David," she beamed happily. "'Tis entirely a blessing to be seeing you again."

"Hello Miss Witton," David responded with a Cheshire catlike grin of his own. "Indeed, how wonderful to see you, too. Allow me to introduce my wife, Hanna. We were married a mere five days ago." David couldn't let that special piece of information pass by.

"My congratulations," Elaine smiled, "and pleased are we all to make your acquaintance, Mrs Langbourne," Elaine said as she bestowed upon Hanna a short curtsy.

Of course, this was the first time – apart from in the synagogue on their wedding day – that someone had called Hanna by her new surname, and it felt good to hear. She quickly flashed a pleasant smile at Elaine. "Why, thank you. And who may these young lasses be?" she asked, turning all their attention to the babies.

Elaine hoisted her children a little higher on her hips in response. "These are my twin daughters," she proudly proclaimed, "Amanda and Fiona. She nodded in the direction of the man in the field, who had placed his hoe on the ground and was busy making his way to greet the new arrivals. "I've been married to yonder Adam for just over a year now, so I am now officially to be called 'Mrs O'Grady'."

"Our congratulations to you," David responded. "Morris asked me to send you his regards. He speaks very highly of you."

"Oh, I think the world of him. He has changed my life completely, that is for sure," said Elaine, just as Adam arrived at the gathering. "Adam, this is Mr David Langbourne and his wife, Mrs Langbourne."

"Ahh," Adam exclaimed. "We are mighty pleased to welcome you to the farm, indeed, sir. I'd shake your hand, but I'm totally covered in this precious mud from the field."

David didn't hesitate and immediately reached for Adam's hand, and shook it firmly. "I have spent years of my life covered in mud," he grinned. "A bit of dirt has never done anyone any harm."

Adam laughed heartily. "Well, it's then certainly very good to meet you, sir."

"Mr David is the brother of Mr Morris and is the one brother who can read very well, wouldn't you know?" Elaine smiled, causing David to blush slightly.

The day David met Elaine was the day he distracted her by reading to her so that Morris could extract O'Connor's hidden treasure from his library books. He had hoped to forget that day because he wasn't altogether sure if what they had done had been legal or not.

He had been further concerned that they had not left any money for Elaine, although they had tried to fake a will in her favour. If it hadn't been for the nefarious antics of a corrupt policeman, the scheme might well have worked. In the end, Morris' deception of the former cop had finally placed the farm legally into their company's books, and as a result, it had become a place for Elaine to live, a home for her. Morris had been the one to decide on Elaine's employment with the added condition that she receive an equal share in any future sale of the property.

Although feeling a little uncomfortable with the morality of the games Morris had played, David had placed the entire matter behind him because, in fact, it had probably achieved the best outcome from a bad situation.

"I know Mr Morris very well," said Adam. "We worked together before O'Connor got smacked on the head by the barn door and died."

"Yes, he did tell me the story," David said, then quickly changed the subject as he cast his eye over the property. "The farm is now profitable, I hear."

"Do come in," Elaine insisted. "Have a cuppa tea with us, and I will tell you all about it. You can wash that all-too precious mud off your hands while you're about it, too" she smiled, winking at David.

"We'd be delighted, thank you," said Hanna, accepting the invitation on the couple's behalf instantly. "I dare say I could use a cup of tea. The Langbourne family send their best to you, by the by, and thank you for the vegetables you provided last week. Here, let me hold Amanda for you. How adorable your girls are…!"

The women chatted freely as they all walked towards the homestead with Adam. David waited a moment to give them a head start while he took a good look at what lay around him.

"I can't believe we own this farm now," he mumbled to himself. "What will my crazy brother do next?"

No doubt, David would find out soon enough.

CHAPTER FOUR

Johannesburg – 1900

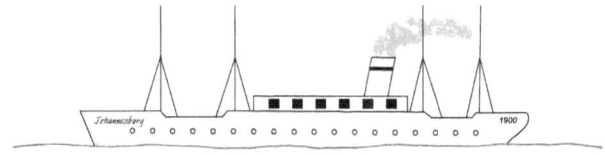

Louis Langbourne strode briskly in the gathering dark towards the entrance of the Johannesburg Club. Due to meet Danie Coetzee at six o'clock sharp, he was already about two minutes behind schedule, but sighed with relief when he realised that he had arrived ahead of Danie. Straightening his evening suit and adjusting his necktie, he stood expectantly at the large wooden doors, looking left and right as he waited for his family's business partner.

Although really a business partner in name only, Danie was an established friend of Morris and David's. He had been quite happy, therefore, to agree to sit on the Langbourne Brothers' Board of Directors. In return for imparting his knowledge in business, Danie had further agreed that they might use his name on their letterhead and company correspondence. In essence, this was a business tactic that Morris had devised when he felt that the strained relations between the British and the Boer governments would likely deteriorate into war. "Coetzee" was a well-known name from both republics, while "Langbourne" was obviously British in origin. Morris had the bright idea that, by placing the two names in close association, it might allay many sensitive feelings, no matter who won the predictable war between the opposing armies. Of course, Morris had contracted to pay Danie handsomely for his professional services.

On the other hand, David privately took their reasoning one step further. He knew that the tempers of certain family members, particularly Morris and Harry, were short and volatile, so he wanted someone outside the family to act as a respected arbitrator in the event of a dispute. Thankfully, however, that had not been necessary up to that point.

The name of "Langbourne Coetzee", therefore, had been well established in Johannesburg and London a few years after the original business "Langbourne Brothers" had been formed in Port Elizabeth and Bulawayo. Being the eldest brother and founder along with David, Morris Langbourne had been recognised and accepted by all four brothers as the natural head of the family in place of their father, Jacob. Morris had long taken exception to his father's inability to look for permanent employment when they had been young boys, during which time he had plunged them all into poverty and starvation. Although the brothers still loved their father out of a traditional sense of respect and family values, Morris had nevertheless assumed the lead role in the family, without making any demands, and had been accepted without question by all the siblings.

Yet Morris had not expected his father to remarry after his first wife had passed away from a long illness, and his father's marriage to his wife's niece, who was barely a year or two older than Morris himself, had irked him even more. Morris had later reluctantly accepted this new dynamic in the family, but when the children had subsequently begun to appear, in reasonably large numbers to boot, he had drawn a firm line.

Morris had made it quite clear to his three brothers – David, Louis and Harry – that he and David had risked life and limb in southern Africa to get to where they were, and that the "Langbourne Brothers" indicated exactly what the company name suggested – for the benefit of the brothers. Only the four of them would have access to ownership and equitable shares in the profits and losses of their business ventures, and that their full-blooded sisters would be cared for as necessary. He had conceded, however, that he would be happy to employ his half-siblings, provided they were able to bring some sort of value to the business.

Louis' thoughts were momentarily disturbed by Danie's arrival.

"Sorry I'm late," said Danie.

"No need to apologise, Danie. I, too, was late; I have just arrived."

"Shall we?" Danie gestured as a doorman swung the heavy doors open for them.

Louis stepped back slightly, waving his arm politely towards the door. "By all means, lead the way."

Since it had grown in stature as an extraordinarily opulent product of the gold-mining elites, the Johannesburg Club attracted only the highest class of gentlemen in town. Captains of industry and commerce rubbed shoulders together, exchanging pleasantries or conducting business deals, while some secretly plotted a political advantage. It was the kind of environment that David had trained Louis to excel in, and the younger brother had quickly become comfortable in such high-society circles. He had mastered some essential ways to introduce himself into a conversation, or – without loss of face – be able to excuse himself if he felt the body language indicated that he was not welcome in that particular group.

Although Danie was a long-standing member of the Club, Louis had not yet been invited and thus was obliged to be accompanied by a member of good standing.

"Has your application been accepted yet?" Danie asked Louis under a hoarse whisper after he had ordered two whiskeys from the bar.

"Not yet, Danie. Your proposal received the required second nominations, and it was put before the Membership Committee this morning, I believe. My only concern is my age. At nineteen years old, I might be considered too young for this club."

"Nonsense. The committee regards my proposals very seriously. Come with me," Danie said, as he handed Louis a glass of the amber liquid. "Mr Anderson over there is on the Committee. He is a colleague of mine and is bound to tell us how the vote went."

The two men walked through the hubbub of conversation and cigarette smoke to a distinguished middle-aged man, already quite bald. When he saw Danie, he greeted him warmly with a sturdy handshake and was promptly introduced to Louis.

"Young Mr Langbourne here has submitted an application to the Club,"

Danie raised his glass towards Louis in salutation, "A first-class gentleman; I was his proposer, and I know his family very well."

"Ahh...," Mr Anderson smiled broadly, "I saw your application this afternoon. You are the gentleman in question, are you?"

"Indeed I am, sir," Louis said humbly.

"Well," Anderson nudged Danie in the ribs jokingly, "we were not too sure of this fellow. What are you drinking there, Mr Langbourne?"

Louis decided to play along with the humour, the dig in Danie's ribs had already told him his application had been successful. "Whiskey is my choice of spirit. Only the best though."

"An excellent answer, sir, and in that case, I am quite happy to tell you – in confidence, of course – that your application was accepted earlier this afternoon."

The three men laughed quite loudly at this, while Louis thanked Mr Anderson wholeheartedly for welcoming him into what was then considered the most prestigious club in Johannesburg. As the evening wore on, Danie introduced Louis to many of the outstanding leaders in manufacturing and commerce. Two of the members happened to be hoteliers, and – by the manner they were talking – Louis began to believe that the hotel sector was poised to become a massive regional industry, just waiting to explode.

One gentleman, who introduced himself as a Mr John Hart, had a company that made acetylene lamps for the mining industry, but also a small sideline of domestic and commercial kitchenware. His dilemma was that he could not keep up with the demand in variety of kitchenware - his factory was limited in what it could manufacture; quantity was not a problem - diversity was. Louis suggested that his company should import kitchen equipment to add to his product offering and that his family business was in a position to do this for him. Mr Hart was delighted with Louis' suggestion, a solution to his pressing problem, and immediately invited Louis to lunch the next day to discuss it further.

It didn't take long for Louis to realise that Langbourne Coetzee could easily become one of the most essential suppliers to the hospitality and catering industry over time.

At one stage, Louis looked around the room to find Danie, deeply engrossed in conversation with a tall and rather distinguished-looking man. For a moment, Louis caught Danie's eye, and raised his glass towards him ever so slightly, mouthing the words "Thank you".

Danie nodded back candidly, knowing that Louis was in his element, which was precisely what Morris would have wanted. Langbourne Coetzee was fast becoming one of the most respected companies in Johannesburg.

CHAPTER FIVE
Bulawayo - 1900

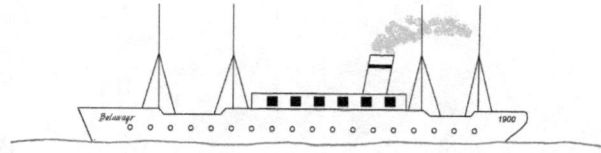

"Morning, Mr Langbourne," Brian Loxton called out cheerfully as Harry walked into the store.

Harry returned the greeting somewhat more seriously, as was his way. "Good morning, Mr Loxton. I see that you enjoyed a reasonable day of trade yesterday."

Although rather pleased with the previous day's results, Harry found it rarely necessary to appear happy or jovial. Brian, on the other hand, understood well by that time, his boss's usual traits. Thus utterly ignoring Harry's adamantine tone, he continued to maintain an appearance of confidence.

"It was a good day for us indeed, Mr Langbourne, and I expect a better day today. The manager of the Maxim Hotel has given me his solemn assurance that he will be visiting to replace much of their dining and kitchen breakages."

"Good, good..." Harry repeated, seeming somehow lost in thought.

"If I may, Mr Langbourne," Loxton continued, "our crockery and cutlery line appears to be gaining great popularity amongst the hospitality trade, and I fear we will run short of stock fairly soon. Any chance…?"

"Indeed…" Harry mumbled, cutting Loxton off mid-sentence. "I have already sent a telegram to our purchasing office in London to address this dilemma."

"Thank you, sir. In a way of sorts, a good dilemma to have," Brian thanked his young boss with a generous smile, and discreetly took his leave, heading for the rear of the store.

Harry was delighted with Mr Loxton's performance, but he didn't like to show it – much. While very perceptive of his customer's needs and their buying trends, Loxton was also well-liked by those customers who he took great pride and effort in knowing personally, thus ensuring repeat business for the company. Although Harry might be civil towards Loxton, congratulate him from time to time, and involve him alone in some private business discussions, he would not share a joke or discuss anything personal. Business, to Harry, was business. His personal life was concentrated exclusively on his brothers and his family in Ireland. Outside of that circle, everything was business.

Harry tugged on his jacket sleeve. "Mrs Collier," he nodded a greeting to their bookkeeper.

"Good morning to you, Mr Langbourne. I trust that you are quite well."

"Indeed, I am, thank you. And I trust that the weekly reconciliation will be on my desk this afternoon, as usual?"

"Yes, Mr Langbourne, already done by the Grace of God, and you may rest assured that I will deliver it exactly as you requested."

An Irish lady with a solid accent, Ivy Collier had been employed more recently as the Langbourne Brothers' company bookkeeper. Although it was in her very nature to find a joke or laugh at just about anything, she knew her saucy brand of humour did not go down too well with Harry. She, therefore, toned down her quips to just above the temperature where Harry would permit a sly smile to creep onto his face, but no more. Being much older than Harry, who was only eighteen at the time, she had gained many life experiences and knew how to handle him.

"I must be as bold as to say, however, Mr Langbourne," Ivy quipped with a playful frown, "that I did manage to drop that horribly giant ledger on my toe yesterday,"

Harry suddenly looked concerned. "Oh dear..."

"A most un...pleasant experience I ought to say," she continued, dragging out the word 'unpleasant', "but I'm further pleased to report on my church's honour that the good ledger survived the terrible ordeal."

Harry couldn't help but let a chuckle escape. He did like Mrs Collier, and her work was exceptional. "As long as you didn't hurt yourself."

"Not at all, Mr Langbourne. Only the good die young, as the popular saying goes, and by that impeccable logic, it follows that I will continue to live to a very ripe old age."

The morning ritual usually began in this vein. After a brief exchange with Mr Loxton and a modest chuckle with Mrs Collier, Harry would wander through the store on Fife Street, scowling and mumbling to himself, while his staff watched in silence. He would then saunter down to the warehouse on Abercorn Street and discuss the various aspects of the previous day with his manager, Michael Johnson. Harry was always interested in how the wagon trading was coming along, which trader had returned, what they had bought, and, more importantly, what they had failed to sell on their last outing.

Harry would then stroll about the warehouse, examining the stock reserves, and continually mumbling and grumbling. He would stop at the cash register and rummage through the coins, notes, and the new Marshall-Hole currency that they were forced to use, making a determined effort to show his displeasure at what was in the till. Even though Harry counted the money correctly, some days he would pretend to find an error and re-count the cash, sending his sales staff, and Mr Johnson, into a bit of a tizz. Finally, at one minute to eight o'clock, he would stand almost to attention at the front door, and consult his watch with a great show of importance. On the stroke of the hour, Harry would adjust his jacket and swing the big doors open.

A brand new day at Langbourne Brothers, Bulawayo, could now begin.

It was almost the lunch hour when Mr Johnson knocked lightly on Harry's office door. "A moment of your time, if you please, sir," he murmured.

"Indeed, come in," Harry welcomed his manager into his sparsely furnished office. "Take a seat."

Johnson sat on the proffered chair and leaned forward in earnest. "I have just had a fascinating chat with one of our wagon traders," he said.

"He has just returned from up north, and called into Salisbury on the way."

"Salisbury?" Harry raised an eyebrow. "That's quite a distance from here."

"Indeed, he is one of our two traders that go that far north. He said that a Mr Divaris is opening a large wholesale business in Salisbury. Now, ordinarily I wouldn't have thought much of it, but our trader didn't spend as much as I had expected him to when it came to re-stocking his wagon."

"Meaning?"

"I think he is going to sell through his stock, and when Divaris opens up for business, he will relocate there."

"I see," Harry mulled over this new information. "I would hazard a guess that Divaris won't be as competitive as we are because the distance to freight goods up to Salisbury would be prohibitive."

"Exactly my thoughts," Johnson looked very concerned, "but with the new rail line from Bulawayo to Salisbury, freight costs are actually not that bad, and the time delay is just one day. I hear, also, that there may soon be a rail connection to the ocean via the settlement called 'Umtali' in the east."

This fresh news induced Harry to bite on his lip in some concern. "Thank you, Mr Johnson. This is certainly something we must consider carefully."

Later, when Harry closed the warehouse for the day, he immediately made his way down to the Charter Hotel to see if he could find anyone he knew with whom he might share a social drink and make subtle enquiries about Salisbury. Since he was a little too early, however, the hotel lounge and bar were still quite deserted at that time. Nevertheless, as the evening wore on, some residents made their way to their favourite watering hole, one of whom was a good friend of the family, Abe Kaufman.

Abe wore a suit that evening, which he looked obviously uncomfortable in. Because he was a prospector, dressing up for an evening's outing was not his idea of comfort, and the resultant effect on his appearance spoke volumes.

"Good evening, Mr Kaufman," Harry greeted the lanky man.

Abe greeted him kindly in return. "Good evening, Harry. How's business?"

"It's alright," Harry said, with typical reserve, before skillfully directing the conversation to his present concern, "I am rather anxious to find out what is happening in Salisbury these days. It is beginning to sound quite forward-looking and I was wondering how its future direction might affect our business."

"Can't say I know much of what's going on out there," Abe said casually. "May I buy you a drink?"

"Thank you, but I'm fine."

"What news of your family? David? Morris?"

Harry knew that – although Abe was very fond of David because they had a close connection – he had always been wary of Morris and his antics. For some unexplained reason, Abe had appeared to be a little intimidated by Morris.

"David should be married by now, and Morris seems very busy in London. I don't hear much from him unless it is business orientated."

Abe chuckled, "I'm sure that's the case. Please pass my best wishes on to David when you next communicate."

"I will certainly do so. And what about you?" Harry asked, "I haven't seen you around for a while."

"I have bought a farm," Abe smiled as he retrieved his beer from the bar counter and paid some money over.

"You've bought a farm?" Harry was surprised. "I thought you were a prospector, not a farmer. Why the change?"

"A farm came up for sale in Essexvale, about twenty miles from here, bordering the rail line to South Africa. I don't intend to plant any crops but might try a few cattle. I did hear, however, that Essexvale is rich in gold so I will be prospecting as well," he winked.

"Well done," Harry congratulated him. "Which side of the railway line? I travel that route quite a bit; I will look out for it. Might even see you in the field, digging away," he teased.

"You do that," Abe chuckled in turn. "If you head out of Bulawayo, it's the farm on the left. You'll get to my boundary about five minutes before Essexvale, and the next boundary ends only 50 yards before you get to the station. Don't bother getting off, there's nothing there, and I don't even have a homestead on the property."

The babble of conversation had by that time increased in volume, while the room began to fill with tobacco smoke. Abe excused himself to chat with a fellow prospector who had come to meet him, and Harry returned to the bar. Others of Harry's acquaintance arrived; some customers, some colleagues in the retail trade, and he was quick to start engaging with them. Although the conversations that evening covered many topics, it was the subject of Salisbury, under Harry's skilful navigation, that kept bobbing up as one of the main themes.

To Harry's surprise, Mr Johnson was absolutely correct, Salisbury was indeed becoming quite a popular destination, and business – particularly in the manufacturing sector – was beginning to expand at an alarming rate. Just as Harry was starting to feel somewhat depressed at the way the conversations were going, he noticed a gentleman who owned a transport business enter the room. His name was Mr Tom Meikle, an acquaintance of Morris and David, and, from what Harry had been told, an extraordinarily successful and dynamic businessman; just the sort of person with whom Morris would sit and talk to for hours on end.

Harry re-charged his glass and made his way to the gentleman, who now stood casually against the bar counter, chatting freely to a man Harry did not recognise.

"Excuse me, sir," Harry sidled up to the men, "Mr Meikle?"

"Yes," he replied and immediately extended his hand. "You are?"

"Harry Langbourne. I believe you know my brothers."

"Yes, indeed. Of course I do. Morris and David. How are they? I believe Morris is in Ireland?"

"England... London, actually," Harry smiled, "a slight change of plan, it seems."

"Forgive me, this is Mr Haddon, a good friend of mine, Mr Langbourne," Tom Meikle introduced Harry.

"How do you do, sir?" Harry shook Mr Haddon's hand and turned back to Mr Meikle. "I'm very pleased you came in tonight. You are in the transport business, am I correct?"

"Yes, that is so," Tom agreed with a smile.

"I was involved in a fascinating conversation over there, earlier," Harry waved his glass in the direction of the group of people he had been talking to. "It seems Salisbury is becoming quite active, commercially that is, and with the new, fast train service linking us to them, do you feel it would affect your business?"

"Not at all," Tom Meikle laughed out loud, "not at all. In fact, it pleases me immensely. I see it as an excellent opportunity for the growth of my business."

Harry was surprised. This was an unexpected view of the matter. "How can that be?" he asked.

"I'll simply open a branch of my business over there. Twice the business, more than twice the profit."

This suddenly made sense to Harry and his concerns were instantly replaced with a sense of excitement. "I didn't think of it like that," Harry confessed.

"To be honest, Mr Langbourne," Tom lowered his voice and smiled, "I'm thinking of building a hotel up there. It won't be long before there are more people in Salisbury than in Bulawayo, mark my words."

"You think so?" Harry asked, but his mind was already elsewhere.

He continued to chat with his newfound friends for another twenty minutes, before politely excusing himself and re-joining the original group of men. A few other gentlemen had included themselves in the conversation, which had now reverted to discussing a cricket match being played somewhere in the Cape Province of South Africa, a town with the unusual name of Matjiesfontein, and Harry was fast losing interest in the entire evening.

"Mr Langbourne…!" Harry heard from somewhere amidst the noise and cigarette smoke. He located the speaker in the group – a short, middle-aged man with ginger hair.

"Yes?"

"Are you a member of the Bulawayo Chamber of Commerce?"

"No," Harry replied shortly. He had no intention of joining a committee that would offer him no benefit and cause him to lessen his attendance to his own business.

"Well you should be," the man insisted. "We are looking to send four members to the Salisbury Chamber of Commerce on an educational tour for a week, all expenses paid. An exchange of information and ideas, a 'look and learn' if you will, and we are short of takers. You interested?"

Harry looked at the man and proffered a pleased smile. "Indeed. How do I join?"

At the beginning of the Twentieth Century, Salisbury was a fairly nondescript town, but from Harry's standpoint at the time, it seemed to him to be bustling with activity. The centre of the town had been neatly arranged in Imperial rectangles, with streets running due north to due south, and avenues running due east to due west. Simple streets appeared also to have been named numerically, while avenues had been named after important or famous people of the recent past, such as "Rhodes", "Jameson", "Speke", and so on. Not much consistency seemed to have been used in the naming process, which Harry found both confusing and annoying.

As for the residential areas, only one main suburb was located on the northern side of town, which – with impeccable logic – ended on the northernmost avenue called "North Avenue". After that, merely open grassland could be seen, earmarked apparently for a new sports field and polo ground. Similar to the town itself, the residential suburb had been laid out in perfect rectangular blocks, its numerous avenues, again, clinging to the four main points of the compass. In keeping with the typical total abandonment of imagination the counterpart authorities had experienced when naming Bulawayo's first suburb, "Suburbs", a Salisbury council member had managed to wink at the name of their first suburb, with the singularly evocative name of "Avenues".

Harry was going to ask their guide where "Street Street", "Road Road" or "Avenue Avenue" were, but since nobody seemed to see the humour in a suburb, adorned with avenues, named "Avenues", he gave his attempt at humour a miss. A short coach ride took the group of commercial businessmen to an industrial and manufacturing area just to the west of the only hill visible for miles around. A brisk walk up the hill and the group had a majestic 360-degree view of the growing town of Salisbury.

The guide from the Chamber of Commerce swept his arm over the vista before them. "As you can see," he intoned, "the Administrators of Mashonaland took great care in designing this new town. If you look over there," he pointed into the distance, towards an area at the approximate centre of the burgeoning settlement, "you can see the flagpole flying the British Union Jack. That is where the Pioneers hoisted the flag on the day they arrived here. As you might notice, the flag is situated in a park, which is called "Cecil Square", in honour of our founder, Cecil John Rhodes. If one were to view this from above, a network of paths exists within the square, and you would notice that they form the layout or pattern of the Union Jack.

"As you can also see, Salisbury is situated on flat ground, the hill we are standing upon being the only prominent landmark for miles around. The hill is called 'The Kopje'."

"What does 'Kopje' mean?" someone asked. "A bit of an odd name for a hill, don't you think?"

I'll bet it means 'a hill', Harry thought to himself.

"It's the Dutch word for 'hill'," the guide stated proudly.

"That makes sense." Harry rolled his eyes and broke away to find some shade. He was getting hot in his dark business suit. He had not brought a hat, he was irritated by the monotonous guide, and he desperately wanted a cup of tea.

The afternoon improved slightly when lunch was served in one of the newer hotels, followed by a visit to the Club Chambers. The group was introduced to the Mayor of Salisbury, Mr van Praagh, and many other council officials. This was, at last, of some interest to Harry, and he had a lengthy and productive discussion with Mr van Praagh.

"I dare say, Mr Langbourne, we could use innovative and motivated people like you in Salisbury," the mayor exhorted. "We have certain concessions in place to make your expansion towards Salisbury less inconvenient. Make use of them, sir."

"Indeed I shall," Harry confirmed. "I will discuss this with my brothers on my return to Bulawayo. I am quite taken with the keen attitude of the people I have met in Mashonaland."

"Well, Mr Langbourne," the mayor held Harry's attention as he lit a stubby cigar and exhaled billows of smoke at the ceiling, "commerce and industry are but one aspect of your tour here. You should see the mining and agricultural sectors of the community."

Harry raised an inquisitive eyebrow. "Really?"

"Yes, indeed. They have found substantial deposits of gold, zinc, and nickel not far from Salisbury. Chromium and iron ore, too, but those are not as near. Tobacco and maize are particularly suited to our climate, and I dare say within a few years we may well have the best quality of tobacco this world has ever seen. Our farmers are most innovative. Why, just to the north of Salisbury we have an enterprising grower who is testing a crop of citrus. When that comes to fruit," van Praagh chortled, "forgive the pun, people around the world who peel an orange in the morning will be enjoying the fruits of Rhodesia at the same time."

When Harry returned to Bulawayo four days later, he was filled with the spirit of adventure, and couldn't wait to put pen to paper to inform Morris in London of what he had discovered. He also wanted to discuss his thoughts and ideas of expanding the business to Salisbury, ideas that he was confident Morris would appreciate.

17th July 1900
   Mr M. Langbourne,
   Flat 12,
   12 Finsbury Pavement,
   London

Dear Brother Morris,

   I trust you are in good health. All is well in Bulawayo, and business continues to thrive, albeit affected somewhat by the difficulties that the conflict in the south creates for us.

   I have recently been concerned at the growth in popularity of the town of Salisbury, which has been affecting our wagon-trading section. Returns have slowed down considerably, and wagon traders appear to be opting to lessen their stock purchase from our Bulawayo store. Mr Johnson believes that some of these traders are planning to move their operation to Salisbury.

   With this in mind, I have been talking to members of the community. Your acquaintance, Mr Tom Meikle (who extends his regards to you, by the way), believes that he may open another branch of his transport business there. He also plans to build a hotel with his brother in Salisbury, so confident is he of the town's future prosperity.

   On a recent visit to Salisbury, compliments of the Bulawayo Chamber of Commerce, I had the opportunity to do a comprehensive study of the town, and indeed, it looks as though they do have the wherewithal to supersede Bulawayo's trading capacity. Agriculture and mining are rather progressive there, too. Having met with the mayor, he also encouraged us to open a branch there, with certain concessions included if we do.

   I am of the opinion that we should seriously investigate the option of opening another branch of Langbourne Brothers in Salisbury, specifically to support our wagon traders, and, with your blessing, would be amenable to conduct such an investigation.

   I await your shipment from Louis with anticipation as our stock levels are depleting rapidly. I expect the shipment to arrive any day now. Louis is in constant contact with me, and I believe he is doing well in Johannesburg.

On a personal front, I trust David arrived in London safely, and I ask that you pass my regards to him and Hanna when you see them.

Please advise soonest regarding the possible expansion to Salisbury,

Fondly yours,

Harry.

Harry re-read his letter while he waited for the ink to dry, then, taking great care to fold it so that all the corners lined up perfectly, he placed the folded page in an envelope and addressed it to his brother in London.

He was pleased with both the letter and himself as his mind raced to work out the logistics of running two shops, one in Bulawayo and one in Salisbury. It would not be easy, but with David's help, it would be entirely possible. He was also satisfied that he had found a way of averting the looming disaster of their wagon trading arm to the aggressive intentions of the town to the north. In fact, he had turned a negative situation into a very positive one, and he was sure his brothers would give him much credit for his foresight.

CHAPTER SIX

Paris - 1900

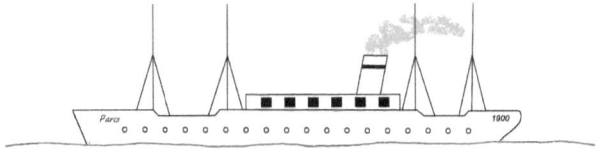

Hanna lovingly squeezed her new husband's arm. "David," she sighed, "do we really have to leave so soon? What a perfect place to spend our honeymoon! We truly have been blessed."

The young couple stood on a quaint bridge overlooking the River Seine, admiring the landscape of this eternally romantic town. The Eiffel Tower stood before them in all its majestic glory, casting an ever-watchful eye over the citizens of Paris.

David smiled at Hanna. "We have Morris to thank for this suggestion," he responded, "and it has been a wonderful trip even with the necessity of including a day or two for business."

"Oh, I think we can forgive him, just this once," she giggled. "After all, Monsieur Paul Follot and his family were so hospitable and generous they were a pleasure to spend time with. I must also admit that I really did enjoy shopping in that huge departmental store while you were talking to the manager."

"Le Bon Marche," David mulled as he stared out at the iron-latticed tower not far away. "It was actually quite fascinating, come to think of it. They really do know how to make their merchandise attractive. I thought we were quite successful in making our customers feel wanted and needed, but they have certainly come up trumps on that one. A good lesson for me, that was."

It was their last day in the fashionable city, and – after spending an entire month enjoying its monuments, churches, museums, and art galleries; its fine restaurants, street-side cafes and culinary delights – they were not at all smitten on returning to the grey sobriety of London. The thought of embarking on a lengthy return journey to southern Africa failed to spark much enthusiasm either.

With a great deal of reluctance, therefore, the young couple made their way back to their stylish hotel to pack their trunks and prepare for their departure the following morning. The next day dawned suitably grey and dismal with a wind that howled around them. The crossing of the channel was most unpleasant.

Hanna was the first to experience motion sickness. Feeling positively queasy, she stood on the deck, holding the rail with white knuckles, while staring into the far distance. Her flowing white dress whipped around her in the wind, but she didn't care one fig. Having experienced seasickness of his own on his maiden voyage to southern Africa, David was all too aware of how Hanna must have been feeling. He tried holding her by the waist, while at the same time trying to bring her skirts under control. All in all, he was able to offer little comfort to her predicament.

"I feel absolutely ghastly," Hanna complained, as she stared fixedly at the horizon.

"Don't worry, my lovely," David murmured, trying hopelessly to soothe her discomfort. "We should be on solid ground before dark, and the feeling will pass once you step onto the land."

"Before dark?" Hanna wailed, and then, throwing all dignity to the wind, she leant over the rail and heaved the contents of her stomach into the ocean.

"It's alright, Hanna, you will feel a lot better now," David tried to reassure his bride.

As yet another wave of nausea washed over her, Hanna hung over the rail and heaved uncontrollably. Unsure of what to do for his suffering wife, David was suddenly joined by a mixture of well-dressed ladies and gentlemen who all rushed for the rail, leaned over, and cast their dignity into the sea. This was too much for David, who – already fighting with billowing skirts and an uncontrollable necktie that had escaped his buttoned jacket – unceremoniously pushed Hanna to the side to lean over the railing and join the bilious choir.

The journey was merciless; some passengers not even making it to the railings in time, retching up their earlier meals onto the deck. As the ship entered the harbour and normality began to prevail, however, the passengers started to move normally about once again, taking stock of their state of dress and presentation. David sat slumped on a bench and thanked his Lord for getting them to England safely. He looked at Hanna, who sat beside him, the back of her head resting against the wall with her eyes closed, seemingly in prayer. She was soaked through from the sea spray, her usually flowing hair pasted against her head and neck. The makeup that she had carefully applied before departing the hotel had smeared down her cheeks.

Suppressing his natural inclination to laugh, David attempted to make light of the situation. "Well, at least you are squeaky clean," he grinned

"That's not even funny, David," Hanna said as she lifted her head from the wall and gave him an icy stare through lowered lids.

"There'll be a hotel along the shoreline," he soothed. "We'll check in and spend the night. We can't travel to London in this state."

"Really?" Hanna said sarcastically, tilting her head back and closing her eyes again, utterly disgusted by the entire journey.

David turned his attention to a sailor who was busy belaying a stout rope. Accidentally, he bumped the foot of a bedraggled man who was sitting next to him on the deck.

"I beg your pardon, sir, you alright there?" the sailor asked apologetically.

David watched as the man begrudgingly shifted his position.

"That journey was shocking," the passenger grumbled.

"Yes, not pleasant, I must agree," the sailor replied, "but not the worst I have made."

"I have to make this trip again next week. Is there anything one can do to avoid this seasickness?"

"Yes, there is!" the sailor exclaimed excitedly, drawing David's attention immediately. "Just have toast and strawberry jam for breakfast before you board the ship. Thick toast with lots of strawberry jam. Put as much jam on the toast as you can. It must dribble down the sides of the crust, it must."

"That will help?" the passenger asked, somewhat curious.

"Nah," the sailor exclaimed, "it won't make any difference at all, but it will taste a lot better when it comes up." He then walked off, laughing raucously.

David started to chuckle and cast a glance at Hanna, but she was staring at him with such venom that he merely cleared his throat and looked to the approaching shoreline with a severe frown creasing his forehead.

"Tea is served," Rose Bertha almost sang out as she placed a silver tea service on the lounge table.

Morris and David were deeply engrossed in their business conversation next to the window that overlooked Finsbury Pavement, but stopped talking immediately and smiled at the cheerful young lady.

"Perfect timing!" Morris exclaimed in delight.

Hanna appeared right behind Rose Bertha, carrying a plate that was positively overflowing with shortbread, the aroma of which had been playing havoc with the brothers' appetites for the last half hour.

"Fresh out of the oven, and made from my mother's own recipe," Hanna proudly announced. "I hear from reliable sources that shortbread is your most favourite thing in the world, Morris."

"David, you are letting out my secrets," Morris jokingly scolded his brother.

"It's no secret, Morris," David laughed. "From Mafeking to Bulawayo, everyone knows that shortbread is the weak spot of Morris Langbourne."

David and Hanna had returned from their honeymoon three days before and had been staying at the behest of Morris in the guest room of 12 Finsbury Pavement. As was quickly becoming the norm, Rose Bertha would arrive in the morning and spend the whole day with them, especially enjoying Hanna's company, before Morris would escort Rose back to her parents' home after the evening meal.

During the day, Morris and David would spend countless hours discussing business plans between short excursions around London, while the ladies shopped or enjoyed the culture of the modern city. Morris was relishing his brother's company, and more particularly, hosting the newlyweds in his flat. David got the feeling that Morris needed this family diversion as he seemed to soften towards Rose Bertha somewhat and even enjoyed a bit of humour.

When they had all settled down in the lounge, and Rose Bertha had poured the tea, Hanna passed the shortbread around, continuing to joke with Morris and David. She was thoroughly enjoying her time with her future sister-in-law.

"You're not going to have any shortbread, Hanna?" Rose Bertha asked with a frown. "After all the effort to make it?"

"No, I'm afraid I haven't quite got over that journey across the channel, and the remnants of the sea sickness have not left me fully yet."

"My, it must have been a very rough journey. We go over to France at least twice a year, and I have never had a problem with the crossing."

"It was rough," David said. "We experienced something almost as bad when Morris and I went to southern Africa in 1891, but this was far worse."

"Worse than our journey?" Morris raised an eyebrow. "Well, I'll be…. I can't say that was very pleasant. I was ill for almost a week."

After their morning tea, the boys adjourned to the window to "talk business", as Morris liked to call it, while the ladies returned to the kitchen to tidy up.

"Hanna," Rose Bertha spoke quietly, "I noticed you didn't eat much dinner last night. Usually, seasickness will leave you after a few hours and a good sleep."

"Oh, Rosie, you have no idea how bad that crossing was. I thought I would die twice, once from the sickness, and once from the treacherous waves. I'm not at all surprised I'm still trying to find my sea legs."

"I don't think it was just the voyage that has made you ill," Rose Bertha said with a wry smile.

"Really?" Hanna asked. "And what makes you think that?"

"Is it not six weeks since you and David got married?"

"So?" Hanna laughed, "Do you think I am lovesick?"

Rose Bertha grinned mischievously. "In a manner of speaking…" she murmured.

Hanna first looked at her blankly, before a look of horror crept over her face. "No, surely not..." she said, quickly covering her mouth with her hand.

"Yes, but why not indeed? I think you are with child, my dear Hanna." Rose Bertha was now grinning widely.

The ladies were interrupted by a sharp knock at the door, and Rose Bertha immediately went to see who it was. Standing to attention was a postman at the door in a smart uniform and a cap which he immediately tipped when the door was opened.

"A letter for you, mar'm," the postman barked.

"Thank you kindly, sir." Rose unconsciously gave a barely discernible curtsy as she took the envelope from the postman and closed the door behind her. She then took the letter directly to Morris.

"A letter from Rhodesia for you, my darling," she beamed. She knew it would make Morris very happy to hear from his brothers overseas.

"Excellent, thank you." Morris took the envelope and quickly tore it open as Rose Bertha returned to the kitchen, and to her secret ladies' talk with Hanna.

"What does it say?" David asked impatiently.

"Hmm... from Badger." Morris almost grunted. "He says..."

'Badger' was Harry's code-name. The brothers only used it between themselves, and in telegrams (which in those days could be read by just about anyone). It was a tactic that Morris had devised and insisted upon to keep their business matters private and confidential. Over time, their code system had become second nature to the brothers, being used almost daily in their various communications. It also had the effect of making the brothers feel exclusive, by having their own language that no-one else could understand.

Morris became lost in thought as he read the contents, forgetting that David was standing right beside him, impatience eating away at him.

"And?" David couldn't contain his curiosity.

"Seems that Salisbury..." Morris broke off again.

David decided to wait for Morris to finish reading the letter because he knew that he would get nowhere until Morris had done so. He reached instead for a piece of shortbread and popped it into his mouth.

"Hmm..." Morris looked up from the letter, then passed it to David. "What do you think of that?"

David took the letter and read it quickly. By the time he had finished,

Morris had taken a seat at his desk, which prompted David to pull up a chair and sit opposite his brother.

"Interesting…" David said, passing the letter back to Morris who read it once more.

"Seems like our wagon-trading arm is threatened," Morris muttered and tossed the letter onto the desktop.

"But Badger has found a solution. I must admit he is quick to act when he needs to," David smiled.

"Yes…" Morris agreed, hesitantly, "he misses the point entirely, though."

"Really?" David was surprised. He always thought that both Harry's actions and his reasoning were always first class.

"Wagon traders only make up a small part of our business now when compared to the warehouse and retail store on Fife." Morris waved a dismissive hand in the air. "No," he said, "let them go I don't want to compete amongst other wagon-trade suppliers. If we do, we will have to buy or build a huge warehouse in Salisbury and staff it and stock it. It will cost a fortune just to compete for pennies in the wagon-trade market."

"But, we do make a good profit out of the wagon-trading arm," David objected.

"David, David, David," Morris said condescendingly, raising his hands in the air, "look at the big picture. You are addressing this problem like Badger, without really thinking it through."

David was about to protest but realised it would be in vain. He knew that what his brother was about to tell him would be unorthodox, to say the least, so he decided to hear the man out instead. "So, Morris,' he said quietly, "how do you see this… this big picture, then?"

"Sell the wagons as soon as possible, get out of the business of course."

"Go on," David leant back in his seat and crossed his legs.

"Right," Morris spun Harry's letter around with two fingers and jabbed his index finger at the word "Salisbury".

"This town has found mineral wealth," he continued, "and the climate for agriculture seems to be perfect for it. If they have good agriculture, they must have good water reserves, too. Badger is right, people will flock there. It is geographically much further away from all the hostilities and political misery of the South African republics, so people will feel safer, again drawing them to Salisbury.

"Wagon traders will begin to gravitate there, because the population will grow, both in the settlement and in the outlying areas. Mr Johnson and Badger have already noticed this; it has begun.

"Salisbury, in my opinion, will become much more significant than Bulawayo. If you remember, we intended to go to Fort Salisbury, as it was known back then, but after walking through the bush for three months, only to arrive in Bulawayo and be told to keep going for another two months, we stopped there. We always knew Salisbury was the place to be.

"Now, suddenly, we have a rail line, something we never had before. It won't be long before all major settlements are linked, and with this will also come a telegraph line. I see no reason to build another warehouse in another town if we can service them all by rail and telegraph from Bulawayo.

"Furthermore," Morris continued, "Bulawayo is closer to Johannesburg."

"So," David uncrossed his legs and leaned forward, "if I get this right, you want to give up the wagon-trading side of the business and effectively turn our Johannesburg and Bulawayo warehouses into distribution centres?"

"Precisely!" Morris retorted, leaning back in his seat this time. "Why supply wagon traders when we can supply those that will supply them? Let everyone else build expensive warehouses, fight amongst each other, and haggle relentlessly over prices. I'll tell you something else," Morris leant forward and lowered his voice slightly, "with the expansion of rail and road networks, I believe the future of the traditional wagon trader is doomed. I don't want to chase after a doomed enterprise."

David shook his head slowly as he tried to comprehend what his brother had predicted. "What if wagon trading is not doomed? We will lose the initiative; we will miss out on a thriving industry."

"Look around you, David," Morris almost scolded his brother as he waved his arms in the air. "Do you see any wagon trading in England? No. The road and rail networks have eradicated it, and so, in the future, Rhodesia will go that way too. It is an extremely progressive country, and those Rhodesian settlers are an unusually determined lot, you cannot deny that."

"True," David agreed, still deep in thought. "So you want to pull out of the wagon-trading side altogether?"

"Yes!" Morris exclaimed again and immediately stood and walked to the window. "We need to tell Badger to sell the grinders, one by one, without making it obvious what we are doing," Morris referred to the wagons using their code name. "The oxen have to go too. Badger needs to put some attention into Salisbury, get to know business operations there, join their Chamber of Commerce, if necessary. He must do what Giraffe is doing in Johannesburg. I have huge plans for Langbourne Brothers, and chasing pennies is not part of it. My plans are much bigger."

"I don't know how Badger is going to react when he discovers you have scuttled his brilliant solution to a serious threat to the business," David said.

"I don't care what he thinks," Morris waved his hand in the air again.

"Maybe I'll tell him his exploration up to Salisbury created other solutions and opportunities," David mused aloud, for he was far more diplomatic than Morris.

"Whatever you wish, it is of no concern to me what you tell him. You need to return to Bulawayo as soon as you can. When can you leave?"

"Excuse me, Gentlemen," Hanna entered the lounge with Rose Bertha. Both ladies were smiling broadly and donning their coats. "We're going down to the Langham. I need to see my mother."

David stood quickly to help Hanna with her coat. "Shall we meet you there later?" he asked.

"Yes, indeed. We will have dinner at the hotel. Don't be late," Hanna smiled.

"Good show. I will need to discuss arrangements with you and your parents about our imminent return to Rhodesia," David kissed Hanna lightly on the cheek.

Hanna smiled and turned to leave, hooking her elbow into Rose Bertha's. "We will be returning after the winter, David," she said over one pert shoulder. "We don't need to rush these things. March or April next year will be just fine. See you boys later."

And they were gone.

Morris and David stood in silence, staring at the empty corridor that the women had just exited.

"What was that all about?" Morris asked his brother. "March next year won't do, that's about eight months away.

"I have no idea what she is on about," David said and carefully took his seat. Swivelling in his chair, he stared down the empty corridor behind him once more, then back at Morris.

They both sat in silence, confusion etched all over their faces.

On finding out that he was soon to become a father, David's life took on a whole new meaning. His stride took on a mild swagger, the swing in his folded umbrella became a little more pronounced, the tilt of his Derby slightly more exaggerated.

The argument as to whether to have the child in Rhodesia or England waged for three days before it was agreed that they would have the baby in London, under the constant care of specialists in Harley Street. Although this arrangement frustrated Morris in that he wanted David to leave immediately, it didn't worry David much as he was basking in pride. It was a very different story for Hanna and her mother. Their plans having been thrown entirely to the wind, every consideration was now being given to purchasing baby items to take back to Rhodesia, a new country that didn't have much in the way of goods to buy for young families.

Although Morris was annoyed at the newlyweds' altered arrangements, he did find their preparations somewhat interesting, if not amusing. It gave him the chance to witness what a young family would consider buying for the impending arrival of a baby, and therefore he began to find suppliers who dealt in these type of goods, concentrating mainly on perambulators and baby cots.

Morris sent a letter to his friend and business colleague in Nottingham, Frank Bowden, who owned Raleigh Bicycles, to inquire if he sold baby perambulators, and if not, would he consider manufacturing a range with the same large wheels like those used on his bicycles, designed explicitly for the rough, un-surfaced streets of southern Africa. If the response was positive, Morris had already decided that a large consignment of these contraptions would be on his next shipment to Rhodesia.

David returned to the Finsbury Pavement flat one afternoon without Hanna. As he entered and hung his hat on the peg in the hallway, Morris noticed he looked somewhat flustered.

"Rough day?" Morris asked.

"I've had enough baby shopping to last me a decade. We now have nine entire trunks packed to the hilt just for the baby. Hanna has almost as many for herself, and don't get me started on Mrs Rubinstein!"

"Come in and let me make you a pot of tea," Morris chuckled. "How many trunks do you have?"

"One, and if hadn't been obliged to purchase three suits and an extra hat, I would have but a single tote bag to my name. Here," David handed Morris an envelope, "I bumped into the postman downstairs. He had this telegram for you. It looks like it's from Giraffe in Johannesburg."

"Splendid!" Morris retorted and started on Louis' message as the two boys walked through to the kitchen.

"What's it say?" David asked, instantly forgetting about his anxious day.

"Huh," Morris grunted, "only two words, 'Hotel Equipment'."

"Hotel equipment?"

"How odd…" Morris broke off in thought and suddenly turned to walk back to his desk.

"What's wrong?" David asked, now forgetting even the promise of tea. He could see a familiar look on Morris' face, the one present when his mind went into high gear.

"Look at this," Morris rummaged in a drawer and retrieved Harry's letter about Salisbury and the threat to their wagon trade. "Here," Morris stubbed his finger at a point in the letter.

David turned the letter upright so he could read it correctly. "'With this in mind,'" David read the letter aloud, "'I have been talking to members of the community. Your acquaintance, Mr Tom Meikle, who extends his regards to you, by the way, believes that he may open another branch of his transport business there. He also plans to build a hotel with his brother in Salisbury, so confident is he of the town's future prosperity.'"

"Isn't that curious," Morris said. "First Harry tells us that Tom Meikle wants to build a hotel in Salisbury with his brother, then Louis tells us, from Johannesburg no less, to buy hotel equipment. Doesn't that tell you a story?" Morris asked with a wry smile.

"It certainly does," David frowned. "I wonder what's going on in southern Africa?"

"I can tell you one thing," Morris sat down heavily in his chair, "I know Tom Meikle well, and he is very astute. If he wants to build a hotel, then we need to sit up and take note. He is a brilliant man, and he does nothing in small measure, that is certain."

"Hotel equipment?" David repeated. "Kitchen equipment, knives, forks, spoons, cups, saucers…"

"Sheets, towels, pillowcases," Morris filled out David's sentence. "What are those bells they put on the reception desks?"

"Curtain fabric, tablecloths, trays, glassware…"

"Stationery, pens, paper," Morris cut off David again. "We need to take a trip to Sheffield and Manchester where the factories are located. We can leave tomorrow," Morris rattled off, his brain moving to the next level.

"Hold up, brother," David threw his arms in the air, "I have commitments with Hanna and her parents over the next few days."

"Can't you postpone them?" Morris grumbled, "I need you. This is important."

"No, Morris," David sighed and smiled at the same time, "you do this without me. You are quite capable of managing on your own."

Forcing himself to face reality, Morris had to agree with David. He would have to do it himself, and he conceded that he was competent. The problem was that he was becoming very accustomed to his current living arrangements, and travel didn't hold much appeal.

"Alright," Morris succumbed, "I'll go. All the stock I purchase will take a good two to four months for the orders to arrive at my warehouse, then another six months to land in Cape Town or Port Elizabeth. I might have to purchase some of it from my agent in Hong Kong, depending on prices, in which case the consignment will become split. If that's the case, it might arrive in East London."

"I should be back in Bulawayo by then. Send me all the details, as you did last time. I'll travel down to the various ports and arrange the transfers to Louis in Johannesburg."

"There is a problem, though," Morris eyed his brother sternly. "This increase in our inventory will demand a huge outlay in cash to pay for these purchases. We don't have this sort of money right now, so I will have to borrow from the Standard Bank."

"I hate borrowing," David complained, but he knew there was no other way of doing it.

"I do too, but we have no choice," Morris insisted. "Are you in agreement?"

David sighed. "Yes, let's do it."

"Good," Morris leant back in his chair. "One more thing; there will be no dividend this year. All available cash will go into this."

"The brothers won't like that," David scowled. "They have just bought a plot of land each and have commenced building a home on it; so have I. I'm sure they will have something to say about this decision."

"Tell them to use their salaries to build their houses."

"Morris, none of us gets paid a decent salary, you and I included. We all depend on the annual dividends," David objected. "I have to complete building my house as I have a family to support now. I can't house my wife and child on the warehouse floor."

"So, stay with the Rubinstein's for a while until our sales pick up."

"I might remind you that the South African War is beginning to resume," David countered. "Contrary to popular opinion, the Brits have not won the war yet. It may be some time before the hotel industry, any industry in fact, recovers. Who knows how long our money may be tied up in sheets and towels before normality returns?"

Morris sighed and looked pensively out the window. When he looked back at David, he had a very determined look in his eyes. David knew the mood had changed.

"Even if the war drags on for a while, this is the perfect time to progress and take risks, because everyone is holding back waiting for a result. We need to be well ahead of the pack. Our brothers have to learn that sometimes a small sacrifice will bring big rewards," Morris almost hissed. "Take that back to them, David."

David knew there was no point in arguing the matter with Morris once he set his mind to something.

"I'll do that, Brother," David grumbled.

"Good. Do we have a quorum, Mr Secretary?" Morris asked, the fire burning in his eyes once again.

"Yes, Mr Chairman," David reluctantly agreed, reaching for a pen in his jacket pocket, because he knew what was coming next.

"Excellent. Please minute this meeting."

CHAPTER SEVEN
Rhodesia - 1901

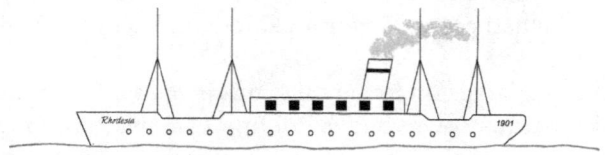

The journey from Southampton to Cape Town had been relatively pleasant, as enjoyable as the rail excursion to Johannesburg that had followed almost immediately afterwards. After settling into their luxurious hotel suite on Commissioner Street in downtown Johannesburg, David had walked the two blocks with Hanna to see Danie Coetzee, and to introduce his new wife and two-month-old daughter, Ettie, to his old friend. Hanna had borne him a beautiful, healthy little girl, and David couldn't be more proud of his new family.

The welcome at Coetzee and Coetzee Accounting had been very warm, and Hanna had taken immediately to her husband's friend and business partner. She could tell why David and Morris liked the man; stately, learned, and exceptionally well-turned out in his pinstriped suit.

When David and Morris had first met Danie, he had been working in Julian Weil's procurement office, situated in a wooden shed. That had been back in Port Elizabeth, in the early days of the boys' southern African venture. Back then, Danie had been very tall and thin, almost gangly in appearance, and would usually have thought deeply before passing any comment on the topic of conversation. At that time Danie had a mild Dutch accent, and David assumed that English was not his first language. Because of this, he had guessed that Danie would have had to translate mentally from Dutch into English before he opened his mouth. David hadn't been certain that this was true and had felt it impolite to ask, but Danie's slight pause before answering questions or commenting in a conversation had suggested such an explanation. Thus Danie had come across as rather a learned man whose opinions ought to be carefully considered, someone whom people would listen to with close attention.

That had been ten years ago, but now – having become a partner in his uncle's accounting firm and thus earning a good income – Danie had filled out quite well. His broad set of shoulders and imposing size (all draped in such immaculate attire) and his usually profound and calculated speech all served to portray him a formidable businessman, which contrasted sharply with his gentle and kindly demeanour.

Thrilled to be seeing his friend again after such a long absence, as well as meeting David's lovely bride, Danie took the young couple to a new and elegant coffee house in a prestigious hotel nearby, to catch up on the latest news about Johannesburg. While sipping an exceptional coffee and sampling the delightful pastries, the two men spoke intently. Hanna sat listening quietly while rocking Ettie gently in her perambulator. The young mother had thought that she might have had to endure a rather dull conversation, but she was pleasantly surprised to find that the topics the men discussed were all extremely interesting. So intense was the discussion that at times Hanna was sure that David and Danie had forgotten she was even there. Hanna really didn't mind at all, because she found it all so enlightening.

Danie, for example, was clearly well versed in the political and financial situation of the South African Republic and confirmed that the South African War was indeed not yet over. The Boers had been regrouping and had been staging guerrilla-style attacks on various military targets throughout the region. The man at the centre of the current Boer offensive was a General De La Rey. He was highly regarded in the Boer ranks and was an exceptional strategist and military man. Groups of Boer commandos had formed around him including other generals from all over the republics, his personal popularity being far more significant than even President Kruger's.

Led by Lords Milner and Kitchener, the British Imperial forces had realised that the Boer commandos – being mostly farmers – had been using their own farms for food and supplies, as well as for medical treatment. As a result, the British had adopted a "concentration" strategy by focusing on one district at a time, rounding up the Boer women and children remaining on their farms, and interning them in so-called "concentration camps". The Dutch farms, their homes and their crops, would then be burned down or blown up to make the commandos lives as painful and uncomfortable as possible. The plan was to narrow the Boer commandos' field of operation and force them, by a "scorched-earth" policy, into unconditional surrender. As was said by US General Sheridan on his southern march into the Confederate states a generation before, "They must have nothing left but their eyes to weep".

Rumours abounded that the Imperial British Army had been giving these captured women and children such little care and support that they had been enduring much hunger and outbreaks of diseases. Nevertheless, now under British occupation, the life of the major South African towns seemed to continue as usual.

As part of their overall concentration strategy, moreover, the British Army had constructed a series of "blockhouses", fortified outposts placed at a set of intervals around the cleared district, connected by tightly-strung wires and a signalling system. These blockhouses stretched for many miles across the countryside. Whenever a Boer commando tried to cross or cut their way past an outpost, the British Army would be alerted, and they would engage the Boers, sending survivors on the retreat. It had thus quickly descended into a war of attrition, a slow but methodical method of cutting the resistance down over time, severely impairing their movement, and hampering their ability to restock arms, ammunition, food, clothing and medical supplies.

On hearing this, Hanna spoke out for the first time. "All a bit cruel, don't you think?" she said quietly. "Why don't the Boers just give up? So many lives lost, so much pain and suffering, and so many people separated from family and home."

Danie paused and took a slow sip of his coffee. "I don't like it either, my dear, but I am helpless to do anything about it. The Boers are not just fighting for their country; they are fighting for their very existence as an autonomous nation. They have a passion for keeping their culture and history alive, a passion that the British cannot understand. I fear this war will go on until the very last Boer commando is captured or killed."

The conversation was becoming very depressing, so Danie tactfully swung the discussion to business. It seemed that, despite this new phase of the war, business was now progressing well in just about every sector.

"Now tell me about Morris," Danie finally asked. "How is he?"

"He is well. Because he refuses to slow down, as usual, he has a new strategy for our business."

"How so?" Danie asked, raising an eyebrow. "I am a silent partner of yours. Perhaps I should be aware of these new plans," he smiled.

"I was getting to that," David chuckled.

David told Danie how Morris had decided that Langbourne Brothers, and Langbourne Coetzee, were a little over-exposed to the continuing instability and dangers of southern Africa and wished to diversify among different countries. Firstly, they would be selling off the wagon-trading arm, returning the stock to the warehouse, and investing the cash from the wagon sales into new lines of inventory. Furthermore, Morris was looking at establishing a strong presence as a wholesaler in England and Europe.

"What new lines of inventory are you thinking of?" Danie asked.

"Hotel and catering equipment. We feel there is a big demand from the hospitality trade. Also for young ones - infants and children," David said, casting a quick glance at Hanna.

Yet again Danie changed the subject. "When will you see Louis?"

"Immediately after our meeting," David answered, sipping the last of his coffee. "We will take a buggy down to Railway Road and I'll show Hanna our Johannesburg warehouse."

"You won't find Louis there, I am certain of that. He spends the afternoons and evenings in the various establishments where businessmen habitually meet."

"That is good to hear," David smiled, "it is something Morris encourages, and something I have tried to instil in him."

"Allow me to send him a message to meet you at your hotel," Danie suggested. "It will be more convenient all round. The warehouse area is not a suitable place to take an infant. Louis is well liked by the business community, and I have had good reports about him. I dare say he appears to have made quite a few influential connections in Johannesburg. In fact, I think he may outperform your Bulawayo enterprise."

David smiled broadly, pleased with this report. "That's wonderful to hear, Danie."

"I personally feel he is working too hard on the business, and this may be detrimental to his health. He never stops."

"He needs another interest," Hanna interjected, "a lady on his arm, perhaps."

Danie laughed. "I hate to say this, but there is quite a line-up of suitors seeking his attention, as he appears to be most attractive to the fairer sex. But I fear he is too committed to the Company. Perhaps encourage him to slow down a little."

Having walked into the hotel just on six o'clock that evening, Louis announced his arrival to the clerk at the reception desk. A bellhop in a crisp white uniform was dispatched on the double to Room 27 to advise Mr and Mrs Langbourne that they had a guest. Taking a seat in the opulent lobby, Louis helped himself to a newspaper, but found that it consisted mostly of advertisements, so he quickly tossed it back onto the table.

In the meantime, David and Hanna had arranged a babysitter for Ettie and emerged from a stairway within fifteen minutes. After David had greeted his young brother with a firm handshake and a broad smile, Hanna gave him an embrace, which Louis reciprocated with an extra peck on both cheeks.

"You are looking absolutely splendid, Hanna," Louis gushed. "So good to see you, too, brother."

"My word!" Hanna took a slight step back and looked Louis up and down. "You look so handsome and dignified in your new suit. No wonder the womenfolk won't leave you alone."

Louis couldn't help but laugh. "You've been talking to Mr Coetzee, haven't you?"

David suggested they get an early dinner as he was famished, and the trio adjourned to the hotel dining room to enjoy the culinary delights that were on offer. The food was indeed most delectable, and David quickly filled Louis in on the news of the family (and all the new half-siblings that were appearing in Ireland) while they enjoyed a hearty meal. They had a few laughs at Morris' expense, knowing his dislike for the new family Jacob and Helena were happily producing.

"Helena is looking absolutely wonderful, you would hardly recognise her," David smiled. "She makes father very happy. And Bloomy is married now…"

"Married?" Louis exclaimed as he was about to put a fork of food into his mouth.

"Yes, and three children already."

Louis tried to absorb all the changes to his family in Ireland. "Great Heavens!" he exclaimed. "And who do you suppose we should hold responsible for all of this, I wonder?"

David poked his fork in the air as he quickly swallowed his food. "Bernard Zieder. Nice enough fellow, nothing really to complain about."

"David!" Hanna scolded her husband, "He's a lovely person."

David ignored Hanna's reprimand. "Morris did buy that farm, would you believe? Got it for a song, and we managed to visit it. Elaine, by the way, runs it quite well; makes a tidy profit, and she has gone and married the farm hand that worked there in Morris' time. Adam, I think his name is. Elaine herself has had twin girls."

"Well, at least the farm makes a profit," Louis grumbled.

"And provides your family with fresh produce," Hanna quickly added.

The conversation continued, with David describing Morris' flat on Finsbury Pavement, and his engagement to Rose Bertha. Hanna spoke very kindly about Rosie and occasionally hinted that Morris needed to pay more attention to her. Before dessert was served, Hanna excused herself to powder her nose and to check on Ettie, tactfully leaving the two brothers to talk privately between themselves.

"Morris got your telegram about supplying hotels. We are going to follow that lead aggressively."

"I'm very pleased to hear that," Louis replied with a frown. "I try to keep my ear to the ground here, and I can tell you that this is an industry we cannot afford to ignore."

"Well," David leant closer to his brother, lowering his voice even further, "Harry sent a letter in which he mentioned a very prominent man by the name of Mr Meikle, someone who is talking about moving his transport business to Salisbury and building a hotel. When Morris read your telegram and Harry's letter so closely together – with the same message – it made him take notice."

"Mr Tom Meikle …yes, I know him quite well. He was here a few weeks ago doing business, and we had a couple of drinks together. He hinted at what he was planning. Nevertheless, I think his ideas are a little ostentatious."

"Well, I hope it works out for him," David said. "Getting back to the hotel supplies, Morris is going to borrow to the hilt to purchase catering equipment, hotel linen, cutlery, crockery, and everything he can find to supply all these emerging hotels."

"Excellent!" Louis grinned. "Splendid news."

"We are going to drop the wagon-trading side of the business, though. Harry will have to gradually start selling the wagons and oxen to get some extra cash into the bank. It also means, furthermore, that we cannot afford a dividend this year," David looked hard at Louis expecting a robust objection.

"I expected that," Louis sighed.

"Well," David leant back, looking somewhat confused, "you took that better than I expected."

"It's clear to me that if we get this right, the dividends the following year will be more than double, so I'm not concerned. In fact, I am excited, this year is going to be memorable."

"Huh," David grunted, "I was anxious you would be upset about suspending the building of your home in Bulawayo. I wonder if Harry will take this news as well as you have."

"Oh no, he won't," Louis likewise leant back in his chair, but he was smiling. "Harry will be very unhappy. But, if you explain everything to him as you did to me, he will understand. It may take him a week or two to get over it, but he will. Perhaps suggest he rents a house for a while - get him out of the warehouse and into a real bed. Give him some independence. It will take his mind off matters."

"Good idea," David agreed. "I certainly won't tell him how Morris is living, cor blimey, that is opulence at its best! Once Harry finds a place to call his own I'll tell him."

"David," Louis leant forward, a serious look crossing his face, "Do you think we, as a company, would look at buying shares in the Stock Exchange?"

"Why," David was suddenly curious.

"As you know I spend a lot of time in gentlemen's clubs and places where businessmen meet, and I hear a lot of very interesting things from a variety of interesting people. Curiously, this allows me to see trends forming, or I can put two and two together."

"Such as?"

"Well, some people here want to open a cement factory in Rhodesia. Cement will be found everywhere soon, but why buy shares in a factory when we can buy shares in that company on the Stock Exchange and sell it whenever we need to. It goes for any business, really."

"Hmm…" David gave this some thought. "I'll talk to Morris about it, but first we need to deal with this hospitality inventory and recover our investment. Perhaps then."

"Yes," Louis mulled, "that would make good sense, and the timing would be right."

David looked curiously at Louis and wondered exactly how much he knew. It indeed seemed as though he had his finger on the pulse and was playing a very crafty game within the commercial and industrial circles of Johannesburg. Morris had taught the brothers that knowledge is a potent tool, and it seemed like Louis was taking that information very seriously, and with good effect.

David saw Hanna enter the dining room and stood to pull her chair out. Louis also stood to receive her.

"Prepare yourself for a lot of stock from Morris," David whispered, "It's going to be an avalanche."

Louis smiled and nodded at David. "I'm already prepared."

Louis was right. Morris' heavy-handed change of tactics did not amuse Harry. The only thing that brought his fiery outburst under control was when David pointed out that it was Harry's insightful letter that had prompted Morris' decision.

David quoted his elder brother for support. "'A little sacrifice now will pay big dividends later.'"

"I know," Harry grumbled, "but now I have to tell my builder to stop work. That is so annoying, for both of us. And you also want me to sell the grinders."

"Slowly, slowly; one at a time, and intermittently. Don't let people know what we are doing. Start with the lesser performing ones, of course. You have six months to move the wagons off our books," David instructed. "Feel free to let the traders have preferential pricing, discounts if you will. Just move them off."

"What about Mr Johnson, when all the wagons have been sold? Are you going to fire him? I sure as hell won't!"

"Not at all. We will need him when the hotel inventory arrives, and then some."

Harry grumbled something inaudible and began to walk away, but suddenly turned back. "You know we are very short of stock because of that war down south. Two more months and we may have to close the Fife Street store."

"Yes," David sighed, "I know. Four weeks and we should have a small shipment arriving. We just have to hold out for that, it will keep us going."

"And all this ridiculous hotel equipment?"

"I'm not sure. I estimate a month or two later." David shrugged. "Come to the Rubinstein's after closing time and join us for dinner. I'd like you to meet your niece, and – besides – we need to talk about finding you a home to rent until our finances settle."

"A room at the Charter Hotel will do me just fine," Harry grumbled as he walked out of the office.

David cocked an eyebrow and thought about what Harry had just said. It made perfect sense.

CHAPTER EIGHT

Port Elizabeth - 1901

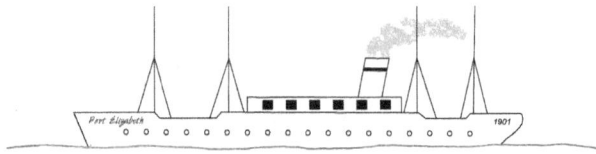

When David's bare feet touched the stone floor, his toes automatically curled up like sea anemones. Although the winters in Rhodesia could get uncomfortably cold, they were mercifully short, while the residents of this new country preferred a cool, un-insulated slate floor, which was more suitable for the long, hot summers.

I really need to buy some slippers, David thought to himself as he stood up and stretched. Turning around, he smiled as he looked at Hanna, curled up snugly among the blankets. Ettie, now four months old, was equally cuddled up comfortably in her mother's arms.

Since the previous year had flashed by far too quickly for David, he reflected briefly on what he had achieved since his return from England. Business had been brisk, despite the constant shortages of stocks. The Anglo-Boer War was continuing to worsen. Even then, for him to travel to Johannesburg by train required a special permit from the British South Africa Police (or the BSAP) in Rhodesia, which allowed him to move about, not only from town to town, but also often within a specific town. Apart from shortages of just about everything, including hard currency, however, Rhodesia had been little affected by the war.

Bowing to Morris' experience in business and worldly affairs, moreover, Harry had carried out his instructions to the letter, even while suppressing some anger that Morris had not recognised his ingenious solution to an impending commercial disaster. Harry nevertheless had methodically sold off their wagons, often getting an exceptional market price for them, and had accepted with a pleasant smile the returned stock, which he and Mr Johnson had quickly re-priced, and so replenished the warehouse through their own sales effort.

Both Bulawayo and Salisbury had continued to prosper, although not at the cracking pace they had kept up before the war. Other settlements such as Fort Victoria, Gwelo and Umtali had begun to feature more in business circles, thanks to the expanding rail and telegraph networks in the country.

David quickly shaved, changed into a grey suit, and – kissing Hanna lightly on the cheek so as not to wake her – slipped out of the Rubinstein home. The 25-minute walk to the warehouse in the fresh, winter air was exhilarating. Entering the premises from the rear, David found Harry already at his desk.

"Morning, Brother," David chirped, "you're in early today. Sleep well?"

"No," Harry grumbled, "damn mosquito kept me awake most of the night. I thought they only came out in summer."

David simply laughed. Harry often sounded grumpy, but David could sense his brother was actually in a reasonably good mood.

As the day progressed, a telegram was delivered, which Harry opened very carefully with the finely sharpened blade of a new letter-opener he had purchased, and one of which he was particularly fond. Letter opening, for Harry, had become a bit of an art, and a little pomp and ceremony was always called for when an envelope crossed his desk.

Having read the contents of the telegram, he looked up in time to see his brother walk past his open door. Harry gave a very distinct click of his tongue, which stopped David in his tracks, and he entered Harry's office with an expectant look on his face.

"Have you received your travel pass from the BSAP Administration?" Harry asked without any expression.

"I need to renew it. Do I need one?" David smiled, knowing what Harry had in mind.

"Yes. It seems the stock has arrived in Port Elizabeth. Lots of it, according to Jack Shiel."

"Good-oh," David took a seat opposite Harry, "I have an extraordinary feeling it's going to be pandemonium there. Morris never does anything in half measures. I suggest that you travel to Johannesburg fourteen days after I leave and help Louis prepare to receive the shipment."

"Are you happy to leave the warehouse with Mr Johnson and Fife Street with Mr Loxton?" Harry asked.

"Well, Mr Loxton is already in full control down there, and Mr Johnson is pretty much out of a job now that he has sold all the wagons, plus he knows what to do here, don't you think?"

"Yes, he does," Harry agreed, "I have total faith in both gentlemen. I would enjoy a change of scenery, too, and it would be good to see Louis."

"Good!" David exclaimed. "Then it's settled. Let's call Mr Johnson in and have a chat."

Harry glanced over David's shoulder. "There he is. Mr Johnson, if you please?" he called out.

Michael Johnson came in and was offered a seat. The boys noticed that he sported a light bandage around his right wrist, but did not mention it just yet. David explained that he would be travelling to Port Elizabeth and would be away for about a month. Harry would be following and would likewise be absent for a month or so. David then quickly came to the point and asked if he would be prepared to manage the warehouse in their absence.

"I must say," Mr Johnson smiled and seemed to relax slightly, "I thought you were about to let me go, now that we have no wagon traders to attend to."

"Well," Harry smiled, "we are offering you a permanent promotion instead."

"Indeed," Mr Johnson chuckled. "I would be delighted to manage the warehouse for you. Thanks to Mr Harry's supervision, I already know how you like the business run."

David also relaxed a little now that everything was falling into place. "Very good," he grinned. "What did you do to your wrist?" he asked.

"Tennis, sir. I have joined a small tennis group at the sports club with

Brian Loxton, and we play a social every Thursday evening. I tripped last night while reaching for an opponent's overhead lob and sprained my wrist."

"Who was your opponent? Anyone I know?" David asked with some curiosity.

"The new pharmacist in town, sir, a Mr Albert Bondi. He says he met Mr Morris in Ireland last year."

"Well, then..." David chuckled, "you had better let him win, I suppose."

"I'll have to play him left-handed next week, but I still doubt he would beat me," Johnson said, laughing heartily. David and Harry couldn't help but join in the hilarity, they were thoroughly pleased that the man remained part of their team.

For a change, David's journey down to Port Elizabeth was rather eventful. The stop in Mafeking was even more horrifying than his last had been. When David had left the town during the now famous Siege of Mafeking, it had appeared ruined beyond repair. Now, as he alighted from the train for the standard two-hour refuelling stop, the settlement was in even worse shape.

A few months before his arrival, a cyclonic whirlwind had torn through the town, lifting roofs off the houses, and knocking walls and water towers over like skittles. Entire homes had been completely obliterated in some places and, to make matters worse, the devastation was followed almost immediately by a severe hail-storm. Hail-stones, the size of cricket balls, had smashed every last remaining pane of glass, stripped every leaf off the trees, and flattened any piece of vegetation that had dared to stand up to the previous whirlwind. Almost all of the traditional houses in the African village associated with the town had been destroyed, and the ferocious hail had even killed several goats.

Mother Nature had proved once again that – in two minutes – she could do more damage than two opposing human armies could have done over seven months, the entire duration of the siege.

David found the rest of his journey interrupted by British soldiers checking travel passes and identity documents. He also noticed the blockhouses, straddling the landscape from end to end, connected by strands of fence-wire, while British troops practised military drills, or stood guard at certain vital points. It intrigued him that the Boer armies could still remain active within the country, out of sight of the vast military network, and even survive at all without proper support, resupplies, and logistics. Yet, somehow, they managed to continue, and the war of attrition carried on in its guerilla or "hit-and-run" phase.

On his arrival in Port Elizabeth, David went through his routine of checking into the Grand Hotel and greeting Mrs Bunting, Shadrek and other staff members, before making his way to meet Jack Shiel briefly at The Standard Bank. As usual, they arranged to meet back at the Grand for dinner, where they could catch up in a more relaxed environment.

David then found the shipping agent who had cleared his goods when they had arrived off the ship, presented his paperwork, reluctantly paid the demurrage fee, and was then escorted to a large, dilapidated warehouse. When the cumbersome doors clad with corrugated iron sheeting were swung open, he was greeted by a higgledy-piggledy mix of boxes and crates, piled almost as high as the roof, and in no noticeable order. The warehouse itself was in a total shambles, from front to back, and top to bottom.

"Which of this is my stuff?" David asked, nervously peering into the gloom.

"All of it, mate," the clerk said.

"All of it? All this?" David's stomach churned. "No, surely…"

"Yip, it sure is. I hope you have lots of help."

David stared at the mass of crates in disbelief. He was dumbstruck. He was expecting a lot of stock, but what lay before him was beyond ridiculous. Not only was the quantity overwhelming, but there was no semblance of order. Boxes and crates of all sizes and materials were strewn haphazardly throughout the warehouse.

"Surely there is someone else's stuff in here, too? This can't be all mine, can it?" David's voice suddenly lost its confidence, and a strange feeling close to hopelessness began to set in.

"I'll tell you what, mate," the clerk said, handing David the padlock key, "you can keep this key. When the shed is clear, you can return it to me, and I will charge you the daily rate. I know you'll be good for it. Now I suggest you get some bleedin' good help as soon as you can."

David thanked the man and locked the door. Pocketing the key, he walked briskly over to the Post Office, ripped a telegram form from a small, wooden box, and scribbled a message to Morris. His handwriting was firm but untidy, and the last full stop was imprinted so hard on the paper that the lead in the pencil actually snapped. David read his script several times over, then, leaning on the counter, he rested his head on his forearms and stayed that way until he could compose himself.

Looking up at the ceiling, David whispered to his Lord for strength and guidance. Then, screwing up the pencilled note, he threw it at the bin, turned on his heel, and strode out of the Post Office.

The ball of paper bounced off the lip of the bin and rolled towards the foot of an elderly lady. Having witnessed David's obvious anguish, the lady watched him storm out through the swing doors, before bending down to pick up the discarded message. Out of pure curiosity, she opened the crumpled paper and read what was written on it.

'For heaven's sake Lion, have you lost your mind? How much did you borrow? This is madness.'

The old lady shook her head a few times, clucked her tongue in sympathy with the poor harassed young man, and then, screwing up the note, tossed it into the bin.

Dinner with Jack later that evening was most enjoyable, although – out of pure embarrassment – David, refrained from mentioning anything about the quantity of stock Morris had purchased. He knew Morris would have had to borrow a vast amount of money to procure the volume of goods stashed in the warehouse, and when the bank loans had run dry, Morris (in his usual way), would have bought even more stock, using further lines of credit and promissory notes. It bothered David that his brother would have risked so much. It wasn't that Morris had over-committed the company finances, but that he appeared to do so without due regard for his partners – his brothers – and the effect that such risk-taking might have on the rest of the family; those who still depended upon the business for their livelihood.

Finally, as the meal ended and strong coffee was served, Jack looked David in the eye.

"I know you well, David, and you are apprehensive about something. May I hazard a guess and ask what Morris has done now?"

David laughed and shook his head. "Is it that obvious, Jack?"

"Go on, spill the beans. It can't be any worse than what Morris did last time."

"It's worse," David stared at his empty plate, a cloud of gloom seeming to descend upon him.

"Tell me," Jack encouraged.

"Morris has bought so much this time that he has filled an entire warehouse down by the docks. I have no idea what's contained in there, and I don't know where to find the paperwork. It is a shambles."

Jack was momentarily inclined to burst out laughing, but David looked in such a sorry state that he quickly restrained himself. "I would assume you are not really concerned about the labour involved in transporting it to the railway station, but more with the cost of purchasing the goods?" Jack asked.

"Exactly," David grumbled loudly. "There must be tens of thousands of pounds worth of stock in that warehouse. We don't have that sort of money. How on earth...?"

"David..." Jack began, but David cut him off.

"I know what you are going to say, Jack, and – yes – this all worries me immensely."

"Something Morris may not have taken into consideration while he is in England," Jack continued, "is that the war here has put a damper on investment. People are scared to invest; to take risks,"

"Well, Morris does take risks, huge risks. We well know that," David sighed. "May we change the subject, please?"

The early-morning sunlight on the harbour made for such a delightful vista that, standing outside the rented warehouse, David was able to take a fresh look at his situation. When he saw a tall African man walking by, he spoke to him in isiXhosa.

"I see you, my friend."

"I see you," the man responded with a smile, "the morning brings us a good day."

"You are right, my friend. I see a good day, too, with a promise of rain on the morrow." David had no idea if it would rain the next day or not, but he felt it would be a polite conversation starter.

"It is possible," the man agreed and smiled broadly, stealing a glance at the sky.

"I look for an old friend, and I ask if your eyes have seen him."

"My eyes are good. They see many things," the friendly man replied.

"The man I seek is Nguni. He is the brother of Daluxolo, who is the husband of Nkosazana."

The man now grinned broadly. "My eyes have seen him yesterday but one. In truth, the man you seek called Nguni is my uncle from my mother's side."

David could disguise neither his happiness nor his relief. "This news makes my heart sing for joy."

"My uncle's village is quite close. I will be happy to send a message to him, or we can go there together."

"Let us go together," David chuckled. "I will be happy to greet him in his village and see his children."

"Then we go now," the man insisted, still smiling.

Nguni's village was just short of an hour's walk to the north-west of the port. Moments after they had commenced their journey, David's guide spoke to a young man along the path, who promptly sprinted off in a slightly different direction, which David found somewhat confusing. It all made sense, however, when he entered Nguni's village and found that the villagers were expecting his arrival and had prepared tea and a meal for him. The famous "African bush telegraph", David realised, had been working at its most efficient.

Nguni was delighted to see David, as was Daluxolo. The fourteen cattle David had arranged for each of them to receive for their loyalty and dedication when looking after the lost wagons in the Rhodesian bush had multiplied considerably, as had the wives and children of the two men, which had all helped to establish a prosperous village. The men sat under a shady tree as the womenfolk brought refreshments, and much was discussed. News was shared, stories embellished, and old memories turned over with a great deal of laughter.

By the time David had been escorted back to Port Elizabeth late in the afternoon, he felt good. An aura of well-being surrounded him, and all his fears and apprehensions had vanished. In two days' time, Nguni and Daluxolo would arrive at the harbour with a team of relatives who would help David move all the new stock to the railway station.

Before they came, however, David needed to arrange the rail logistics. He would need to limit his concerns to transporting the goods safely to Johannesburg and Bulawayo, and then selling them profitably. Morris alone would have to handle the financial stresses and headaches, he thought, as he drifted off to sleep, it is what made Morris the person he was.

Another pristine morning greeted David once again, totally contradicting his prediction of rain. After a hearty breakfast at the Grand, he made his way to the Railway Station, to be the first inside when the doors opened, and immediately began negotiating the transfer of his abundant cargo with the clerk.

Although one-and-a-quarter rail wagons were available the following day, David wanted all the stock to travel up at the same time, so he decided against splitting the consignment. With all the hullaballoo, he was anxious that some cartons and crates might go missing. The only other option was to wait for three days, when four carriages would be available.

Not being sure how many carriages were needed to accommodate a warehouse full of stock, David tentatively booked and paid for all four rail carriages, on the proviso that he would be refunded for any space not utilised. If he needed more than the four wagons, the admin officer agreed that he could make six carriages available the following week, but the caveat was that he had to repack all his stock in the warehouse as the railways would not have room to store it in their limited holding area.

Although David agreed to these terms, he knew it would never come to that, and – if a problem were to emerge – he knew that renegotiating the conditions would be a simple matter. After finalising the rail-freight arrangements, David hired a wagon and a team of mules, which would be used to assist Nguni and his team. He also sent a message back to Nguni, postponing the intended removal date by an extra two days.

Spending a few hours in the blazing hot warehouse a little later, David rummaged through all the purchases trying to make sense of what was contained in all the boxes. Since none of the codes and markings made any sense to him, frustration joined with the intense heat to force him to a stop, and he spent the rest of the day in visiting friends and acquaintances. Sonja Du Plessis was high on his agenda.

The removal day presented itself with as much glory as the previous days, and, just after the sun had made its presence known on the horizon, Nguni, Daluxolo and a team of fourteen men arrived. A human chain of men was formed to carry the crates (mostly atop their heads), and one wagon, used to transport the extra-heavy boxes, snaked its way from the harbour warehouse to the railway station.

Four railway carriages awaited the men, and, loading the wagons with precision, making use of every available square inch of space, they successfully relocated the goods from the warehouse into three rail wagons. The wagons were covered by a heavy tarpaulin that was coated with a foul-smelling bitumen to offer some waterproofing and securely tied down with thick, cumbersome ropes.

Having arranged his refund for one wagon, David shook hands with the railway official in thanks for his excellent service and took his leave. Although Nguni and Daluxolo refused to accept payment for their work, David insisted they be rewarded, and a simple negotiation which converted coins into livestock left everyone smiling and content.

Settling the demurrage fees with the shipping agent, David handed back the key and returned to the Grand Hotel to prepare for his own departure. It had been a good day, and he was mightily pleased. Only one more task remained, and that was to send a telegram to Louis, warning him of the impending arrival of the railway wagons, and to send another one to Hanna, letting her know she was constantly in his thoughts and would be home soon.

LANCOE
JOHANNESBURG

EXPECT 4 RAIL WAGONS STOP REG NOS SA321, SA542, SA117, SA743 STOP
10 MEN TO MOVE STOCK WILL BE REQUIRED STOP
PREPARE! STOP
WILL FOLLOW TOMORROW STOP
EAGLE

CHAPTER NINE

Somewhere in the Cape

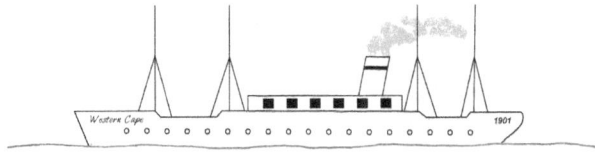

The morning before his departure from Port Elizabeth, David received a telegram from Louis to say that Harry had arrived and that they were making preparations for receiving the rail wagons. Eight men had been engaged to commence on the day the goods were scheduled to arrive. Furthermore, a small consignment had arrived in Cape Town, and David had been required to go there first before returning to Johannesburg. Demurrage fees were frighteningly expensive, and the urgency was stressed.

It annoyed David that the Port Elizabeth shipment was not the last of it, and he had to change his travel plans, but Cape Town was a lovely city, and he would make the most of this deviation.

David bade his friends farewell, checked out of the Grand Hotel, and walked down the hill to the railway station from where he boarded a train for Cape Town. The journey would take him back past Graaff-Reinet to join the main north-south line at De Aar, where he would change trains and head south. Because he was now anxious to get to Cape Town, the journey seemed painfully slow and monotonous. What did capture his attention, though, was that British military camps dotted the countryside all along the line, the soldiers wearing the distinctive khaki uniforms of the British Army.

"I've never seen so many soldiers," David commented to a fellow passenger.

"Well, the Boers have changed their tactics and have undertaken a sabotage type of warfare now. Didn't you know?"

"Yes, I had heard that," David conceded.

"They are destroying railway lines, water supplies, and all that. It seems very disruptive and unnecessary. The army has remained behind to thwart their activities. They have built these clever fortified outposts along the railway lines that they call 'block houses'. It's only a matter of time before the Boers will have to give up; the British are strangling their every move."

This unsettled David. He could not understand why people would fight to the bitter end. Surely the war was over. The Boers had been defeated, he thought, and now it was time to reconcile and rebuild; to get on with life. The train pulled into a station called Klipplaat to refill with water, but the wait seemed to drag on far too long. Suddenly, he heard loud, authoritative voices barking commands from a carriage further up front. Passengers began to emerge from their compartments and make their way to where the commotion appeared to be located. When David saw that the British soldiers were causing the disturbance, his heart sank.

A gentleman in a business suit walked back up the carriage towards David, grumbling to himself and shaking his head in disgust. David stopped him and asked what was going on.

"Damn Boers, that's what's wrong! They have blown up the line outside Graaff-Reinet, and a train has been derailed. It's going to take months to open the line again. They're turning us back."

"Oh no…" David groaned. It was the last thing he wanted to hear; it would really upset his plans. He grunted, almost growled, and walked to a window, looking down at the passengers who were slowly clambering off the train. Some men had walked a short distance away and were relieving themselves.

"I can't believe this!" David hissed and thumped his fist against the wall of the train in frustration. Yet almost immediately, he began to consider alternative ways that might allow him to successfully complete his journey from Port Elizabeth; every day was costing his company money, a lot of money! He could catch a cargo ship to Cape Town, David mused, but it might be weeks before a ship was due to depart from the harbour, and that would make the storage fees at the shipping agent hideously expensive. In fact, he thought, a delay of just one week might completely eat up all their potential profits. He could ride there by horse, but that, too, would take weeks – if he could locate a horse.

David wracked his brain to think of whom he could call on in Cape Town to clear his goods for him, but to no avail. He would have to return to Port Elizabeth as soon as possible, send a telegram to Morris, and work a plan through his friend, Yoni Goldberg; it had worked once before.

The whistle sounded, and the conductor called for everyone to board the train. Within a few minutes, the carriages began to shunt and gradually pick up speed as they headed back to Port Elizabeth, only this time in reverse. The countryside spread out on either side of the train in vistas of open fields of swaying grass, and, after about an hour, David started to nod off to the soporific sounds of the wheels on the tracks. Sometime later, he was jolted awake by an alarming explosion which jerked him back to reality.

The carriage began to shudder and the brakes slammed on, causing the metal to screech horribly in his ears. The sound of the distressed metal became mixed with the noise of women screaming, and a terrible grinding sound, along with other noises that David had never heard before. The world started to twist and turn, his balance was upset, and, when he looked out of the window, he saw grass and stones whipping past in a blur. They were tipping over, and David realised that if he didn't brace himself quickly against some metalwork, he would be sucked out of the window and crushed between the chassis of the train and the fast-approaching ground.

He reached for the door-jamb and held on tight. The carriage side-wall finally hit the ground and skidded, sending the shattered window panes instantly under the train. Accompanied by a ghastly noise, a collection of rocks, stones, and clumps of turf tore past underneath him like a sheet of giant sandpaper, and he realised he was now hanging from the doorway directly above certain death. With fear and adrenalin racing through every fibre of his body, he held on for dear life, while it seemed to take forever for the train to finally come to a standstill. It was not a moment too soon as David's grip finally gave way and he dropped onto the ground below.

He remained crouched in the dim light of the compartment in the eerie silence. David pressed the palm of his hand on the cool surface of the flattened grass. He was still a little confused as to what had happened. It slowly dawned on him that it wasn't silent at all, a fresh cacophony consisting of shouts of agony, screams of fear, hissing steam, and people banging furiously on metal walls broke out. Reality hit home with a vengeance.

David stood up and gave himself a quick check over; he appeared fine. There was no blood, and he was in no pain. He tried to reach the door above him but it was too high, so he stood on the arm of a seat that was protruding at a peculiar angle and managed to wriggle himself out of the compartment and into the passageway above. A man lay next to him, unconscious. David attended to as many people as he could, in whatever way he was able. Over the next hour or so, the wounded were assisted by the able-bodied, and the conductor of the train made every effort to get the situation under control.

It soon transpired that the Boers had deliberately sabotaged the line after the train had passed en route to Graaff-Reinet. Some concern was expressed that they might still be in the area and so attack the civilians. A quick foot patrol by a handful of British soldiers proved, however, that the Boer commando had left the area.

Five passengers lost their lives that day.

Nightfall came quickly, and the wounded were cared for as best as was possible, using medical supplies that belonged to the train crew, and whatever the soldiers could muster from their provisions. Very few people received much sleep that night, while David didn't sleep a wink.

When dawn broke, help had still not arrived and, feeling both exhausted and frustrated, David walked around to the far side of the train wreckage, not only to see the extent of the damage but also to watch the sunrise in relative privacy. To his surprise, he saw a small group of older men tending to six horses. The horses did not have saddles but were haltered.

David approached the men. "Good morning, Gentlemen. I didn't know there were horses on the train. They didn't get hurt, did they?"

"This one did," a man sighed, nodding his head at one of the horses. "Fortunately, the livestock cart didn't tip over, but some metal catapulted from somewhere and got her in the eye. She's lost her right eye and part of her ear."

"Oh dear," David commiserated and noticed the dried blood that had caked down the horse's face. "Any idea when help might arrive?"

"No idea," one of the men grumbled, "we were just talking about that. The way we see it, the line is blocked somewhere near Graaff-Reinet so help can't come from that side, therefore, a rescue team will have to be sent up from Port Elizabeth. They might be able to get within about one hundred yards of us before they hit the sabotaged line over there," he pointed over his shoulder with his thumb.

"The problem is," another of the men took over, "someone has to ride back there and tell them we need help. It looks as if the telegraph lines are cut, too."

David looked at the closest telegraph pole and noticed that the wires were missing.

"Well," David suggested, "one would think that, if no telegrams are being received, someone at the Post Office might think that a problem exists somewhere along the line and send a crew to fix it."

The first man picked up the conversation again. "That's not the problem," he said. "Two of us here both noticed there was no locomotive at the station when we left. When we pulled out of Port Elizabeth, we were the last, pending the arrival of the next. And with what's happening here, it looks like Port Elizabeth won't be getting another locomotive until this debacle is cleared. Even if they knew we were in trouble, they would have to send ox-drawn wagons up to collect the injured."

David's heart sank. He was well and truly stuck in the middle of nowhere with no help arriving for a very long time. He had to find a way out.

"If I could borrow one of these horses, I could high-tail it back to Port Elizabeth in about two days."

"A team of soldiers have already left. No point in you following, chum."

David sighed in frustration. For every day he was stuck out here, the storage fees at the Cape Town agent were mounting like rocks at the bottom of a landslide. When help did eventually arrive, moreover, it would be the sick and injured who would be evacuated first, followed by the women and children, then the elderly men, and he would be in the group that was stone-cold last.

Yet suddenly he had an idea.

"Are these horses privately owned, or do they belong to the military?" David asked, stroking the injured horse tenderly on her neck.

"Private at the moment, but the army has requisitioned them. Why?"

"I wouldn't mind buying one off you. I'm desperately trying to get to Cape Town."

"Cape Town is hundreds of miles away. You'll never make it on your own. What's more, there's a war raging out there and you, sadly, will be a marked man."

"I've done Mafeking to Bulawayo several times on a horse," David laughed, "even walked it once. Cape Town from here should be simple enough, especially if I have some urgent business that's waiting for me," he grinned mischievously. "In any case, I have an official pass from the BSAP in Rhodesia; it proves this is not my war."

"Sorry, son," the man shook his head sadly, "but the military has offered top money for these horses. They are at a premium, you know. I doubt you can afford them anyhow."

"How much? Just as a matter of interest," David asked casually.

"£70 each, and the saddle is extra."

David gently stroked the injured horse again. He spoke softly and compassionately to the poor beast as he carefully studied her wounds.

"The army won't want damaged goods. I'm willing to offer £70 for this old girl, inclusive of the saddle."

"Sorry, not for sale, son," the man said bluntly, but with a sly smile hovering about his lips.

"Done," the third man, who had not said a word yet, cut in. "She's my girl, and you can have her for that. But there's one condition, you have to find your own saddle. It's somewhere in that carriage over there," he nodded at a wagon on its side.

Smiling in appreciation, David turned slowly, calmly walked up to the train, and found a way in through the door at one end. It didn't take long to locate all the saddles, and – not knowing which one belonged to which horse – he retrieved them all. Before emerging from the wreckage, David extracted £90 from an inside pocket and relocated it to his trouser pocket. Once outside again, and with the correct saddle identified, David counted out £70, making a deliberate show of placing the remaining £20 back in his pocket.

"I'll need a sidearm, for protection against predators," David said. "I have £20 left if anyone knows of someone who might want to sell me theirs."

"You can have mine for £20," the man who had sold David the horse said quickly. "It comes with six rounds of ammunition. That's all, sadly."

"You have a deal, sir," said David, exchanging his £20 for the old revolver and ammunition.

"Do you even know the way to Cape Town?" one of the men asked sarcastically.

"Not yet," David smiled confidently, "but I will. Thank you, Gentlemen, I wish you a safe onward journey."

David walked off with his new, albeit damaged, prized possession to the other side of the wreckage. Most of the passengers and crew were huddled there in relative safety. He found a group of British soldiers and asked if he could borrow a map. One of the soldiers promptly obliged.

David spread it out on the ground and pulled his compass from his pocket. He orientated the map once the needle had stopped swinging, and took a bearing on a little black dot that said "Cape Town". To his dismay, however, no towns or settlements appeared along the most direct route. He worked out that, if he took a bearing of about 265° west, he ought to pass through a settlement called Willowmore. There, he hoped, he would find some food and provisions.

Continuing to draw an imaginary line from Willowmore to Cape Town on the same bearing, he would pass just south of Prince Albert, then just north of Calitzdorp before arriving at Ladismith. He intended to stop there for more provisions, and, hopefully, board a train or carriage on to Cape Town, if they had a connection. If those options were not available, he would just have to continue his journey on horseback.

He thanked the officer and returned the map. Another quick scrimmage around some of the upturned wagons found him some food he could take, and, most importantly, a sack of oats for his horse. Then, explaining his intentions to the conductor, David took his westerly bearing and left the misery of the wreck for the rescuers to find.

The first day was a lot tougher than David had anticipated. In his hurry to leave he had forgotten to take a hat or bedding. He also hadn't thought to bring a container for water, so he found himself having to stop at every river, spring or stream that he came across. The sleeve of his shirt, torn off roughly at the shoulder, served as a hat, fashioned with the sheath knife that he was grateful to have on his person.

Just before dark, David stopped by a stream and let his faithful horse graze contentedly while he cut some dry grass to devise a makeshift mattress, which he positioned under a leafy tree. Hungry and cold, he didn't sleep at all well that night, so sunrise saw him already continuing his journey, heading for the farming community of Willowmore. He finally arrived late that afternoon, but the only person in residence was the priest of the local church who very kindly offered him a place to sleep for the night and some food. He purchased an old blanket from the kindly man before setting off again at dawn, following his chosen bearing. His next stop would be Ladismith, and he calculated that it was a two to three-day trip from his present position.

Although hunger would be a problem, he knew how to deal with that because he had experienced hunger and starvation more than once in his life. In any event, his horse did him proud, and he made sure that he always approached her from the left to avoid startling her. It was the constant thought of Hanna that kept him going and in reasonable spirits, along with the knowledge that his final destination was getting closer with every passing hour.

One afternoon, he found himself riding through an immense valley with extremely rugged mountains rising on either side of him. David was annoyed with himself, as he had not included rough and mountainous terrain in his calculations, having imagined that the journey would be mostly flat. These mountains, however, were rather formidable.

Having estimated that he must have passed Prince Albert to his right, he reasoned that Calitzdorp would be to his left and slightly in front of him. The valley zig-zagged as far as his eye could see and a small river gurgled happily alongside him, indicating to David that he was at the very base of the sheer mountains on either side. The bush was luscious and green, fresh and inviting, so he decided to follow the valley, which, he hoped, would come out at Ladismith.

"This place is like the Garden of Eden," David said excitedly to his horse. The contrast between the lush valley and the dry, harsh, rocky ground beyond the valley walls was stark. His memory of the soldier's map back at the train suggested that he was miles from any form of civilisation. He wondered if anyone else had ever seen this place of pure magic, and was beginning to think that this should perhaps be his Nomandudwane.

Then something caught his eye.

Nothing significant, but something curious. Just to his left, he saw a small piece of grass that had been bent over. David almost ignored it, but something didn't seem quite right. He pulled his horse to a halt and dismounted, studying the curious stem intently. He saw that it was very slowly trying to straighten to its original position. A little further into the bush was another stalk of grass, about the same size and also trying to straighten up.

David looked around, thinking he might see some animal, hoping it was not a predator, such as a leopard or a lion, but he noticed, rather oddly he thought, that no animal paw-prints were visible, anywhere. He was about to abandon his inspection of this anomaly and merely continue with the journey when he stopped short as he was about to rise. In between the two stems of grass was another one, already upright, but the kink near its base was quite visible.

Fear clutched at his entire chest. "Someone has been here recently and is deliberately trying to hide their tracks", David thought to himself. He remained crouched and looked for more evidence. Although none appeared, something just did not feel right.

Carefully standing up to his full height, he turned to face his horse and give her a pat on the neck. Then he swung himself into the saddle and scratched his head. In reality, however, he was looking at the ground for clues on both sides of his mount. Nothing was evident to his right, so he looked back to the left again. Another bent piece of grass stood just a little further in, and he could see the faint outline of the heel of a foot; not a boot, but a bare foot. Although perplexed by what he saw, David could not help congratulating himself for remembering so adroitly the bush-tracking skills that Daluxolo had taught him. He could not understand why someone – even someone whose ancestors arose in Africa – would want to cover their tracks so far from anywhere.

Yet curiosity gained an advantage over David, as he swung his horse to the left, urging her into the foliage. Indeed, more footprints became visible and even more signs of their being cleverly covered up. He dismounted again, and dropped to his haunches, studying the barely discernible imprint on the ground. "This is quite bizarre," he thought to himself.

Looking ahead at about shoulder height, he saw unmistakably that a spider web had been disturbed, the little arachnid busy repairing the damage. David picked up a small stick and took another few paces towards the web, gently lifting a loose strand of silk that was lightly drifting on the breeze. "Whoever they are, they are very good", David thought, "but not good enough to fool me." Standing in silence, he looked into the near distance at the craggy rocks at the base of a towering mountain and suddenly froze in pure fear.

Standing a mere ten yards directly in front of him was a wild-looking European man dressed in sacking. His hair was long and unruly, with grass and twigs entangled in the knots. Dried mud was smeared all over his face, forearms, feet, and shins. His dress and dishevelled appearance were well integrated with the surrounding bush. What frightened David the most was that this man was pointing a rifle directly at his face.

David very slowly raised his hands into the air, while the man in front of him didn't even flinch. Then, without any warning of sound, David felt the cold steel of a rifle barrel gently pressed against the back of his head. He would normally have jumped in fright, but already he was frozen in fear, his heart pounding uncontrollably in his chest. A menacing raspy voice in a half whisper instructed him to get to his knees very slowly. David obliged without saying a word.

A dark sack was thrown over his head, his hands bound behind his back and his sidearm forcibly pulled from his belt. He was roughly frisked, and his knife, compass, and other items were removed from his pockets. Not a word was spoken as he was manhandled to his feet and forced to walk forward. As he stumbled along, David took note of the heat on his one shoulder, and roughly worked out that he was being marched in a southerly direction. The only sound he could hear was from the hooves of his horse, so he knew she was coming along for the walk, but he could not hear any human footsteps.

He presumed that his captors had been well trained in bush-craft. They walked on in absolute silence, and, soon after they began a slight incline, the sun's heat suddenly disappeared, being instantly replaced by a pleasantly cool draft.

We must be in a barn, David thought to himself, but the slight echoes of his shoes on the uneven floor made him realise he was in a cave. After he had been harshly pushed to the ground, his back hitting a cold rock wall, he sat still, surrounded by silence.

At one point, he thought he heard some fabric move close to him, but then all went eerily quiet. David thought to call out and say something, but – not being sure what to say in such a situation – he chose to remain silent, in case his talking solicited a violent blow to the head with the butt of a rifle. He was convinced that these men were Boer guerrillas, but the man he had seen, dressed in sacking, barefoot and looking like the character of a castaway on a forgotten jungle island, confused him.

David sat for about an hour, silent, cold, and uncomfortable on the stone floor, his hands starting to lose sensation. Finally, he heard movement close by, and the sound of a fire being lit. He began to smell the smoke, and finally, without any warning, his hood was whipped off his head. What he saw made him gasp in fright; he saw three British soldiers and five Boer guerrillas.

"Who are you?" a soldier in British fatigues demanded, as he crouched down to bring himself to David's level.

"David Langbourne, sir," David answered as politely as he could, but he was so confused, he wasn't sure if he had been courteous.

"Why are you here?" the soldier asked, but he had a rough accent, the accent of a Boer.

"My train was derailed about half way from Port Elizabeth and Graaff-Reinet. I need to get to Cape Town urgently, so I bought a horse and took a bearing to the west. Are you British or Boer?" David couldn't help but ask.

"I ask the questions!" came the stark response. "Why are you here?"

"I was travelling in a straight line from the derailment towards Cape Town."

"Are you British?"

"No sir, I am Rhodesian. I have a pass issued by the BSAP Administration in Bulawayo. It confirms I am a civilian, not a soldier, and not part of the war. Your men took it off me when I was detained."

The soldier looked over his shoulder. David peered into the gloom and noticed a total of five men in the firelight, all pointing rifles at him, and that he was definitely inside a cave. His interrogator motioned with his head for someone to bring him something, and the man who wore sacking for clothes handed over the paperwork he had taken off David.

"You say you are not British?" the man asked again, but this time there was a menacing smile lurking at the corners of his lips.

"No, sir," David repeated.

"And is this the pass that you were issued with?" he said while opening a folded piece of paper with the BSAP coat of arms imprinted across the top.

"Yes, sir, that is the one."

"Tell me," the captor paused as he flipped the page over, "Mr David Langbourne. Tell me, what does BSAP stand for?"

"British South Af…" David broke off because he could see where this conversation was going.

"British South Africa? Go on?" the man sneered.

David hesitated. "It's the name of the police force in Rhodesia. They have nothing to do with what's going on down here."

"I beg to differ, Mr Langbourne. I believe they are very involved down here. If my memory serves me correctly, it was Dr Jameson who was the administrator of that organisation at one time, the very one who started this war."

"Yes, he was a fool," David said with some venom. "You have no idea what hardships he caused us in Rhodesia as a result."

The soldier sniggered, then promptly forced the hood back over David's head, plunging his world into darkness once more. He heard a short hiss, and then something hard slammed into his face.

The darkness became complete.

David woke with a splitting headache. The darkness and silence were still absolute, but his hands were now tied in front of him, not behind his back. When he tried to move into a sitting position, he heard chains rattling, and it didn't take long for him to realise that he was shackled, not just by his hands, but by his legs as well.

Understanding that his situation was dire, he lay still for a moment, gathering his thoughts, before attempting to sit up. It wasn't easy, and he allowed a grunt or two to escape, which stirred someone in the cave. Finding it virtually impossible to sit, he gave up and lay back with a sigh. David heard some mumbling in the local variant of Dutch, which he didn't understand, but he supposed that his return to consciousness had been reported. His muscles were stiff from the cold floor, and his back ached. With the hood still covering his head, David lay quietly and waited for something to happen. After what seemed like hours, coupled with the oppressive silence and darkness, he drifted into a shallow sleep.

A sharp kick to his hip woke David with such a start that, briefly not knowing where he was or why his movements were restricted, he wriggled desperately, trying to sit up and make sense of his situation. His circumstances rushed back to him in a flash, and he calmed down, breathing heavily from his exertion. He braced for another impact, but it didn't come. Instead, his hood was violently torn from his head, and squatting in front of him was another Boer commando, dressed in civilian clothing, and holding a Mauser rifle. He pulled David into a sitting position.

"Why are you here?" he asked with a guttural accent.

"Please, may I have some water, sir?" David asked in a parched and croaking voice. He glanced to his right and noticed that a faint glow of daylight was trying to sneak into the entrance of the cave.

"Later. Why are you here, man?"

"I'm trying to get to Cape Town. My train was derailed on the way to Graaff-Reinet."

"You don't travel to Cape Town from Graaff-Reinet this way. Why are you here?"

"I went to Willowmore first. Then it is a straight line from there to Ladismith. I was hoping to catch a train from Ladismith."

"It looks to us that you are a British subject. Your papers prove you are," the soldier said with a menacing grimace.

The interrogation went on for quite some time, with the guerrilla repeating his questions over and over again. David answered as best he could and several times asked for water, but without any luck, as the constant questioning wore him down. After what seemed like hours and hours, David's hood was finally pulled over his head again, and the cave went silent. About another hour later, David heard several men enter the cave, mumbling in their Dutch dialect among themselves. One man deliberately kicked David's leg, as he passed, but David did nothing; he was in no position to complain.

Suddenly, something was said in the mumbling that caught David's attention – his surname. It wasn't quite so much his surname being mentioned, which he had always expected, but someone repeating his name in surprise, a sound which set his senses on fire.

"Langbourne?" the man exclaimed again, this time a little louder. "Wat is sy voornaam?"

David understood this to be a question as to his first name.

"Ek dink dis 'Dawid'," someone said.

"'David Langbourne'? Agge-nee...," the first man said, approached David immediately, and whipped off his hood.

David blinked at the man in front of him. He was dressed like the first Boer he had seen, a gunny-sack for clothing, barefoot, unruly hair, and clutching a rifle. He was very thin, and missing a front tooth.

"Piet van Tonder?" David croaked, "from Patensie?" David couldn't believe who stood before him.

Piet looked at David in horror. "What are you doing here, man?"

"Ken jy hierdie vent?" one of the Boers asked.

"Ja, I know him," said Piet over his shoulder. "What are you doing here? You could get killed!"

"I'm trying to get to Cape Town, then I will return to Rhodesia. I live there now, Mijneer," David used the Dutch title for "Master" out of respect. "Please, may I have some water?"

David could not believe his luck; someone he knew personally. Piet van Tonder had been a tobacco farmer in Patensie, a three-day walk from Port Elizabeth. He had extended his hospitality to David and Morris when they had first walked to his farm to buy tobacco for their cigarette business. While his wife Hennie had cooked them some marvellous meals, Piet had taught David how to shoot a rifle and how to hunt. It was Piet who had sparked David's interest and love for birds, and had shared so much of his knowledge of the other animals, insects, and plants of the African bush.

Piet stared in horror as he pulled a water bottle off the belt that held his sack in place. "I cannot believe what I am looking at," he exclaimed. "Are you fighting for the British?"

"No, not at all. I'm just a civilian from Rhodesia. I'm not a fighter," David insisted.

"Drink!" Piet commanded, thrusting his water bottle at David, before walking towards the exit of the cave.

Just as he was about to walk out of sight, however, Piet turned to face his comrades and, shaking a warning finger at them, said something in the local language. David assumed – or even dared to hope – that Piet had warned his fellow fighters not to hurt him, but then again, it could have been a command not to let the prisoner out of their sight. Through the long slugs of cold water, David relaxed slightly.

His Lord had given him a reprieve.

CHAPTER TEN
Captive

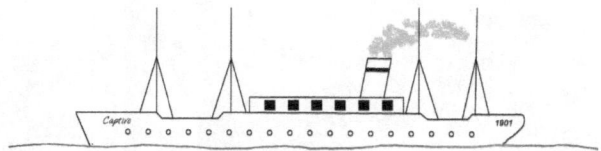

Hours seemed to pass before the light at the entrance to the cave dimmed slightly as someone entered the opening. David's guards stirred and stood as two men walked in and stood before him. One was Piet van Tonder, the other was someone David had not seen before.

"This is our commandant," Piet said sharply.

David could tell that Piet was trying to be civil, but the anger in his raspy voice was palpable. David stared at the commandant from his semi-lying position, legs and hands still shackled. He could not hide his fear. The commandant was dressed in a British officer's military uniform, but with no boots. He carried a rifle with a belt of ammunition over his left shoulder. Like all the others, he had a very unruly and unkempt beard; his hair was in bad need of a haircut, and dried blood splattered his uniform.

He got down on his haunches and spoke softly. "Your name is David Langbourne?" he asked.

"Yes, sir," David replied. He was feeling very weak as he had not had anything substantial to eat for a while now. The water had soothed his voice a little, but it was still croaky.

"Mijneer van Tonder tells me he knows you. How did you find us?" the commandant asked politely.

David was taken aback at the courtesy offered to him, as well as the soldier's excellent command of the English language. His accent was distinctly local Dutch, but he spoke English well, and – surprisingly – he looked even younger than David himself. David explained how he had unintentionally stumbled across their camp while attempting to navigate a straight line from Willowmore to Cape Town after his train was derailed.

"I see," the commandant scratched his chin through his beard. "And was anyone killed or injured on that train?"

"Yes," David replied nervously, suddenly realising that it might have been the commandant himself who had been responsible for that attack. "About four or five people, and several more injured. There were horses on the train, too," David volunteered. "The horse I was riding was injured in the derailment. I purchased her to make this journey. I had not initially intended making the journey on horseback."

"I was not involved in that derailment, about which I am sure you are wondering. Nevertheless, those that were there will be joining us in a day or so, and they will be interested to hear what you say. You say you are not British, yet you carry a pass stating that you are."

David sighed. "It looks that way, but for me to travel through these South African states, I need permission from the British South Africa Police in Rhodesia who administers the law of that country. I want nothing to do with their dispute with you. I am a businessman in Bulawayo, with a branch in Johannesburg, and I have stock I need to send north from both Port Elizabeth and Cape Town."

The interrogation went on for about an hour, during which time the commandant showed David a modicum of compassion, releasing the shackles from his feet, and allowing him to sit on an upturned wooden crate. He sat across from David on a similar box, while three of his men pointed their rifles at David loosely, but with cautious suspicion. The commandant made it clear that David's relative freedom was only temporary and that he would soon be re-shackled and back on the floor. He questioned David so politely, that – if it hadn't been for the cold cuffs on his wrists, and a splitting headache – David would have thought that they were enjoying a social meeting over a cup of coffee.

Eventually, however, curiosity got the better of David. Believing that he had answered all his questions fully and frankly, he decided to pose a query himself.

"I can't understand why you are showing me this respect, sir, when your men are obviously agitated at my presence. Can you explain why that is?"

To David's utter surprise, the commandant chuckled heartily and answered his question without reservation. "Firstly, I don't believe you are a soldier, nor a spy, and I think you are telling the truth. Mr van Tonder spoke very highly of you, yet he has grave suspicions. He is very bitter about the British, you understand."

"I am sure all Boer commandos are angry at the British," David replied quietly.

"Ah, yes, indeed they are, Mr Langbourne, as I am. But you see, the British soldiers took his family into captivity and burnt his farm down, even his crops in the field. He has nothing left, and he cannot locate his family. What kind of people do this?"

David grimaced because he did not like what he was hearing. "I have met Hennie van Tonder and her children in their home. She provided my brother and me with one of the most delicious meals we have ever eaten. When I leave here, I will do all in my power to locate his family."

"Ahh…" the commander rocked back on his crate slightly, "sadly I cannot release you from your captivity. You see, you have stumbled across, although unintentionally, a secret camp we have. The British have no idea we are here, and they have yet to find this valley. It is totally secret, and about the only place we have left to hide. I cannot risk letting you go and advising the British Army of our whereabouts."

"But, I promise you, I would never do that," David insisted.

"I may believe you, but I'm sure, if you were in my position, you would not risk it. Far too much lies at stake; too many lives at risk. Even if you said nothing, they might follow your tracks back here."

David's heart sank. In the depths of his gut, he knew the commandant was right and, now that the British had taken to burning the Boer farms down and transporting their wives and children to unknown locations, this war had become personal as well as political.

"May I ask your name?" David asked tentatively.

"You may, you have a right to know who I am. Commandant Reitz."

"I have heard the name."

"My father, probably. He is in politics. It was he who signed the Declaration of War. My name is Deneys Reitz."

"Why are some of your men dressed in sacks? And why are you dressed in a British Army uniform?" David asked as a sudden realisation hit him.

"My friend," the commander became serious, "they are uniforms of British soldiers we have killed or captured. We have been reduced to wearing sacking, as you can see, and we need clothing to keep us warm, so this will have to do under the circumstances. Now, we have spoken enough for one day."

Commandant Reitz abruptly ended the conversation and stood up. "My men will make you as comfortable as we are able, but sadly the food is in very short supply. We will provide, when we have, but be assured we will not harm you. Also be assured that not only will you remain our prisoner, but also that if you try to escape, you will be shot and killed. My men have their orders."

"I understand," David sighed. "I thank you for affording me your time and for your understanding of my situation."

Still bound in shackles, David sat in the shade of a tree, savouring a crust of bread. He was barefoot and dressed in sacking, his clothing having been stripped from him and shared among various commandos who were able to fit into them. His routine over the last ten days had been the same, an hour or so in the sun during the morning, shackled in the cave most of the day, then an hour or so outdoors in the afternoon. Scraps of food were provided while he was outside, and he had to do his ablutions at gunpoint.

David had only seen Piet van Tonder twice since his conversation with the Veldkornet. He assumed that Van Tonder was on point duty somewhere in the surrounding hills, protecting the secret Boer camp and sleeping rough. It seemed to David that a network of Boer soldiers had been carefully set in place, who would report back from all over the vast valley, keeping the Veldkornet well informed.

On this particular morning, Van Tonder had assigned himself to watch over David while he was outdoors, the Veldkornet's eyes glaring, a menacing look hidden behind his dark pupils. Even now the man was a shadow of his former self. Once a prominent and burly farmer with the forearms and shoulders of a hard labourer, he now looked as if he had wasted away from starvation; he was skeletal, unkempt, filthy, and splattered with months of dirt. David wasn't too sure whether or not some of the mud spatter on his face, chest, and arms was actually dried blood. One of the men, who still wore a semblance of a farmer's clothing and not sacking, definitely had a large bloodstain on his chest. Whose blood it might be was not obvious.

"It troubles me to see you this way, Mijneer van Tonder," David said. "When we met on your farm in Patensie you were a large and powerful man. I am very saddened to see what this war has done to you and your people."

"Ja," Piet sighed, "this is a terrible war." Suddenly he changed the subject, all the while carefully scanning the bushes suspiciously. "Why did you leave Port Elizabeth?"

"My brother decided we could make better money in Rhodesia. We had sold our cigarette business, so we decided to try our luck up there."

Piet seemed to relax slightly as he stared at David, inquisitively. "Was it good for you?"

"Yes, overall. We had some problems with the Matabele rebellion. But it also caused our business to be successful after it was over."

"How so?" Piet asked. He seemed more at ease and sat gingerly on a small rock at his feet.

"There was this administrator up there, a Dr Leander Jameson. He was the cause of the rebellion. He took all the soldiers away and left Bulawayo utterly vulnerable to attack. The town was put under siege by Matabele warriors for about three months, and we were nearly killed. I don't like that man. When I met him, I thought he was a gentleman, but he was only interested in himself. He caused starvation, sickness, fear and death in the community.

"Anyhow, we lost a lot of wagons in the bush – for a whole year – while the fighting continued. When we eventually found them, the prices of everything had jumped so high we made a lot of money. Overall, we did alright but at great initial cost."

What David said seemed to catch Piet's attention. "Do you know why Jameson took a force of men out of Bulawayo?"

"Of course," David sighed, "he tried to overthrow the Republican Government of the Transvaal."

"It caused a great deal of mistrust between the British and the Boers, and resulted in this war." Piet almost spat out his anger.

"Isn't it sad that one man can cause so much death, destruction, and loss?" David shook his head in despair.

"No," Piet pointed a menacing finger at David, "not just him. The British wanted this war. The British were looking for this fight. Jameson was just the trigger. They want our land, our gold and our diamonds, and they have come here in hundreds of thousands to take it all."

David didn't have an answer. He sat in silence, staring at his former friend, a man he admired immensely, a man who had taken a liking to him and taught him all the basics about the African bush, how to shoot straight, and how to survive.

"Now," Piet sat straight and pointed into the bush, "they have taken my wife and children and thrown them in a camp under terrible conditions ... and they destroyed my farm. What are the British thinking? Is this fair?"

After this outburst, the remainder of David's time outside was very awkward; hardly another word was spoken. David didn't have answers, and he felt sick to the stomach about Piet's situation. He saw before him a once powerful man who had been physically, emotionally and mentally gutted. And now, because his entire family was in the hands of his enemy, he was driven by a force that could only end in raw hate, or death.

As Jack Shiel surveyed the hustle and bustle of the Port Elizabeth harbour, his face was etched in concern. Approaching a thin, Xhosa-speaking man who was sitting on an upturned box, wearing a mixture of tribal robes and ill-fitting Western clothing, Jack tried to converse in a combination of English and hand signals. Since Jack had never needed to use isiXhosa, he had never bothered to learn it.

"Nguni?" he asked, making some vague gestures depicting a muscular man by gripping his own forearm and pushing his bicep up as high as possible. He also tried puffing out his chest and extending his elbows in an attempt to improve his physique. Although he knew that he looked quite comical in his business suit, Jack didn't care. He was in a quandary and felt that his only hope of a solution was to find David's long-standing and faithful friend, Nguni.

The thin man nodded and grinned broadly, before rattling off a few incomprehensible phrases, punctuated frequently by the sharp clicks of the language. Jack picked up the international signal of "yes" when the man nodded briefly and looked quite pleased with himself as he waited for another round of charades.

Jack promptly pointed towards the central part of the town. "Standard Bank. You know Standard Bank? Standard Bank," he repeated forcefully, jabbing his finger in the direction of the business district each time he uttered the phrase.

"Stun-dud Bunk," the Xhosa said, smiling still.

"Yes," Jack nodded in agreement. "Standard Bank. Nguni," he pointed to town again, then to himself, "me".

The man smiled, repeated the words "Stun-dud Bunk," and waited for more instructions.

"Good. Thank you," Jack said forcing out yet another, unfamiliar smile, while awkwardly grasping the man's hand, and started walking back to his office, totally unsure if the message had been understood at all and if it would get through to Nguni.

At about three o'clock that afternoon, however, a large man in the traditional robes of the amaBhaca stood silently in the banking hall, against one wall. He barely moved, but his curious eyes followed everyone's movements as they conducted their daily business.

"Sir," a teller popped his head into Jack's office, "I'm terribly sorry to trouble you, but I think that Xhosa man you were looking for is here."

Jack leapt to his feet and strode into the banking hall, immediately gripping Nguni's hand in a firm handshake. The relief on his face was evident.

"I see you, Nguni," he said in English. "Thank you for coming here so quickly."

Nguni returned the handshake. "I see you, Boss," he said. He had never spoken to a bank manager before, but he knew that this 'mlungu' was a friend of Boss David and Boss Morris, because he had seen them with this man on several occasions, and each time they had seemed quite happy in each other's company.

Jack took Nguni by the shoulder and led him to a quiet corner of the hall. "Nguni," he murmured, "I am worried about David."

Immediately, Nguni's forehead was creased with worry. "Where?" he hissed.

"I don't know," Jack sighed. Speaking carefully and slowly so that Nguni might understand his English, Jack explained that, about two weeks beforehand, the train that David had been travelling on had experienced an accident. When David had not returned with the other passengers, Jack had ferreted out that David had purchased a horse and headed for Cape Town. When the manager had made further enquiries, a preacher in Willowmore had informed him that David had spent the night there and had left the following day on an injured horse, but nothing more had been heard of him since. Jack had then telegraphed his brothers in Johannesburg and Bulawayo, but they, too, had not heard from him.

"Boss Louis will go to Cape Town to wait for him," Jack said, "but I worry because there is a lot of fighting over there."

"I go look," Nguni said without hesitation, and almost turned to walk out of the bank.

"Wait," Jack put a hand on his shoulder. "You don't know where to go, but I will get you to Willowmore. Maybe you can track him from there?"

"I track him," Nguni's deep voice rumbled through the stark hall. "I take Daluxolo. He track Boss David. My brother, he be best tracker."

Jack pointed at the floor, indicating the spot where they stood. "Meet me here tomorrow morning," he said. "I will arrange for a coach to take you to Willowmore, with a letter for the preacher," Jack frowned. "I cannot come with you. The Boers do not like me, but you, Nguni, they do not worry about."

"It is good," Nguni agreed, but the worry etched on his face was telling.

As Jack returned to his office, anxiety fiercely aggravating his heartburn, he feared the worst for his good friend David. He knew David would have made contact with his brothers had he been able to, yet it had been two weeks now without any sign of him. Jack couldn't face waiting another inactive day. He had to do something, and Nguni was his only hope.

David had lost track of the number of days he had been in captivity but felt sure it had been at least a month. Similar to when he had been held under siege in Mafeking, his biggest worry was Hanna and what she might be going through. He knew it was not fair on her – a missing husband and a four-month-old daughter to care for – by this time she must have been beside herself with worry; barely married and believing she was already a widow.

His concern for the business took second place. He knew his brothers would take control and sort out the Cape Town problem. Why, under the circumstances, Morris may even come out himself, the shipment was massive enough as it was, and Morris, with his extraordinary gift for numbers, knew exactly what items were in which crate, as well as their cost price and retail sales price. It made sense, David thought, that Morris would come out, especially now that he had gone missing.

David was also fully aware that he might be thought of as being dead and how that would place Hanna under severe strain. He kept putting that thought out of his head as it distressed him, too. He thought back to the last time he had seen Piet van Tonder, which had been about two weeks previously. It had been such a depressing conversation that it had left him feeling utterly helpless for days. Assuming that Piet had been reassigned somewhere else, David missed seeing his familiar face, despite Piet's horrifying condition and the depths into which his life had sunk.

Other Boer commandos assigned to watch over David during his morning and afternoon breaks were in similar situations to Piet. They looked like farmers, but they were all dressed in scraps of clothing and sacking, anything they could find, while beneath their glaring anger, could be seen their hurt and deep despair. On some days there were too few commandos in the camp to take David out into the sunshine or to feed him, but David kept his peace and bided his time, confident that one day he would be released.

The Boer soldier who entered the cave that day to let David out into the sunshine and to do his ablutions was none other than the commandant himself. He apologised for the delay that morning, which he explained was due to a shortage of men, most of whom were out on a critical operation. David found the commandant to be unexpectedly gentlemanly and civil, not just to David himself but also to his men. What was even more surprising was that he seemed to David to be barely eighteen years old.

"My friend, Mijneer van Tonder," David said, as he stood up with some effort, owing to the stiffness of his joints, "I have not seen him for a couple of weeks. Do you know if he is alright?"

"Come," Commandant Reitz helped David to his feet. "I saw him two days ago. He is doing an essential job for me, and I left him in good health."

"Thank you. I have been worried."

The young men walked into the sunlight, David, as always, shielding his eyes for the first minute or so to adjust to the harsh daylight. He was thin, and the joints of his elbows and knees were starting to show clearly under his skin. A rugged beard had formed on his face and, dressed in sacking and barefoot, he could easily pass as one of the commandant's men.

"Sit," Reitz invited as they arrived under the tree that had become David's outside sanctuary. He unshackled David's hands but kept his legs in irons.

"I'll stand, if you don't mind," David stretched and rubbed his behind, trying to get some blood moving again. "I tend to sit a great deal in the cave."

"As you wish," the commandant said, as he pulled some dried beef from a pouch that was slung over his shoulder. "Biltong?" he asked.

David accepted the gracious offer gladly. "Thank you, sir," he said.

"Tell me," Commandant Reitz said, "Mijneer van Tonder told me about the conversation you and he had last time. He told me your sentiments towards the British."

"About Dr Jameson," David corrected him. "My sentiments have not changed," David said bluntly as he savoured the salty, dried meat.

"I think you are a decent citizen, Mr Langbourne, but I hope you can understand why I cannot risk letting you go."

"I understand," David accepted the situation without hesitation. "I'd probably do the same if I was in your position."

"No hard feelings, then?" Reitz smiled.

For the first time in what seemed like months, David laughed. "No hard feelings, Commandant."

Reitz grinned. "Are you married?"

"Yes, I am, and I have a four-month-old daughter. Her name is Ettie."

"Congratulations. I'm sure your wife must be concerned about you, and I do feel for her."

"She will be upset, yes," David looked sad, but then straightened up and smiled at his captor. "She will also be furious with me when she eventually sees me. Sometimes I am afraid to be released."

Commandant Reitz burst out laughing but quickly checked himself, casting furtive glances into the surrounding bush.

"Commandant," David became serious, "why do you and some of your men wear the uniform of the British army?"

"It is simply a matter of keeping warm. This uniform," the commandant patted his chest, "was taken off an officer who was shot and killed not far from here." Commandant Reitz lifted his left arm slightly, and with his right finger prodded a hole about four inches below the armpit. "The bullet went in here, and straight through his heart."

David was on the brink of asking Reitz if it was he who had killed the officer but thought better of it. "Does it not feel demeaning to be wearing the uniform of your enemy?" David decided to ask instead.

"My friend," Reitz said with a calculating look in his eyes, "sometimes the winter in the Cape can get very cold. Water on the ground will turn to ice at night. For us burghers, if we are not dressed correctly, we would die out there. It has almost happened to me, I can tell you. I have already lost two good men to the cold."

"I don't understand, and please forgive me, Commandant," David quickly apologised for asking questions that he probably should avoid, "but why is it that you are not correctly dressed in the first place?"

The commandant cocked his head slightly so that he was watching at David through the corners of his eyes. He seemed somewhat surprised at the question.

"It is obvious to me that you have not been following the events of the war very closely."

"No," David admitted hesitantly.

"Let me tell you a story, Mr Langbourne. Take a seat," he invited David once again, and this time David obliged as Deneys Reitz likewise took a seat on a small rock.

Deneys' father, Francis Reitz, was the State Secretary for the South African Republic who had agreed to the signing of the Declaration of War against the British Empire. Although being underage at the time, Deneys had been given permission by President Kruger himself to enlist and was handed a rifle and ammunition. Along with his brothers, and using his own horse, he had joined the forces that were heading east to invade Natal. The early stages of the war had subsequently become extremely fierce, and he had seen many of his friends and colleagues killed. He had also been part of the group that had enforced the Siege of Ladysmith in Natal until they had been overrun by the British Army. Without horses, his commando had begun walking towards the Cape Colony to join forces with General Koos De Le Rey outside Colesberg, a fearless leader and tactical soldier extraordinaire.

"You walked?" David interrupted Deneys. "That must be almost eight hundred miles!"

"Yes," Deneys sighed, "and now you know why many of us do not have boots. We walked so far that our shoes broke apart and were abandoned along the way. Of course, without boots, it makes our journey more difficult and slows us down. In fact, being barefoot in the bush is a very dangerous hazard. It is hard to outrun an offensive force, and, if a man's feet should become cut in the process, you could be certain that the British trackers would easily hunt him down and find him. Not to mention the chance of stepping on a puff adder. Boots are vital, as are saddles. Without a saddle, one cannot ride too far, especially at speed."

"So where did you get your saddles?" David asked incredulously. He had noticed that there were many stashed in the cave.

"We carried them on our shoulders."

"Hold up," David put a hand in the air, "you carried your saddles on your shoulders for eight hundred miles? All the way from Natal?"

"And a rifle," Deneys chuckled, "and a bandolier of ammunition. You can't use a horse in a conflict without a saddle, they are vital, as everyone knows. We would also have to help our walking wounded as we had no hospitals. Those that could not walk we would leave for the British to find. We knew that the British would tend to our wounded in their medical facilities; mercifully, they are good in that way. Not having a saddle is like not having boots."

"You amaze me, sir," David shook his head in fascination. "I have never come across a tougher group of people than you Boers."

"We are tough," Deneys chuckled again and stood, quickly casting an attentive eye toward the bushes. "We Boers use bush medicine, and mostly it works just as well as the fancy British medicine. A colleague of mine was crouching just as an attack commenced, and as he raised up to charge, a bullet hit him in the top of his shoulder by his neck and travelled through his torso, exiting near his groin. But he lives today. In fact, he was the man who watched over you two days ago; he is on light duties."

"My word…" David trailed off as he stared at his captor in awe. He did not know what to say.

Deneys pulled a little silver object out of his pocket, no bigger than his thumb. It looked like a lady's high-heeled boot with intricate engraving all over it. There was a lid on the top which he flipped open with his thumb and, gripping his rifle between his legs, tapped out some brown powder into the palm of his hand.

"Snuff?" he offered his palm to David.

"No thank you, sir, but thank you for the offer. That's a curious-looking snuffbox."

Deneys pinched some snuff between his thumb and index finger and sharply inhaled a small quantity into his nostrils. "It is," he said as he exhaled and passed the trinket to David.

David turned the exquisite piece of craftsmanship over in his hands, and even flipped the lid open, taking a quick whiff of the pungent ground tobacco contained within. "There are some initials on the top," David noticed. "JWR?"

"I took it off a British captain whom I had shot. He wasn't badly injured, but his fighting days will be no more. I recall his surname was Reid or something similar."

David looked up at the commandant, somewhat horrified that he could discuss the shooting of a man so casually. Then he noticed something behind him in the bush, just over Deneys' shoulder. About halfway up the tree was a twig that had been broken. It hung lazily, attached by a small piece of bark.

"Why did you take it off him?" David carefully brought his attention back to the commandant.

"We are compelled to take everything we can from our enemy, food, ammunition, field-glasses. I found this in the captain's pocket, and took it for myself, because of his ungrateful attitude."

"If I had been shot and had a bullet in me, I would also be somewhat ungrateful," David said, then suddenly laughed at his own joke.

Commandant Reitz also laughed at the comment. "Indeed, Captain Reid did not have a good day that day."

David smiled and handed back the snuffbox. As he did so, he stole another quick glance at the broken twig in the tree behind him.

"Tell me," David continued, sensing that both he and the commandant were a little more relaxed in each other's company, "are there any lions in this area?"

"Why? Are you scared you won't be able to run away if there were?" Deneys chuckled.

"Something like that," David smiled, somewhat embarrassed.

"Yes, I am sure there are, but I haven't seen any here. Leopards, certainly. Giraffes and elephants could never walk down these slopes." Deneys waved a hand at the steep and rocky valley walls surrounding them."

"That's what I thought," David mumbled and cast another furtive glance at the twig in the tree. It could only have been broken by an elephant or giraffe as it was so high up. "I must ask you this, sir – " David began.

"You ask a lot of questions for a prisoner." Deneys had cut David off, but he was smiling as he did so.

David quickly put up a hand in defence. "This will be my last for today," he chuckled.

Deneys feigned a sigh in return. "Go on, my friend."

"I know you wear the captured uniforms of the British soldiers for warmth, because your clothes, like your boots, have worn through to nothing."

"That is true," Deneys nodded solemnly.

"Are you aware that in rules of war, if you are captured impersonating your enemy by wearing their uniform, they can execute you without trial? No transfer to a prisoner-of-war camp, no discussion - just a summary execution in the field?"

"Is that a fact?" Deneys grinned menacingly, but David saw grave concern suddenly wash over his face. "It doesn't bother us any. When we win this war we will give these uniforms back," he laughed feebly.

"Be that as it may, sir, but I am only telling you what I have been told by a colonel in Rhodesia. It is accepted international law. I tell you this because I have a concern for you. If you or your men get captured, you will be executed before nightfall, no question about it."

"I must be honest, I have not heard that said before," the commandant mused aloud, appearing more deeply concerned.

"I also cannot understand," David quickly added, "why you continue to fight to the bitter end when a negotiated settlement would save many lives."

Reitz suddenly became very earnest. "Perhaps you don't understand," he said. "We will win this war. General De la Rey has a plan, and it is working. We are not fighting just to settle a dispute; we are fighting for our country and our heritage, our language and our culture. Now we are fighting for our farms, and our women and children, too. We are fighting for our very future. This is no longer a political war, the British have made very sure of that."

David sighed in desperation. "Sir, I have no answers for you, or for this war. I do not understand it; nor why it has to be so brutal on both sides. There are civilians like me on each side who do not want to fight but to live in peace and harmony amongst all dividing lines, racial, cultural, political, tribal, and religious. I plan to leave here alive, whether you let me go, or I escape, but I can assure you one way or the other, I will not allow the British to know where you are hiding. We are all human, and some of your men are wounded, tired, and drained. I could not live with myself if I showed the British where to come and slaughter you.

"We may never meet again," David continued, "but I would like to take this opportunity to thank you for treating me well, and for showing me kindness when some of your men very rightly wished to kill me. I have enjoyed our conversations, and when this war is over, and if we are both alive, I would prefer if we could find a way to become friends."

Deneys looked at David carefully. He frowned as he took in what his prisoner had said. He changed his rifle to his left hand and extended his right to David, who likewise did the same. Deneys helped David to his feet and then held his grip for just a fraction longer than necessary. He gave David's hand a hardly noticeable shake.

"I enjoyed talking to you, Mr David Langbourne," the commandant said softly, "but I doubt very much that we will ever be friends. I will never accept British rule in this country. If the British win and I live to the end of the war, then I will leave this land."

"Let's hope there is a mutually agreed settlement, sooner rather than later," David said, wobbling slightly because he stood up too fast. Holding onto the trunk of the tree for support with his right hand, he held out his left hand for the shackles to be reapplied. Deneys skilfully locked one on, then the other. What he didn't notice was that David's fingers had twisted a little twig that was attempting to grow into a branch. He didn't break it but bent it hard enough for it to be bruised. Then, walking back to the cave with the commandant, David prepared for another long day in the damp gloom of his current home.

Louis and Harry had not spoken to each other much in the days since Harry had joined Louis in Johannesburg. The stock had been released from the warehouse at the Cape Town harbour, and Louis had travelled north to assist Harry. The whereabouts and fate of their elder brother overshadowed the sorting and shipping of the mountains of merchandise that had arrived on the trains. Now, with most of the preparation and allocations done, and the Rhodesian stock safely on its way, their minds were continually drawn back to David.

"Shall we check with the Post Office again?" Harry murmured.

"We were there only a few hours ago," Louis responded rather gloomily.

The brothers sat in silence once again, gazing at the half-empty warehouse. They had looked at the same boxes so often they had begun to feel some attachment to them, almost as if they were their only connection to their old life.

"Come on," Harry said and stood up abruptly, causing his chair to scrape in anger. "We have to get out of here. Let's revisit Danie."

Without objection, Louis stood up and donned his jacket, before both boys walked out of the gloom of the oppressive warehouse walls and into the sunshine. They spoke brief sentences to one another, not saying much until they had reached the offices of Coetzee and Coetzee Accounting. Danie welcomed them into his office, but his mood was equally sombre.

"No news, Gentlemen?" Danie quietly asked.

"No," Louis replied. "Morris contacts us from London daily, but we have no further news for him."

"Indeed," Danie nodded, "Morris sends me a telegram daily, too. He is very distraught, and I think he may well come out here."

Harry straightened his tie unconsciously. "I doubt that," he sighed. "We have done everything he has asked, and there is nothing for him to do. I have to return to Bulawayo very soon. Our shipment will have arrived, and our managers will have their hands full."

"When will you leave?"

"I should have gone three or four days ago. I am uncomfortable with having to face Hanna, so I am putting it off."

"Poor woman," Danie shook his head solemnly. "Such a lovely young lady; the perfect wife for David."

"Do you suppose there is any chance that David might be alive?" Louis asked anxiously.

Danie answered with grave concern in his voice, "It is hard to tell. The British have not reported a casualty that could be identified as David in any way, so we can only pray to the Good Lord that he is lost in the bush or has been captured by the Boers. Yet it has been a month now, and it doesn't bode well, I'm afraid. We can only continue to pray. Harry, I feel, for the sake of your business, you should return to Bulawayo now."

"Can't you go?" Harry addressed Louis, "you're older than me."

Louis shook his head, sorrow seeping from every part of his body. "I'll go if you want me to."

"With all due respect, Gentlemen," Danie said with authority as he looked at Louis, "Morris needs you to start approaching your business contacts and sell through the stock. Given that he appears to have grossly over-committed himself to the banks and the passage of time, your commitment to increased sales is absolutely essential. May I, therefore, make a suggestion?"

The two brothers stared at Danie, unblinking. Danie indeed commanded some authority within the small family group, and it was an unspoken agreement that when Danie spoke, they would listen.

"Go back to Bulawayo, Harry. Visit Hanna and let her know that we are all still in the dark. I actually think she would cherish a visit from you. Louis, you start moving within your commercial circles and get the word out of what you have to sell. I will visit Cape Town tomorrow, where I have some business in hand, and conduct more enquiries with the military regarding David's whereabouts. But you two need to get back to your business and start operating, hard. Morris is counting on you."

This was precisely what Louis and Harry needed, the encouragement of a man with authority and direction, a man who would lead them when their mentor was missing. Fraught with despair, but with a clear idea of what had to be done, arrangements were made, and a plan of action initiated. Harry boarded the train that very evening, and Louis made arrangements to meet at the Johannesburg Club for an evening of conversation, and to perhaps clinch a deal or two.

CHAPTER ELEVEN

The Tracker

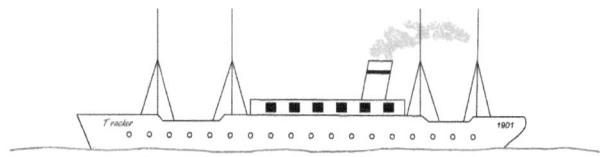

David's mind was racing; the vision of the broken twig, about ten feet up in the tree, would not leave him. He knew that there were no elephants or giraffes in the valley, the sides were too steep and broken, making it too dangerous for them to clamber down, and a leopard would certainly not have left that damage. Neither could an adult man reach up to break that twig; it was too high. A man on a horse, perhaps, but then the rider would have had to stand in his saddle and reach up to snap that twig. Perhaps a man, standing on another's shoulders, might have done it.

Someone had deliberately broken it, David thought. It was as if someone had sent him a message, a signal. It had been perfectly positioned, directly in front of where he would stand or sit during his outdoor excursions. There was no chance he would have missed that sign. But he questioned if it was indeed a signal; at the very least he needed to believe it was.

He cast his memory back to when he and Morris took three months to walk to Bulawayo with their six wagons. That was back in 1893, a long time ago. Because the old pioneer track had been so vast, they had snapped twigs at shoulder height while sitting on a horse to indicate that the path they had tested was not passable. Tebogo, the Motswana, had taught David the trick at the time, but he had not seen Tebogo again since that trip. Morris certainly could not have done it, England was too far away for him to be anywhere near this part of the country. In any case, Morris hated the bush.

David sighed. His mind was playing games with him. He was so desperate to go home that he thought he might believe in leprechauns if they ever existed. The reality was that he was held captive in a valley so inaccessible and remote that even the British army did not come down there. In fact, he believed the British did not even know of the valley's existence. David did imagine, however, that a small farming community might live somewhere nearby, because on two occasions he was sure he had smelt the aroma of freshly baked bread coming from further down the valley. He suspected that this was where his captors had been getting their scant food.

He therefore reluctantly dismissed the broken-twig signal from his mind and closed his eyes, allowing a long sigh of resignation to escape. Yet, as he closed his eyelids, the image of that broken twig appeared once again. He could see every little splinter, the pale yellow-green fresh wood under the grey bark. He opened his eyes again and stared at the cave wall in front of him, unfocused. The image continued to torment him.

Was it Nguni? Perhaps Daluxolo? David wondered. They had spoken about the broken-twig signal once before, but they had not needed any use for it back then. How would they even know he was missing? His thoughts plagued him. Well, if it was a sign, he thought, then he had left a message to say he had seen it. He could do no more.

David's afternoon session in the sun seemed to take forever to come around. Beginning to doubt having ever seen it, he desperately wanted to take another look at that twig. The Boer soldier who was his guard that afternoon was a surly man, filled with hate and the desire for revenge. Having expected a rough handling that afternoon from this man, David was not disappointed. After the shackles on his wrists had been roughly removed, David was shoved in the back, but his legs in chains could not keep up with the momentum, causing him to crash to the ground. Because this particular soldier always behaved in such a savage manner, David simply accepted his fate.

Once he had picked himself up off the ground, however, David shuffled over to his tree trunk and – not wanting to alert his captor in any way – tried desperately not to look at the opposite tree for the broken twig. When David reached the allotted shady patch, therefore, he put both hands against the trunk and stretched his legs. While doing this, he looked at the little twig he had bruised earlier that day to see how it was doing. To his utter surprise, it was missing. It had been plucked carefully from its socket and removed.

David continued to do his stretching exercises against the tree, before turning to place his back against the trunk and starting on some half squats. He was too weak to do a full squat, but he knew the movement was good for him. As he did so, David stared at his guard, who stared back menacingly. Yet the moment the Boer began to survey the bush for danger, David took his chance to look into the tree ahead of him. There it remained, the broken twig, precisely as he had seen it earlier, only this time it was accompanied by a second broken twig, just to the right of it.

David's heart leapt!

This was definitely man-made; someone had been here and had surely left a sign for him - there was no mistaking it.

Immediately, David's heart started racing. He checked the earth below the tree for a hoof print or a human footprint, but saw nothing. Whoever was doing this was very good at bush-craft. He concluded that, without a doubt, someone was going to rescue him. Nervously, David looked back at his guard, who had once again turned his full attention on the captive.

The question that filled David's mind was how this rescue might be made possible and who would be carrying it out. Was he supposed to do nothing, or was he expected to cause some diversion? All signs pointed to the fact that he was expected to initiate something to indicate that he had seen and understood the message, but what? What could he do without alerting his captors?

His opportunity came when the Boer cast another cautionary look into the bush around him. David quickly, but casually, pointed his index finger into the air and drew a quick imaginary circle.

It was something he would do to signal Nguni or Daluxolo in the morning when they were driving the wagons to say, "Let's go", or, after a long day on the trek, the same signal would take on a different meaning. It could mean "That's enough", or "Put the wagons into a laager", a protective circular formation for the night. It had always amazed David how bush signals such as these – a type of whistle or click, the nod of the head in one direction, or the squint of an eye – could have such exacting and understood meanings without a word being said.

As the Boer soldier seemed to relax just a fraction and return his gaze to his subject, David carefully allowed himself to slide down the trunk into a sitting position. The instant his hands and backside touched the ground, David leapt up, hissed a cry of pain and shook his hand furiously, staring intently at the ground he had sat upon, and totally ignoring his guard.

The Boer, quick as lightning, trained his rifle threateningly on David and took up a stance that meant business, one leg slightly in front, bent at the knee. David continued to ignore him but flailed his hand madly about him, stomping at the ground as furiously as his chains would allow, pretending to kill whatever had caused him so much pain. Then, looking at his guard, whispered the word "scorpion" several times, still thrashing his hand about and pretending to be in severe pain.

Then, the incredible happened. The Boer lowered his rifle and started laughing at David. From where he was, he looked at the ground at David's feet, expecting to see the squashed remains of a scorpion in the dust. Instead, a look of pure terror crossed his face when he felt the cold point of a sharp spear touching the back of his neck.

It all happened very quickly. Even David had not seen Nguni appear behind the Boer's back, and at what seemed the very same moment that the Boer froze, a mound of earth and dried leaves to his side erupted menacingly. Covered in dust and debris, Daluxolo snatched the Boer's rifle away. Before the dust settled, Daluxolo had rammed a cloth into the Boer's mouth, then pushed him to the ground, neutralising him in an instant and without a sound. It was all over in a blur.

Both David and the Boer were so confused by the speed of events that they were almost paralysed in shock. Nguni quickly applied the shackles to the Boer's wrists, then using the key that locked them in place, strode over to David and removed the restraints from his legs. Daluxolo then pulled the soldier to his feet and handed David the rifle.

Without a word, Nguni led them out of the clearing in a northerly direction, while frog-marching the Boer in front of him. Daluxolo remained behind to cover their tracks. It was a difficult task, but once he was satisfied with his handiwork, Daluxolo silently melted into the bush with a determined scowl.

Because the valley was less than half a mile wide, it didn't take long at all – barely minutes – for the men to reach the steep incline of the rugged mountainside. As they rounded a large boulder that had fallen to the valley floor (a geological event that must have been spectacular when it happened), Nguni forced the Boer onto the ground and made him lie face down. He then stepped over to David, who was still in a slight state of shock, but obviously very relieved by the turn of events.

"I see you, Nguni," David whispered in isiXhosa so that his captive could not hear them.

"I see you, Boss David," Nguni whispered back, flashing his white teeth in joy.

"Where is Daluxolo?"

"He hides our tracks. He will be here soon-soon. We will wait for darkness."

"We should make more distance, should we not?" David was concerned because they were barely a few hundred yards from the camp.

"We cannot climb in the sun. The men, they will see us for many miles. We need darkness."

"Nguni," David put his arm around the big man's shoulder and whispered into his ear, "the camp is too close, and in less than an hour, they will see I am missing. There are still two or three hours before dark."

Nguni put his lips close to David's ear. "Daluxolo and me, we have made a trail that goes the other way. By the time they find that the trail ends at nothing, it will be dark."

David shook his head in awe and smiled in fascination. "You are very clever, Nguni."

"It is Daluxolo who is clever. I am strong."

David suppressed a laugh and then looked at the hapless Boer lying on the ground at his feet. He reached down and tugged at the sacking the man wore as clothing and tore off a lengthy strip. Lifting the man's head slightly, David wriggled the cloth strip into a position over his gag and tied it off at the back of his head, so that he could not spit or dislodge the cloth. David knew that any sound out of the ordinary would completely unravel the planning of his two amaXhosa friends.

"We talk later," David nodded at Nguni, who merely nodded back.

An hour later Daluxolo arrived at the rendezvous, and in total silence the men sat, waiting patiently for sunset. David reached over and clasped Daluxolo's forearm, a silent but powerful form of thanks; words were not necessary. Just before dark, Nguni moved the Boer to a large tree and made him sit facing the trunk, tying his feet around the tree securely. Then, with some dexterity, shackled his arms around the tree as well. With the gag firmly in place, Nguni was satisfied that neither would the man escape nor would he raise the alarm.

"His people will find him tomorrow," Nguni grinned.

"They will find our tracks too. Will we be able to outrun them?" David asked. He knew the Boers were fast on their feet, but he was sure Nguni had an answer.

"We walk that way," Nguni pointed to the top of the valley, "then will be near the camp of your people who wear uniforms."

"Not too far?" David was pleasantly surprised.

"Over this mountain, but two, and for two nights we walk, then we will see the cooking fires. It is near-near."

"We go," Daluxolo said with authority.

"Show me the way, Daluxolo," David smiled and gripped his shoulder firmly.

Clambering out of the valley barefoot had been almost unbearable for David. Sometimes, Nguni would wrap his large hand around David's emaciated and chafed wrists and haul him over a boulder, but It was evident that David had lost most of his strength and fitness. Without the help of Nguni and Daluxolo, he would never have made it out of the valley.

The ascent had taken over four hours, and by the time they had crested the summit, David's feet had become lacerated and bled badly. Although he knew he should not have been surprised, he had seen how his two friends had been unscathed, owing to their lifelong experience of walking barefoot. Although they were quite ready to continue, therefore, they also recognised David's plight and insisted on resting so that he might regain some strength.

Exhausted, David was sure that, if he had carried a square meal inside of him, he would have thrown it up by that time. The journey was not over though; they had another valley to clamber down and another steep, jagged climb back out. In fact, David wondered how many of these valleys were ahead and understood in a flash why the British troops would never venture into these canyons.

David could not go any further. As much as his mind willed him to keep going, his strength had wasted away. The month of minimal food, consisting mainly of dried meat and scraps of bread had taken its toll.

"I can't," David managed to say between gasps of breath as he carefully lowered himself and sat on the ground.

The instant he sat down, however, Nguni lifted David over his shoulders and began the descent. "We go," Nguni rumbled and started walking into the valley.

"You can't carry me," David grunted his objection, being too tired to manoeuvre himself into a more comfortable position.

"My goats are heavier than you," Nguni said flatly.

The two brothers chuckled to themselves as they set a hard pace, mindful of the hazards of loose rock and gravel. David gratefully allowed his saviours to continue unimpeded with their escape plan.

Just before sunrise, the escapees settled under some thick bushes to rest and to sleep during the coming daylight hours. To David's surprise, Daluxolo rummaged under some dead leaves and pulled out a calabash – a formerly bulbous fruit, whose shell had been dried hard and filled with water. He passed it around, and they slaked their thirst. David slept quickly and soundly.

When David awoke, it was almost sunset. Nguni sat by his side and offered him some more water.

"Thank you, my friend. How did you find me?" David asked for the first time since his rescue.

"The boss from the bank, he was looking for you."

"Jack Shiel," David sighed as he tried to gather his thoughts. He would ask more questions later as he suddenly remembered the Boers would be looking for them, too. "Where is Daluxolo?"

"He is near-near. He looks for the Boers behind us."

Right on cue, Daluxolo appeared as silently as a leopard and crouched, a broad smile spreading across his face.

"The men, they have gone back," Daluxolo grinned.

"They will not track in the dark," Nguni muttered. "The road is clear. We will see your people when the sun greets us."

David tried to stand, but he flinched as soon as he put pressure on his lacerated feet. Without hesitation, Daluxolo stood up and swung David over his back.

"You can't carry me all the way," David tried to complain.

"Ghaw!" Daluxolo hawked in disgust as he tossed David once to settle him on his shoulders, "my chickens are heavier than you," he said with a chuckle and stole a mischievous smile at his brother.

With that, David fell silent, but there was a cheeky grin on his face. From time to time, the brothers shared their load, and at regular intervals, they stopped at a place they had previously scouted and unearthed some simple nourishment, including more calabashes of water. It was obvious to David that the Xhosa brothers had planned his escape very carefully. During their assessment of his captivity, they had noticed that David had no footwear and just the basics of clothing. They had seen the state of his health and had planned to have nourishment breaks on the two-day race ahead of the Boer hunting party.

The men crested the last ridge of valleys and looked out over the Great Karoo, a massive expanse of scrubland that was classified as a semi-desert. Fires dotted across the vast landscape, as far as their eyes could see. About ten miles away was a concentration of these fires.

Nguni's deep voice rumbled for the first time that night. "That is the camp of your people," he said.

"I didn't realise," David looked out into the distance, somewhat taken aback at the number of British camps scattered about. "We can get to the main camp before sunrise."

"No," Daluxolo countered, "that camp is a town. And there, and there, and there," he pointed off into the dark in various places, "the other people lie and watch the people with flags. We must walk off this mountain and wait for the sun. It is too dangerous to walk to the town in the dark."

"Alright," David agreed, realising that the Boers from the hidden camp were secretly watching what the British were doing. "We will do that. I would like to approach the town from the side, not from here so that the men in that town don't know where we came from."

The amaXhosa brothers looked at each other in silence, not quite sure why David requested this.

"That is good," Nguni agreed solemnly.

"We go around. There are other men straight down there," Daluxolo pointed directly down the mountainside.

They reached the base of the mountain and rested, waiting for daybreak. David drifted into a fitful slumber several times before Nguni woke him for the final push to the camp. With David shared between the sturdy shoulders of his faithful friends they made good time over the flat ground, and after walking for about two hours, they encountered their first British outpost.

Two soldiers demanded at gunpoint that Nguni put David, resembling a wounded Boer soldier, on the ground, before approaching him very cautiously to ask him who he was.

"David Langbourne, sir," David replied. "I have been held captive by the Boers, but these men have rescued me."

Barely conscious, David was loaded onto a cart and transported into the camp, where he was handed over to a medical orderly, while Nguni and Daluxolo sat patiently under a tree nearby, watching the entrance to the hospital tent like two hawks.

When David awoke, he looked around, momentarily bewildered and lost, before he remembered that he was in a hospital tent. He sighed in relief when he heard a man's voice and saw a medical officer standing at the end of his bed. He also noticed that his own feet had been heavily bandaged.

"Ahh…so you're awake," said the medic.

"Good morning to you, sir," David replied.

"I think that ought to be 'Good afternoon'. You have only been out since this morning. Your feet are a pretty mess. I dare say you will be on crutches for the next week or two. What is your name, please?"

"David Langbourne. Where am I?"

"You're in a British Army camp at a settlement called Prince Albert. Where are you from?"

"Rhodesia," David said quietly.

"You are a long way out of town," the officer chuckled. "What brought you here?"

"Oh, a long story. Tell me, sir, the two Xhosa men who brought me here.

Do you know where they are?"

"They're outside, waiting to see you. We have given them food and water, and they will be adequately taken care of tonight."

"Good. Thank you, sir. One more thing; is there a telegraph office in Prince Albert?"

"Not yet, but I can arrange a message to Kruidfontein tomorrow. It's about 30 miles from here. There's a telegraph and rail station there."

"Please, may I see my friends?" David asked.

The medical officer nodded and walked out of the tent to summon Nguni and Daluxolo, while David closed his eyes and smiled.

Everything was going to be alright.

```
JACK SHIEL
STANDARD BANK
PORT ELIZABETH

AT PRINCE ALBERT STOP PLEASE ADVISE BROTHERS AND HANNA STOP
WILL RETURN TO JOHANNESBURG SOON STOP
NEED THREE DAYS RECOVERY STOP
WITH NGUNI AND DALUXOLO STOP
PLEASE ARRANGE SOME MONEY AT KRUIDFONTEIN STOP
I WILL COLLECT FROM RAILWAY STATION IN 4 DAYS STOP
ETERNAL THANKS TO YOU STOP
LETTER TO FOLLOW STOP
DAVID LANGBOURNE
```

Wearing a mismatch of second-hand clothing and leaning heavily on two walking sticks made of crooked saplings, David limped with Nguni and Daluxolo at his side towards the coach that would take them to the Kruidfontein railway station. Just as David was being helped onto the coach by his companions, however, he noticed on his left four Boer guerrillas, guarded by a group of soldiers. Bound by the wrists and sitting on the ground, all four prisoners were dressed in hessian with their distinctive unruly, unkempt hair and bushy beards.

David took a closer look at one of the men and realised with some shock that it was none other than Piet van Tonder.

David put a hand on Nguni's shoulder "Wait, wait ...", he said. "I know that man."

"I remember him," Nguni said in surprise, "he is the boss from the farm we went to."

Piet van Tonder noticed David hobbling over to him, accompanied by Nguni, but he did not smile. When he recognised Nguni, he gave a barely discernible nod of recognition.

"May I speak to this man?" David politely asked one of the guards, "I know him."

The guard nodded as he tightened his grip on his rifle. "Go ahead, but be quick about it," he growled.

David stared at Piet for a moment, but could not find any words. The two men simply locked eyes and looked at each other. Finally, Piet looked away, and David noticed a tear in the corner of his eye.

"I will ask them to look after you, Mijneer van Tonder," David finally said, his voice croaking slightly.

"I don't care what they do to me," Piet sighed, still looking into the far distance. "They burnt my farm to the ground, destroyed my crops, and imprisoned my family. I have now received word that many people in that camp have died without medical care. Word is that Hennie and all my children are among the dead."

Piet suddenly looked David in the eye with a glare full of hate. Both eyes were welling up in extreme sadness. "They can do with me what they want. They have taken everything I hold dear. I have nothing left to live for, but revenge."

Finally overcome with grief and weakness, David's knees buckled. Nguni caught him before he fell and gently lowered David to the ground. There he also crouched, level with Piet, and allowed the tears to well up and flow down his cheeks. There was nothing he could say, the sadness of this brutal war was just too much for both of them.

When David eventually stood, with the help of Nguni, he turned to face the guard. "May I speak to the officer in charge of these prisoners?"

The British soldier gestured towards a lone officer, sitting at a makeshift desk under a tree, shuffling and sorting the inevitable paperwork. "You'll find an officer over there, sir, sitting at that desk under the tree," he said, a little less aggressively. "Speak to him."

David thanked the man and limped over to the officer, appearing to hold the rank of a captain, who put his papers down when he saw David approach.

David grimaced, as he leant on his sticks. "Good morning, sir," he said, "that prisoner over there ..."

The captain cut David off mid-sentence. "What about him?" he barked.

"I know him. His name is Piet van Tonder. He is a farmer in the Patensie area. He helped me with my business operation before the start of the war, and when I was captured he saved my life. My captors were going to kill me, but Mr van Tonder recognised me and asked his commandant to spare me. Because of him, they treated me well and shared their food with me. I would ask that he be given the same consideration."

The captain cast a quick glance at David's feet, swaddled in heavy bandages. "Forgive me for saying so, sir," he sneered, "but it looks to me as if they did not treat you well at all."

"This was my own doing, sir. I was in good health until I escaped. I fled barefoot over these mountains. Until then I was treated by them as well as they could manage under the prevailing conditions."

The captain frowned. "Very well then, so be it. I will ensure he is treated with respect. What did you say his name was?" he asked as he flipped a piece of paper over on his desk and dipped his pen in a bottle of ink.

"Piet van Tonder. All those men over there were in the same camp. They all treated me fairly and correctly. I don't know their names, I'm afraid."

"Very well, Mr...?"

"Langbourne. David Langbourne. Thank you, sir."

After a bone-jarring coach ride, David boarded the train at Kruidfontein destined for Johannesburg. Helping him aboard, Nguni and Daluxolo stayed with him for the journey as far as De Aar, where they disembarked. Jack Shiel would arrive four hours later to escort the two amaXhosa brothers back to Port Elizabeth.

As far as David was concerned, the parting was emotional. Few words were spoken, but much was said through eye contact, vague frowns, and firm handshakes. As his train pulled away, David leaned back in his seat and reflected on his life in southern Africa, and all that had happened around him during that time. His thoughts turned to the two amaXhosa brothers, and what an integral and significant part they had played in the lives of the Langbourne family.

Without Nguni and Daluxolo they surely would not have survived in this demanding land, let alone achieved what they had so far. Nguni and Daluxolo had trekked thousands of miles with them, transporting their wagons and guarding them with their lives, above and beyond what had been expected of them. They had taught David their language, the customs of their clan, the identity and behaviour of the trees, the birds, the insects, and the animals, and how to survive in the bush. They had even taught the boys how to fish.

Having just parted company with the two men he admired immensely, and even though he longed to be in Hanna's arms again, his heart was torn to pieces.

CHAPTER TWELVE

London - 1902

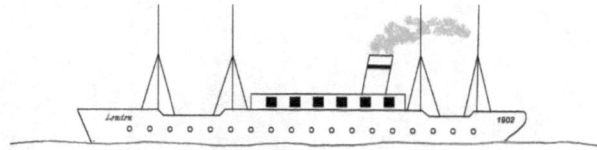

Morris opened the coach door and clumsily unfurled the umbrella as he slid out of the awkward contraption, trying desperately to stay out of the hammering rain. Irritation was rapidly creeping in as he held the door open for Rose Bertha, who extracted herself at an annoyingly slow pace. Slamming the door behind her, his umbrella was lightly deflected in a gentle bounce that caused the lashing rain to splatter the young couple.

"Morris, please!" Rose Bertha complained bitterly and put a protective hand over her head.

"I'm trying. Sorry. Now let's go. Move, stay with me," Morris almost snapped.

By the time Morris and Rose Bertha reached the front door of Yoni and Ruth Goldberg's flat, barely three yards away, they were more wet than dry. Morris was in a foul mood, but Rose Bertha seemed very composed, smiling sweetly as the front door swung open.

"Come in, come in. It's wet out there, come in," Yoni hurriedly ushered the young couple into the warmth and comfort of his home.

In her hurry to get out of the rain, Rose Bertha bumped Morris' hand that held the umbrella causing him to drop it behind him. It bounced clumsily down the steps onto the pavement.

"Oh dear," Yoni sympathised, but before he could offer Morris a second umbrella, Morris had already dashed to the pavement amidst a tirade of grumbles and wordless sounds, where he bent over hurriedly and picked it up.

In the few seconds it took him to recover his umbrella, he had been thoroughly drenched. When he finally entered the household, Morris stood both dripping and fuming, all at the same time. Yoni wanted to laugh but suppressed the reaction because it was clear Morris would not appreciate the joke. Yoni made a fuss over Morris instead, and hung his coat on the rack, then quickly led him into the lounge.

Rose Bertha's parents had already arrived, and Morris was obliged to greet everyone, including his hostess, Ruth Goldberg, with as much civility as he could muster. After a welcome sherry had been served, much jovial conversation quickly emerged from inside the room, despite an ominous grey cloud that hovered menacingly over Morris' head.

Yet Rose Bertha couldn't contain her own excitement any longer. "We have an announcement," she beamed. "Morris and I have set a date for our wedding."

"Mazel tov!" Yoni exclaimed.

A round of hearty congratulations followed, with the men shaking hands and the women hugging Morris gingerly so as not to get wet themselves.

"When, pray tell?" Ruth asked eagerly.

"October," said Morris, wiping some raindrops off his brow with exaggerated gestures, as if he were swatting flies. "Five months hence. Here in London."

"What made you decide on October, Morris?" Yoni pressed, beaming foolishly.

Knowing that he needed to move on from his unceremonious drenching, Morris took a deep breath. "As you know, they will be signing a peace treaty in South Africa next week, thus formally bringing an end to the Boer War. It will thus be safe for my brothers to travel again, and I would very much like them all to return here for an indaba with me."

"An indaba?" Lionel Friedlander raised an eyebrow.

"My apologies, it is the term the people in southern Africa use to signify a very important meeting, usually proclaimed only by the chief of a village. Because I need to set a course for our business now that the war is over, I have asked my brothers to make arrangements to come to London. I don't want them to abandon our business entirely, so I have instructed them to stagger their departure and return dates, and I want a period of three days when they are all here at the same time."

"And that is a marvellous opportunity for us to have our wedding," Rose Bertha cut in excitedly.

"Yes, indeed," Morris concurred.

"Your brother, David?" Yoni asked with some concern. "Is he well recovered?"

"Yes," Morris nodded and took a step over to a luxurious lounger, planting his wet self firmly in the seat. "He is fully recovered and, according to Harry, is putting on weight nicely."

"That must be Hanna's doing," Rose Bertha giggled.

"Indeed," said Morris, frowning darkly into his sherry glass, as he took a slow sip of the warming liquid. "He went through quite an ordeal. I look forward to seeing him again and hearing all about it. He will be the first of my brothers to arrive."

Notwithstanding Morris' undignified arrival, the evening progressed wonderfully well. As always, Ruth Goldberg provided a magnificent spread that received everyone's enthusiastic compliments. During the course of the evening, Morris further advised the group that he would be too busy with his business affairs and the arrival of his brothers, to attend to any arrangements for the wedding. This delighted the Friedlander ladies immensely, and secretly pleased everyone at the dinner table. For Morris, however, the memory of the frustrations his younger brother had had to endure with his wedding arrangements was all too fresh.

At the very end of May 1902, the Boer War finally came to an end with the signing of the Treaty of Vereeniging. Commandant Reitz's father, F.W. Reitz, who was the Secretary of State for the South African Republic at the time, was instrumental in forming the treaty on behalf of the Boers, but refused himself to swear allegiance to the British Empire. He was therefore given two weeks to leave the country and went into exile in Madagascar.

Deneys Reitz, likewise refusing to swear allegiance to the British, immediately followed his father into exile.

It had been four months since David's escape, and his feet had healed well under Hanna's loving care. He had gained weight, and the colour had returned to his cheeks, with his constant smile serving as a magnet to all those around him. Harry, on the other hand, had continued to flourish and excel in business. The business community in turn still regarded him favourably and had granted him much respect.

In Johannesburg meanwhile, Louis had kept his ear to the ground in all vital military, political, and commercial terrains. He had continued, moreover, to rub shoulders with the movers and shakers of commerce and industry, and – with Danie's help – had continued to mingle with Johannesburg's business elite.

When the news that the war was coming to an end had reached them, the business communities in both Rhodesia and South Africa had wasted no time in increasing their commercial drive and enthusiasm. The economies went into overdrive, and Langbourne Brothers rode the wave.

In the September of that year, the young brothers began preparations for their reunion in London and their attendance at the wedding of their eldest brother, who was, without a doubt, the leader of their family. The excitement was tangible. They had hoped to travel on board ship together, but Morris had insisted they stagger their journeys to keep the Langbourne absence down to a minimum.

David, Hanna, and Ettie left Bulawayo first, travelling to Cape Town by rail, before boarding one of the brand new, Union-Castle Line steamships. Getting a berth had not been easy for the civilians as the ship had been loaded with returning, wounded soldiers. Only two cabins were available in First Class when David approached the ticket office, so he secured one immediately for his family. He had not realised that, because the war was over, soldiers and officers who could not contribute further, owing to their injuries, but were stable enough to be moved, would be sent home; a strategy designed to lessen the burden on field and regional hospitals struggling to cope with the after-effects of the war. Realising what was happening, David quickly booked and paid for a cabin for Louis and Harry on a later departure time, and left the tickets with the purser for them to collect. Then, striding down to the Post Office, he sent an urgent telegram to Louis explaining what he had done.

Getting to their cabin required that David and Hanna weave their way along the decks, stepping around or over soldiers who sat or lay haphazardly in their path. By the time they were shown to their cabin, David was an emotional wreck. He sat quietly at the end of the bed, a tear managing to escape from one of his eyes before he hurriedly wiped it away to avoid Hanna's notice.

After she had laid Ettie down, Hanna sat next to David, putting one arm around his shoulders and squeezing gently, because she had noticed the tear after all.

"War is a terrible thing, David," she tried to console her husband.

"Did you see those injuries?" he replied, "I don't think all of the men will survive long enough to get back to England."

"There are good doctors and nurses on board, my darling. They will be well looked after."

"It depresses me, seeing all that hurt and pain. Some of those men cannot be repaired. They aren't only suffering from broken bones and missing limbs, but broken minds as well. Did you see that man…"

"Hush," Hanna held a finger to David's lips. She had seen the man with the wild animal-like stare, rocking back and forth as he sat on the deck.

"I don't think I can go back on deck. It saddens me too much," David said as his voice quivered.

"But we must!" Hanna exclaimed with a surprisingly cheery voice. "These men need people like us to talk to. We need to bring some normalcy into their lives. We may not be doctors or nurses, but we are humans, and just being with them, showing compassion and love, will bring joy into their hearts, and – heaven knows – they need some of that. It's the least we can do."

David sighed. "You're right, my heart. It won't be easy, but I will try."

"That's the spirit," said Hanna, squeezing her husband once again. She knew how difficult it would be for him, but she also knew that if she did not get David to face his demons head-on, they would haunt him forever.

For each of the seventeen days they were at sea making their way to Southampton, David and Hanna joined many civilian passengers, not just talking to the wounded troops, but helping with dressings and assisting the nursing staff as best they could. At some point they began to enjoy what they were doing, because not only did it shorten the journey, but David and Hanna also experienced a welcome, inner peace from doing something to ease the suffering around them.

One morning near the end of the journey, David was sitting on an upturned bucket beside a man who had lost a leg and had also been shot twice in the abdomen.

"Another cigarette?" David asked him.

"Cheers, mate," the soldier replied with a thick Australian accent.

David pulled a pack of cigarettes from a tote bag and passed one to the man. He then cupped his hands and lit a match, carefully guarding the flame against the puffs of wind. When the cigarette was lit, the soldier pulled heavily on it and savoured the nicotine, before exhaling with a loud sigh. David looked over to his right and watched Hanna cradling Ettie and sharing a joke with a man whose head was completely bandaged. The man laughed softly and waved a hand aimlessly at something.

"That your wife there, mate?" the Australian asked, cocking his head in the direction of Hanna.

"Yes," David smiled, "how can you tell?"

"It's quite obvious, mate. I see how you look at 'er."

"She is an amazing woman. I'm very blessed to have her in my life."

"I can see that, cobber," the man agreed, "so where are you from?"

"Rhodesia, north of the fighting."

"Ahh… I've heard of that place. Pretty good there I hear. You're damn lucky you didn't get tangled up in this godforsaken war."

David looked out to the shimmering blue sea and the distant horizon. He thought about the Boer soldiers who had held him captive for so long, living like wild animals with nothing but a fire in their hearts. He wondered if Commandant Reitz had lived to see the end of the war, or if he had ever left that hell-hole of a cave.

"Yes," David sighed and looked at the man with a small smile, "I was fortunate indeed."

The reception area of the Langham Hotel was a familiar and therefore welcome sight to David and Hanna. The last time David had entered the foyer, Hanna and her parents had been among the residents, and David had then lodged with Morris. That had been before they were married, but now they would stay here as husband and wife, along with their adorable daughter. The soft, amber glow from the electric light-bulbs, together with the rich wood panelling and regal painting on the walls, drew the couple inside with a powerful sense of well-being. After checking in, David donned his Derby hat, kissed Hanna on the cheek, and left her to unpack and settle in while he strode off to Finsbury Pavement to greet his brother.

Striding forth with a spring in his step, he fancied he heard the voices of the grand old buildings of central London, while the familiar sights and sounds – even the pungent odours – began to clear from his mind the painful memories of the depressing journey from Cape Town. He was once more excited to see Morris, to get involved in his wedding day, and to discuss the future of their business. David was also keen to see his father and family once more. If it wasn't for Morris being positioned at the end of his brisk walk, David felt he could have kept walking all day, right into the dusk, when the street-lights were lit. He felt safe in London and had a strong sense of belonging.

Such was his joy when he reached Morris' flat that he bounded up the four flights of steps, two at a time, not slowing for a moment, gripping the bannister with one hand while swinging around the next bend in the staircase. Only slightly out of breath, David stood in front of the brass numerals attached to the glossy black door indicating Flat Number 12, and knocked sharply. The door opened a moment later, and there stood Morris, beaming from ear to ear, as he welcomed his younger brother in with a fierce handshake and hearty slap on the shoulder.

"About time you got here," Morris almost laughed. "Come in, come in. When did you arrive?"

"We got into Southampton yesterday, but arrived here in London, just now. Hanna is settling in with Ettie at the Langham."

"Lovely!" Morris led David into his richly furnished apartment. "Would you like some tea?

"Yes, please. So … how are you? Your flat is looking wonderful! What have you done? It looks to me as if you've been moving the furniture around."

"Yes," Morris said as he walked into the kitchen to re-heat the kettle on the AGA stove, "Rose Bertha felt she wanted a new look. So, how was the journey?"

"Terrible," David grimaced.

"Oh?" Morris raised an eyebrow. "Bad weather?"

"No, the weather was fine, but there were hundreds of wounded soldiers on the ship. It seems as if the army is bringing their wounded back for treatment. All the civilian passengers helped where they could, giving the soldiers some form of support but it was truly depressing, I can tell you that. Anyhow, let's talk about that another time. Tell me, are Father and the family coming here for your wedding?"

Morris sighed as he roughly spooned some tea leaves into a porcelain teapot.

"Yes. If I could have had it my way it would have been just Father and Bloomy, but I came under a lot of pressure from Rose Bertha and her mother, by heavens. Mrs Friedlander? Now there's a difficult woman to deal with!" Morris tossed the teaspoon into the drawer with a clatter. "So, it will be Father and Helena, obviously, and all six of their children."

David laughed. "Remind me what their names are again?"

"Well there is Rachel, as you know, then Paddy, he must be about seven years old now, then Ernest, Tillie, Lilly, and Archie, who I think is two."

"That's quite a brood," David chuckled.

Morris scowled. "Ye-es. And would you believe? Helena is with child yet again."

"So that's seven children," David chuckled. "My word! Father has been a busy man." David was now laughing quite heartily at his brother's clear disapproval.

"Yes, now try to guess who has to pay for their journey from Dublin, and all their accommodation?"

"Oh, do try to look on the brighter side, Morris," David grinned. "You know very well you can now afford it, and you only get married once. Just think how lucky you are that you didn't have to pay for Hanna and me to get here, nor for Louis and Harry."

"Yes, thanks for coming," Morris smiled, because he was actually very pleased to see David. "When do the other two get here?"

"There's been a change of plan because of all those military movements going on. Harry met Louis in Cape Town one week after we left, and they will be travelling to Southampton together. They should arrive in London next week."

"Good," Morris smiled again and picked up the tray he had been preparing while they spoke. "Let's adjourn to the lounge and have some tea; we have much to discuss. Now, what happened to you? Harry said you were slightly hurt … on your feet? How did you get captured? What happened? Tell me." As was his wont, Morris asked one question after the other before even the first could be answered.

"I cut my feet during the escape," David smiled inwardly. "Come on, pour some tea. Then I'll tell you all about it."

Morris listened intently as David gave a brief description of his ordeal, and what he had experienced of the Boer side of the war. The younger brother made no bones about his feelings about war, and struck a chord with his older brother in that regard. When David mentioned that he had been rescued by Nguni and Daluxolo, Morris was dumbfounded.

"I didn't know that!" he exclaimed. "How did they know you were in trouble? How did they find you? How did they rescue you?"

"Jack Shiel," David threw his hand in the air, "he realised I was missing, so he contacted Louis and very quickly put two and two together. They then managed to contact Nguni, and together they put a plan into action. I must say, Nguni and Daluxolo are magnificent trackers, they truly are, and masters of camouflage. They were hidden right under my nose, and I had no idea. I knew they were there, because I saw clear bush signs that they had deliberately left for me, but I could not see them until they simply appeared out of the ground … literally."

Morris shook his head slightly in awe, before taking a quick sip of his tea, "You do understand, David," he had a serious tone in his voice, "that without Nguni and Daluxolo we would not be where we are today. We would probably not even be alive."

"I would certainly be dead many times over, if it hadn't been for them," David concurred. "Our business would not be the success it is, if it had not been for them either."

Morris squirmed uncomfortably, being well aware of the facts. "I know that all too well. Tell me," Morris said, shifting the topic of conversation, "how did you injure your feet?"

"Oh, I was barefoot when Nguni and Daluxolo rescued me, and we had to clamber up a couple of mountains and walk about ten miles to the nearest British camp. The rocks were very jagged and sharp in that area. Not being used to walking barefoot, I cut my feet rather badly. I couldn't walk for about two weeks afterwards. That valley really was hell."

"So, did Nguni and Daluxolo have shoes?"

"No, that's the interesting thing; they never wear shoes, as you know, and they were fine. Their feet are accustomed to it. Not us Europeans, that's for sure. In fact, the Boers are well aware of that, too. The three most important possessions for them to fight in the war are firstly a rifle, secondly boots, and third, what do you think?"

"Food and water?" Morris ventured.

"No, a saddle for their horse."

"A saddle?"

"Yes," David smiled and savoured a sip of his now lukewarm tea. "With a gun, you can fight and hunt for food. If your horse gets shot and dies, you have to walk or run. You cannot walk for long in the African bush without boots. Sharp rocks, a snake or the freezing cold will get you. Then, if you do find another horse, you can't ride bare-back for long without a saddle. You would have to hold your rifle, bedding and provisions as well as the reins. You will be outrun by the enemy in no time at all.

"Just look at what happened to me," David leant back in his seat, "I didn't even make it to the top of the first mountain peak without slicing open both soles and leaving a bold trail of blood for them to track me. Nguni and Daluxolo took turns in carrying me out.

"I'll tell you something fascinating," David continued. "When a Boer's horse gets shot, he takes the saddle off, throws it over one shoulder, his rifle over the other, and he walks. Believe me, he will walk hundreds of miles, if not a thousand, to evade the British troops. Can you imagine the weight he must carry? Without boots, he would not make it."

"Boots?" Morris mulled in fascination, "who would ever have thought?"

"The Boer commando that captured me walked from Ladysmith or Colenso up in the Natal area when they were defeated by General Buller, all the way to that valley near Prince Albert. That's a distance of some six or seven hundred miles. By then, many of them had walked right out of their boots, and their clothes. They wore sacking, Morris, sacking! Hardly any of them had boots. It was freezing cold and they were starving. Some were badly injured, but, they all had a rifle, and most had a saddle. Can you imagine what they had to endure?"

"It all sounds too terrible," said Morris with genuine shock in his voice.

"It was horrible," said David sadly, before he sat bolt upright in his seat, and shook a menacing finger at Morris. "Do you know another reason why I am alive? Because the Lord God Almighty was watching over me and sent me a friend."

"A friend?" Morris was beginning to think David was losing his mind.

"Piet van Tonder was in that camp. He was one of the Boer soldiers in that commando."

"Piet van Tonder?" the expression on Morris' face was a picture of disbelief.

"Yes, Piet van Tonder," David repeated, a thin layer of tears starting to make his eyes shimmer in the light from the window. "He saved my life. He introduced me to their commandant, a decent fellow by the name of Deneys Reitz and vouched for me. It was Piet who kept me alive.

"It's so sad, Morris," David went on. "The British rounded up all the Boers' wives and children and put them in what they called 'concentration camps' in a deliberate attempt to cut off supplies to the commandos. The women and children were so badly treated, that all sorts of diseases ran through the camps, and tens of thousands of these women and children died. Piet's wife, Hennie, and his five children were all captured."

"Oh, Lord," Morris sighed in despair. "I hope they are alright."

"No, sadly I heard that none of them made it. Piet's farm and crops were burnt to the ground by the British soldiers. He has lost everything; his home, his entire family... everything." At this point, a tear that had clung desperately to David's lower eyelid finally succumbed to gravity and rolled down his cheek.

"Oh no," Morris shook his head slowly and looked away. "I can't believe this."

"Believe it, Morris," David sunk back into his seat. "War is worse than you think. Never," David shook his finger at Morris, "never must any one of us brothers fight in a war, ever. Not you, not me, none of our family, and none of our children. War must be avoided at all costs."

"So it shall be," Morris said forlornly and stared out the window with David.

CHAPTER THIRTEEN

The Indaba

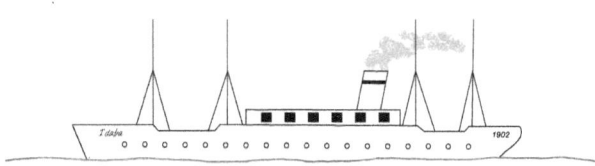

From his rather insignificant podium, the concierge stared blankly out onto the street. Hanna cast another expectant look at the large wood-and-glass doors of the Langham Hotel, which were firmly shut, keeping the gusty chill where it rightly belonged; outside!

Sitting across from her was Morris, who gazed into his half-empty porcelain teacup, deep in thought, perhaps working out a business deal, or planning his next commercial venture. To her left sat her husband, one leg crossed over the other, engrossed in a newspaper, a slight smile playing on his face. She stared at David for a moment, then back at Morris, and marvelled at how – with such widely different characters – they could work so perfectly well together as a team.

Hanna interrupted the two brothers' thoughts. "I might go to the room and check on Ettie," she announced.

"You only checked on her half an hour ago," David said as he folded his newspaper. "I'm sure the babysitter is very capable."

"It's this endless waiting for your brothers that is making me restless. I need to move about some. Do you think they will arrive today?"

"Well, I thought they would be here yesterday, but one can never tell, you know. I now think Father and the family will beat them to it."

Morris placed his cup and saucer carefully on the table. "I expect the Irish family to arrive tomorrow. It will be a bit worrying if Louis and Harry arrive after them. They may miss my wedding."

Sighing in frustration, Hanna cast her eye back to the front door. As he had done so many times that day, the concierge, patted down his lapels, took a step towards the heavy doors, and swung them open. Into the foyer stepped Louis, followed by Harry.

"They're here!" Hanna squealed with excitement and leapt to her feet.

The reunion of the brothers was a most joyous event, with much handshaking, laughter, and pecks on the cheeks for Hanna from the new arrivals. Louis and Harry were particularly delighted to see Morris again. The conversations seemed to pick up immediately from where they had left off as if no time had passed at all. Being somewhat amused by Morris' stylish and rather formal attire, having no relation to the way he had dressed in Bulawayo, they mocked him gently about it, but it worried him not.

"Magnificent hotel," Louis said as he looked at the interior of the establishment in awe.

"I've never seen anything like it," Harry agreed, excitement in his voice. "Is this where we are staying?"

"No," Morris replied, "you two are staying with me in my home."

"With you?" Harry asked, disappointment evident in his voice, visions of a lumpy mattress in a vacant warehouse crowding his imagination. "But David and Hanna are staying here, aren't they?"

"He's married and has a child. I can't accommodate you all. Do you think I'm made of money?" Morris almost scolded.

David discerned his young brothers' unspoken concern and quickly interjected, before an argument erupted. "You'll like it there. But now, you must be starving. Let's have some lunch, then Morris and I will walk you two down to Finsbury Pavement and settle you in. We have a lot to discuss."

Lunch at the Langham was a decadent affair, as always. Although somewhat overwhelmed by the quality and variety of food, the dessert table was of particular interest to the young brothers, who promptly embarrassed Morris by returning for second helpings.

"It is lovely to see you boys together," Hanna smiled as she dabbed her lips gently with a delicate serviette.

"Well, it is lovely to have you with us on this occasion," Louis beamed. "You certainly are a very welcome addition to our family."

"Hear, hear," Morris added as he nodded his approval to David. David smiled back.

"Will Sally be joining Father?" Harry asked tentatively. He was desperate to reunite with his favourite sister.

"Oh yes," Morris smiled through a sigh. "The whole family is coming. Rose Bertha's parents are kindly hosting Bloomy and her family in their spacious home. Bloomy and Bernard now have four children and one on the way…"

"Good heavens!" Louis interjected. "It's hard to imagine Bloomy with children, let alone so many."

"Yes," Morris sighed again. "Father, Helena, and their brood will be staying with Mr Goldberg…"

"Who is he?" Harry asked.

"You will meet him soon, a very learned and influential man for whom I have a great deal of respect."

Harry and Louis looked at David and raised their eyebrows in surprise. David knew what they were thinking; Morris didn't respect many people. In fact, David thought, Yoni Goldberg was probably the only person Morris admired.

"As I was saying, Father and Helena will be staying with Yoni and Ruth Goldberg with their five children. Our sisters," Morris confirmed, "Sally and Rachel, will be staying here at the Langham. David and Hanna have kindly agreed to look after them."

When a distinguished waiter in the light grey-and-white uniform of the Langham staff walked past the Langbourne table, David caught his eye. "I'll get the bill, Morris," he said.

Morris nodded his thanks. "Splendid!" he exclaimed. "Hanna, if you would kindly excuse us, I would like to take the lads down to Finsbury Pavement and settle them in. David, will you join us?" Morris asked, but it was really more of a command.

* * *

With a couple of tote bags in hand, the sum total of their luggage from southern Africa, Louis and Harry walked behind their older brothers, admiring the architecture of London and nodding friendly greetings to virtually every person who walked in the opposite direction. The brothers were delighted to be in such an established city, its multi-storey buildings presenting such imposing solid exteriors, made mainly of grey stone or soot-stained, red brick.

Walking past a rather stately church, Louis and Harry were almost stopped in their tracks as the stained-glass windows caught the light. They were equally intrigued by the fancy, horse-drawn carriages with highly polished, glossy paintwork, finished off with brass. Carriages of this quality were not seen in southern Africa.

As they entered the gloomy stairway that led up to Morris' flat, the inferior paint still peeling off the cold grey walls, David deciphered his younger brothers' thoughts – after all, he well remembered his own first impression of the building.

"Almost there, fellahs," David announced. "This is where you will be living for the next few days."

Louis exchanged a disappointed look with Harry, who looked equally despondent, but they did not say anything. Morris, in the lead, was oblivious to the exchanges.

"Not quite as nice as the Langham," David continued to tease.

"I'll say," Harry mumbled sarcastically.

Ascending the dark, dank, and miserable stairway, David hid his smile, knowing that his brothers would enjoy the surprise when they entered Morris' home. At the fourth level, Morris fumbled with the key in the darkness as his brothers bunched up behind him.

"Welcome to my flat," Morris said with some pride as he swung the door open, "your home for the duration of your stay."

Walking through the entrance hall to be greeted by the sheer luxury of the flat, the younger brothers allowed their jaws to drop, the contrast between the stairwell and the interior of the flat being so extreme.

David could not contain his pride in his older brother's achievements. "What do you think?" he said.

"Well ..." said Harry slowly, "not half as nice as the Langham, but I suppose it will do."

Seeing that Harry was joking, Morris took it as a kind of compliment.

"Not my doing, I have to admit. Rose Bertha did it all."

"When will we meet our future sister-in-law?" Louis asked as he caressed a black marble statuette holding an unlit candle.

"Tomorrow. But first let me show you to your room, then we can freshen up and reconvene in the lounge for our indaba."

"Do we have a quorum, Mr Secretary?" Morris asked authoritatively.

"Yes, Mr Chairman," David said with equal solemnity.

Harry was contemplating the necessity of being so formal and businesslike, especially at a time like this. They had just spent such a pleasurable afternoon together as a family, laughing and joking amongst themselves. He knew perfectly well, however, that Morris was who he was, and that business for him was always business. Harry thus held his tongue, and Louis – who had caught his quick glance and felt the same way – also silently agreed to do the same.

After the brothers had unpacked their meagre belongings in the room they would be sharing and had freshened up in the bathroom, they adjourned to the lounge to enjoy a welcome tray of tea and biscuits made by Rose Bertha especially for the occasion. Before taking their seats on the comfortable chairs, Louis and Harry took a moment to stand by the window and look down from four floors above to the street below. Both had a strange sense of vertigo which they rather enjoyed. When Morris began to clear his throat, however, the younger siblings reluctantly took their seats.

"Firstly," Morris began with a satisfied smile, "I would like to welcome you, my brothers, to London. I would also like to thank you for all the effort, hard work, and sacrifices you have made for the family business, and congratulate you on your individual contributions to our successes.

"David has appraised me of your selfless hard work and of your many accomplishments, and I can assure you that the figures in the financials are reflecting this most admirably. I see, for example, that the hotel equipment is selling very well." Morris cocked an eyebrow at Louis.

Louis was caught momentarily off guard. "Ahh, yes," he muttered. "Sales in Johannesburg are still slow, obviously because of the after-effects of the war, but Rhodesia is forging ahead. Most of my stock has been shipped on to Bulawayo."

Harry instantly picked up the baton. "I can't keep up with the hotel inventory, so I have moved Mr Johnson onto that side of it. He is a true asset to the business. He has managed to sell all the wagons and oxen, and I have been able to close down the wagon-trading arm of the business completely."

"Splendid!" Morris beamed. "Louis, who is in charge of the Johannesburg warehouse?"

Morris' grilling went on for over an hour. The pot of tea was untouched and became cold, but such was the intensity of the meeting that nobody noticed. Despite testing his brothers with complicated, and sometimes ambiguous questions, David, Louis and Harry always had a quick and complete answer for their older brother. Although dreading this encounter with Morris, the younger brothers found themselves enjoying the challenge. The hours quietly went sailing by until, suddenly, they came to realise that the room was becoming quite dim and a candle was needed.

David looked up from his notes, disrupting the flow of the meeting, "Good heavens!" he exclaimed. "It's getting dark. What in heaven's name is the time? I need to get back to Hanna and Ettie."

"Alright," said Morris. "Let's adjourn until tomorrow morning. David, are you alright to come back here tomorrow, first light?"

"Yes," David quickly agreed as he hurriedly folded his notepad. "No, wait. Aren't we supposed to meet at the Langham tomorrow in anticipation of Father's arrival?"

"Oh," Morris looked momentarily confused. "Yes, that's correct. Right-you-are, we will meet you at the Langham for breakfast and then retire to one of the lounges to continue. I'm nowhere near finished with this meeting. Tomorrow, then?"

"Tomorrow," David agreed as he strode to the hallway and donned his overcoat. He was out of the door in an instant.

The meeting continued the next day exactly as Morris had wished. After a delicious breakfast that almost made the boys' eyes water, the brothers moved into a small lounge abutting the foyer, with strict instructions to the concierge to alert them once a bearded man with several young children arrived.

Morris' agenda predictably moved from past and present to the future. He was now plotting a course for the next phase of their burgeoning business.

It was soon evident that the business would need an efficient and effective buying team that could purchase goods from all over the world. Morris wanted to be different, he didn't want to stock the same merchandise as everyone else and so be forced to haggle and to compete in price wars with other traders and retailers in southern Africa. They would take turns in travelling to a mutually agreed country, making connections, negotiating prices, and contracts, and arranging for the goods to be sent back to southern Africa.

The next item on Morris' expansion agenda was to open more wholesale warehouses in different parts of southern Africa. It was at this point that David began to get fidgety and proceeded to interrupt Morris.

"Morris, with all due respect," he reasoned, "there are only four of us. We already have business centres in Bulawayo, Johannesburg, and London, and now you want us to open a wholesale company in each of Kimberley, Cape Town, East London, and Port Elizabeth in the Cape Colony, and another outlet in Rhodesia at Fort Salisbury. You also want us to travel the world to purchase for the company and hold down our existing businesses. How on earth do you expect us to do all of that?"

Louis looked at Morris, cocking his head in confusion. "Yes... how?"

Harry started to raise his hand but lowered it quickly.

"I never said it would be easy, but it can be done," Morris continued blandly. "David, I need you to tackle Port Elizabeth and East London; you already have contacts there. I also want you to look into Cape Town. Louis, you deal with Kimberley. Harry, you already have some experience and connections in Salisbury. I need you to return there and investigate the possibilities.

"As soon as you find something suitable, I need you all to employ competent staff to manage the businesses. Then you will need to visit them regularly to make sure they are trading efficiently."

"What will you be doing?" David asked, almost exasperated.

"I'll be looking after London and all the shipping requirements. Which reminds me, I want to purchase a ship. We will need one to transport the huge quantity of goods we will be importing into southern Africa."

"A ship?" David exclaimed and tossed his notepad onto the coffee table in front of him. A teaspoon clattered across the table and gently thudded onto the plush carpet.

A deathly silence enveloped the meeting. After an awkward pause,

Harry leant forward and retrieved the teaspoon, replacing it ever so gently on the tea tray.

"Well, not immediately," Morris cautiously resumed, "perhaps not a real ship, but a shipping company, or a significant part of one. I believe that, with the end of the Boer War, there will be many shipping companies that thought the war would go on for many years to come and therefore have invested in extra ships to cater for the British shipment of arms, ammunition, oxen, and horses, not to mention the troop movements. Suddenly, the war is over, and – once all the ordinance has been returned or re-distributed around the world, and the British government no longer require their services – there will be a lot of cargo ships lying idle with neither work nor cargo. It won't take long for some smaller ship owners to start feeling the pinch.

"I also believe there are several shipping companies out there who have no idea how to run a business correctly. The odds of that are good, and I wish to pounce on a shipping company that fits my requirements in terms of price, organisation, size – that sort of thing. I believe I can pick up a shipping company at a very keen price.

"What you need to remember is that Danie Coetzee and Jack Shiel taught us a great deal about the shipping industry when we were in Port Elizabeth. Not so, David?" Morris deferred to his brother. "It's not that difficult. Between David and me we have the know-how, although I accept we don't have the experience, yet. Our business lends itself perfectly to being involved in the shipping industry. It's an obvious progression.

"Furthermore, when a new war erupts, we will have the capability to cater to any government's urgent requirements."

"Morris…" David held up his hands to halt the discussion briefly as he floundered for words. "If any other person but you had said this to me I would have regarded it as a joke, but you? Have you…?" David sighed as he composed himself. "Never mind," he muttered, resigning himself to a loss of words. He had a sinking feeling that Morris would have thought out every detail, probably more minutely than even he could imagine, and Morris never joked about business.

Louis scratched his head, a look of total confusion crossing his face. "Excuse me, Brother, but how much does a ship, or more to the point, a shipping company, cost? How will you pay for it?"

"I'm not sure just at the moment," Morris confessed, "but in good time I will find a way. Regardless, we will be taking a loan from the bank to help pay for one."

"No, Morris," David objected calmly. "We've been there before, and I didn't like the risks."

"The risks paid off, didn't they?"

"It nearly killed us," David shook his head. "It nearly killed me," he thumped his chest hard with his index finger to make his point.

Morris knew this was correct and did not have an answer to David's remark. Instead, he suggested they break for a cup of tea, a proposal that was readily accepted by all his siblings.

"There's a lovely tea-room about two blocks from here," Morris said as they walked out of the lounge. "Let's get a bit of air and a change of scenery."

As they were all once again in agreement, the brothers strode casually along the pavement chatting idly. All of the brothers, except Morris, were confused and confounded by the pace and intensity of their eldest brother's approach to the expansion of the business. It all sounded too hard and too complicated, and this little break was most welcome to all concerned. No-one dared mention anything to do with business, in case Morris picked up the thread again, and they were all certain he would if he were to be given the opportunity.

The tea-room was decorated in dainty florals and lace, and along the walls were numerous figurines of porcelain dolls dressed in extravagant miniaturised clothing of high-class fashion. The faces of the toys were painted beautifully and looked almost life-like. After looking at the displays with great interest, the boys received their order of tea and settled down to enjoy the ambience.

David started the conversation by addressing the younger brothers. "Tell me about your journey," he said.

Louis carefully returned his cup to his saucer. "Oh," he sighed, "it was depressing. There were a lot of wounded British soldiers on board."

"Yes, my experience, too," David murmured. "Very sad."

"Strange how they might send all of that ordnance over to southern Africa, then bring it all back after the war is over. You would think they would leave it there in the event that war might erupt again, as it has done many times in the past." Harry observed.

"Maybe they are expecting a war closer to home next time," Morris mused.

"I can understand bringing back guns and cannons and reusable items, but boots, and old torn uniforms?" Louis added.

"Boots?" Morris suddenly looked up and shot a quick look at David.

"Yes, why? What did I say?" Louis knew he had struck a chord with Morris.

"Odd," Morris scratched his head. "David and I were just talking about the importance of boots and footwear during a time of war."

"Well, as we boarded the ship, there was a pile of old army boots on the wharf, ready to be shipped back here I suppose," Louis continued.

"New?" Morris asked.

"Oh no, second-hand, very much so. Covered in mud, some with missing laces, some black, some brown, all different sizes, it seems, in no particular order, a total hodgepodge of boots. The pile on the pier was huge, the size of..." Louis looked around him. "Well, you couldn't fit them into this tea-room, could you Harry?"

"No," Harry confirmed. "You'd probably need two of these tea-rooms to accommodate that pile of rubbish. It beats me why they would want to pay good money to ship them back here. Must be this strange British bureaucracy thing."

"Why do you think they would pay to transport them here?" Morris asked Harry.

"Why otherwise dump them on a shipping wharf?" Harry replied with a smirk.

"Huh, good point. Well, that brings me to another matter," Morris suddenly moved the conversation along. "Under no circumstances may any of our family ever involve themselves in the hostilities of war. Do I make myself clear?"

Louis and Harry bristled at Morris' sudden outburst, but David was expecting this.

"Morris is right," David concurred. "War is a terrible thing. I have seen it from both sides, and it is horrible. They say every story has two sides, and, from personal experience, I know that to be true."

"I have no inclination to kill another person, no matter what my country or government decrees," Louis spoke carefully, "but what if I have a belief that my country needs to be defended to protect my own personal interests, or that of the home and family which I hope to have one day? How do I stand aside while my compatriots go out and die for their country? For me?"

"A good question," David mulled, "Morris, how would you answer that?"

"It is very noble to defend and support one's own country, home and family," Morris replied, "but I am sure there must be other ways to be of service without picking up a gun and killing someone. Perhaps one might volunteer for an administrative role, but I absolutely forbid any of you to pick up a gun and kill another person. It is against God's will, and it is the sixth of the Ten Commandments, 'Thou shalt not kill.'"

The younger brothers sat in stunned silence and stared at Morris. Once again, without question, he had asserted his authority over the family, and they all accepted it without reservation. The fire that burned behind Morris' eyes when he forbade them to fight left the boys in no doubt that Morris had issued an unbreakable family rule to never kill another person, even under the orders of a sitting government.

"One other thing," Morris continued once he was sure he had thoroughly made his point, "as far as our children go, I want them all to be educated here in England. I have found an outstanding school called Cheltenham College. Our children can board there while we brothers are travelling or spending time abroad. Through our company, Langbourne Brothers, we must make provision to ensure a good education for them at Cheltenham College. I have looked the college over thoroughly and have decided that it suits our requirements perfectly. The same applies to our grand-children; we must ensure that they are properly educated in a quality learning establishment.

"Furthermore, if a war breaks out in southern Africa once more, and we feel our families are at risk, they are to be relocated back here to England at once. If war breaks out in England, on the other hand, we will move ourselves and our families out to Rhodesia. War is deadly, and often pointless, usually because negotiations break down for unnecessary reasons. I need you to run our business, no matter what.

"Just look at you three. David, at twenty-seven years of age, has been tangled up in three wars already."

"Four," David corrected. "Don't forget the two Matabele rebellions, the first part of the Boer War in Mafeking, and then down in the Cape during the last phase of the Boer War."

"Exactly!" Morris exclaimed. "How many wars must there be before you lose your life? And Louis, two wars before you are twenty-one, and one war for Harry, and what are you, nineteen?

"Yes," Harry agreed.

"We will accept what you say on these matters, Morris," said David, while his younger brothers nodded in agreement, "but I believe there won't be another war for a long time to come. Too often, and all very recently, the powerful British might has been tested, and every time the British have confirmed their superiority. Other countries will be cautious to test the British armies again after they saw how the colonies around the world united to form a massive force."

"Perhaps…" Morris frowned as he took a sip of his tea, "but I fear there is another war coming, and I want to be ready for it if it does. Right-oh, finish your tea and let's get back to the Langham, I have more I need to discuss with you."

Begrudgingly the brothers drank down the remainder of their tea and exchanged furtive glances with each other while they tried to digest all that Morris had planned for them.

The walk back to the hotel saw Morris chatting with David in the lead, while Louis and Harry kept a respectful distance behind, talking earnestly in subdued tones. As they rounded a corner, David saw their father, Jacob, helping a contingent of women and children alight from a large carriage drawn by two horses.

"They have arrived," David said joyfully. "It will be good to watch the faces of Louis and Harry because they haven't seen the family in many years. I still can't believe Sally is a young lady."

Morris smiled and turned with David to see when their younger brothers would notice the family's arrival. It didn't take long at all. They almost broke into a run the instant they saw the commotion ahead of them and recognised their father. Brushing past their older brothers with faces aglow, Louis and Harry joined the large family gathering with much happiness and whoops of laughter.

Comments were passed, of course about Louis' newfound height, and how dapper Harry looked. Harry wasted no time in embracing Sally, his favourite sister, before standing to attention by her side, almost possessively. The youngest of all the children stood with their backs to the carriage and watched somewhat nervously as they were all but forgotten in the excitement. When Morris finally decided, however, that enough exuberance had been expressed for the moment, he nodded to David and they stepped forward to join the happy gathering.

Jacob suddenly recalled the children and, gripping the eldest two by the shoulders, thrust them forward at Louis and Harry. "You remember Rachel and Paddy?"

"Yes, indeed," Louis grinned, "but you two were mere babies when we left. How old are you now?" he asked his two half-siblings.

"I am eight," Rachael said proudly, "and Paddy is seven."

"My word, you two have grown, but who is this?" said Louis, gently placing his hand on the boy standing next to them, dressed in a miniature day suit and looking very uncomfortable.

"This is Ernest," Rachel replied, taking control of both the situation and the introductions. "Ernest is six, while this is Tillie, who is four, and this Lilly, who is three, and that," she pointed to a baby in Helena's arms, "is Archie. He is the baby and is two years old. He's the naughty one."

When another round of laughter followed, David smiled as he watched Morris beginning to relax and enjoy the moment, since it was not often that he saw Morris laugh. David did notice, however, that Morris always seemed to let his guard down and enjoy a laugh or a chuckle whenever young children were around. David wondered if it was because Morris never felt threatened by children. Indeed, he always seemed to regard people of his own age and older with suspicion, his family excluded.

David touched his father's young wife on the arm, "Helena," he asked, "Where is Bloomy?"

"She's right behind us," she whispered, leaning into David's ear, "we had to take two coaches as there were too many of us."

Right on cue, a second coach pulled up behind the first.

"Ahh…" Jacob announced, throwing both arms in the air in a joyous gesture, "Bloomy and her family have caught up. Bloomy, Bloomy, come and meet your brothers, they have grown!" he laughed aloud.

Bloomy, in her usual fashion which consisted of a long and flowing dress, carefully exited the wagon holding an infant, no more than a year old. David quickly stepped to the door to give her a supporting hand, what with all the billowing fabric and impatient children also trying desperately to get out at the same time.

Louis and Harry stared in fascination at their sister who, when they last had seen her, had been a lot younger, very thin, emaciated, and quite determinedly unmarried. Now, as two of her children escaped the confines of the coach in front of her, when she reached the ground, another one bundled out. As Bloomy straightened up and adjusted the grip of the infant on her hip, it was apparent to the brothers that she was once more with child, her belly being well rounded with more of their abundant life.

"Good Lord," Harry mumbled to Louis under his breath.

"I can't believe we have been away that long," Louis murmured back.

Bloomy hugged her brothers from southern Africa without reservation and introduced all her young children.

"Where is Bernard?" Morris asked Bloomy, a sudden look of realisation on his face.

"Oh, he has gone to America. I meant to tell you, I'm sorry. He has gone to join a friend who has a big deal on the go and which will make us all a lot of money."

Naturally, Morris was suddenly curious. "What deal?" he snapped.

"I have no idea, Brother Morris. Something to do with furniture. Now, Louis, let me look at you!"

After all the introductions had been made, and the small mountain of luggage unloaded onto the pavement, Morris nodded at David to catch his attention. He tapped his pocket where his fob watch was typically located then pointed at the coach. David knew what he meant and bowed in acknowledgement as Morris gathered up the extended family and herded them into the Langham Hotel, and out of the cold wind.

"Harry," David caught his brother's attention and inclined his head at the small pile of luggage on the pavement with a curious look. "If you wouldn't mind?"

Harry grinned and immediately began to pick up some of the cases.

"Could you avail me of your services at six o'clock this evening, sir?" David asked the lead buggy driver.

"Most certainly, esquire. Six on the hour," he responded and flicked the reins of the horses.

After David had made the same arrangement with the second coach driver, he bent down to retrieve some of the abandoned suitcases.

"Come on Harry, let's shake a leg," he laughed.

CHAPTER FOURTEEN

Celebration

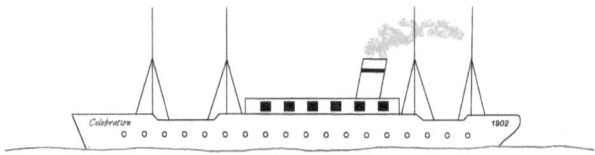

With the Langbourne family billeted out between the Goldbergs, the Friedlanders, the Langham Hotel, and Morris' own flat for five days before the wedding, numerous gatherings were arranged whereby everyone could meet and enjoy each other's company to the fullest. It was also a perfect time to get reacquainted with each other, both old family members and new, while making Rose Bertha's family welcome in particular. Apart from outings to parks, where picnics were held on days with good sunshine, the hotel tea gardens were much enjoyed by all.

Jacob was in his element when thoroughly enveloped by his large family. With Rose Bertha spending many hours fussing around Hanna and Ettie, Jacob was always joking and laughing with his sons from abroad, and even Morris relished the familial company and joviality.

Since it was lavishly funded by Mr and Mrs Friedlander, the much-anticipated wedding day was thoroughly delightful. With the food, wine, and music flowing in abundance, Rose Bertha was the centre of attraction in her outstanding wedding gown, which had been selected and fitted to perfection during a recent trip to Paris.

Although Morris must have been the proudest man in town, Jacob seemed determined to contend, because he was clearly having the time of his life. For the first time in over a decade, he had his entire family together. His sons had left for southern Africa as destitute young teens and had returned eleven years later as successful international businessmen, rich not just in money, but in experience and knowledge as well. His three eldest were married, and now the grandchildren had begun to arrive.

During the time his boys had been in southern Africa, Jacob had re-married, and his new wife, Helena, was an absolute joy. She loved him dearly and loved his children as much as her own. Helena, many years Jacob's junior, made him feel alive, bringing new hope and light into a life that he thought would be dark and fraught with misery forever. The fear of that misery occasionally revisited him in a bleak reminder of where he had once been, but with the loving care of his wife and the family he had around, he usually overcame that visitation and soon came to realise that much more love and life still remained to be enjoyed.

Jacob was well aware that his children were becoming adults and leaving the nest. Of course, his four eldest boys now lived in southern Africa or in London, while Bloomy and her children were due to depart for America in the near future, or as soon as her husband, Bernard, might establish his mysterious business over there.

Soon after the ceremonial smashing of a wine glass, wrapped in a pristine white handkerchief, the wedding ceremonies drew to a close and Morris, together with Rose Bertha, left the venue for an unknown destination for their wedding night. They had planned to return to Finsbury Pavement as a married couple the following day and stay for a week, mainly to see the various family members off on their return journeys, before they left on their honeymoon for New York in the United States.

Morris had booked a passage on a new Cunard vessel that was expected to make the transatlantic voyage in under six days. He had planned to stay in New York with his bride for a fortnight before returning to London. His father-in-law had given him the names of four prominent businessmen to meet while in that progressive city and an introductory letter for each of them. Morris had accepted the offer with great excitement, and Rose Bertha, although a little disappointed at the prospect of mixing some business with her honeymoon, understood what was required and stoically accepted the inevitable intrusions into her special holiday.

Morris had also suggested that Louis and Harry visit Paris before returning to southern Africa. As much as Morris wanted his brothers back on track as quickly as possible, he strongly felt they needed exposure to the wonders of the French capital. Therefore, just as Mr Friedlander had done for him with regards to New York, he provided Louis and Harry with introductory letters to Monsieur Follot and the manager of Le Bon Marche departmental store, Monsieur Andre Hersh.

Louis and Harry left for Paris the same day that Jacob, Helena and Bloomy, accompanied by their various children, departed for Dublin. David and Hanna had a further three days to spend in London while they waited for their ship to southern Africa, during which time Morris made the most of his brother's company.

"I want to investigate these old army boots in Cape Town," Morris said to David as they walked back to the Langham one morning.

"What on earth do you want to do with a pile of old boots, Morris? I saw them, they are only fit for the rubbish pit."

"They might have a value. Let's just see … why not?"

David sighed. "Well, have you any idea where to start looking?"

"Nope!" Morris exclaimed with a grin, "But let's ask around and see what happens."

What started as a simple enquiry ended up being the most intense and frustrating run-around that the brothers had ever endured. They walked into an old brick, government building in the middle of London, which turned out to be an army recruitment office. A clerk in military uniform forwarded the brothers to the south of the city where they would find the ordnance department. It turned out that the ordnance department had moved to new premises two years previously, forcing Morris and David to catch a train to the north. That turned out to be the wrong ordnance department, and they were directed to another location, many miles away.

By that time it had become quite late, so they gave up for the day and returned home. Undaunted, Morris began the search again at first light, alone this time, and was sent to the African War Office back in London.

After a full day of unsuccessfully running around, he went home and collected Rose Bertha before joining David and Hanna at the Langham for dinner.

"Well?" David asked with a smile, "any luck?"

"No. What a muddle! But I finally have the name of someone who might be of assistance."

"You are going to a lot of effort for minimal reward, Morris. Believe me, I have seen that pile of boots, and they are worthless. They will cost you money to store them."

"I've thought about that. We own a farm in Ireland, the one Elaine and her husband are running for us. We will store the boots there until the next war, and then sell them."

"Bad idea, Morris, bad idea," David shook his head, a frown crossing his face. "The cost of freight, the money tied up in the boots, the shipping needed to send them to a future potential buyer – all very expensive. What if the next war is in southern Africa again? Then you will have to send them back there. You will lose money, Morris, believe me, you will lose."

"I haven't finished my investigations yet, David," Morris objected. "It all depends on the purchase price, that is, if the army will actually sell them to me."

By the time David, Hanna, and Ettie had left Southampton harbour for Cape Town, Morris was still no closer to buying his load of old boots, so he put his mission on hold while he and Rose Bertha departed for America on their honeymoon.

As for David, he was itching to get back to southern Africa. The pressure that Morris had put him under was now immense. He was expected to look at business opportunities in Cape Town, Port Elizabeth, and East London. He was also looking forward to introducing Hanna and Ettie to his good friend, Jack Shiel. More importantly, he wanted to introduce Hanna and their young daughter to his closest friends, Nguni and Daluxolo, and Daluxolo's wife, Nkosazana. The seventeen-day journey back thus gave him ample time to look forward to his return to southern Africa.

CHAPTER FIFTEEN
The Folly

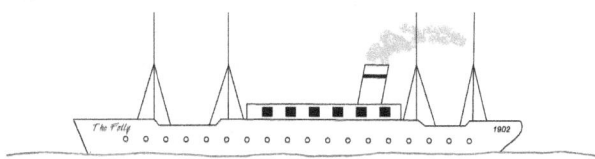

Although Morris and Rose Bertha's honeymoon in New York had been memorable and enjoyable, the return trip by sea had proved to be very frustrating for Morris. As far as he was concerned, the holiday was now over, and he wanted desperately to get back to business. Noticing the change in Morris, Rose Bertha had no desire to confront him but rather let him be, which turned out to be the wisest way to handle the situation.

Morris' first objective after getting back to their home was to check the Post Office for any telegrams from his brothers. As there were none, he resumed his search for someone in the British Army who could tell him who might be in charge of the second-hand boots that had been dumped on the wharf in Cape Town.

Eventually, his search led him to a pompous colonel, whose advice had nevertheless been enlightening; Morris had been looking in the wrong area entirely. Who he really needed to see turned out to be someone in the Ministry of Defence. It took almost a week of searching and asking before he finally found himself sitting in front of a pin-striped suit containing a proper gentleman by the name of Lord Cunningham.

No more than about thirty-five years old, Cunningham had an undeniable air of self-importance which did not escape Morris' attention. Having earlier decided how he would conduct himself in this meeting, Morris quickly changed his tactic and decided to play the ignorant, inexperienced young businessman, filled with hope and grand illusions. It paid off.

"So what brings you to see me, Mr Langbourne?" the suave gentleman asked as he settled back in the extravagant chair behind his desk.

"Firstly, m'lord, thank you for sparing me some of your invaluable time. My brother has a small business in Rhodesia, and he recently returned to London for my wedding."

"Oh, congratulations!" Lord Cunningham smiled.

"Thank you, m'lord. When he was on the point of leaving the harbour in Cape Town, however, he noticed a pile of old army boots on the pier. He seemed to think that, if the British Army was quite finished with them, it might appear to be a waste of money for the British Government to ship them back all the way to England..."

"Yes, that would be a waste of taxpayers' money," Cunningham murmured, "but what makes him believe they are being shipped back here?"

"Absolutely no idea, m'lord," Morris confessed. "I would assume he simply thought that – now that the South African War is well and truly over, and the boots appear to be piled up at the docks – there might indeed be no further use for them. Of course, if they might be required to be used elsewhere in His Majesty's Empire, then such a requirement would negate all my further questions, and I won't take up any more of your time."

"Not a problem, Mr Langbourne, but simply out of mere curiosity, might I ask what in heaven's name you would want with a pile of second-hand, army boots?"

"Well, my brother's thoughts were that – in amongst that pile of boots – there might be one or two pairs that are still usable. He rather thought that he would sort through the pile, find what he could use, then perhaps sell the usable ones for a small profit and dispose of the rest, thereby saving your Government a great deal of money. I believe his logic is that the

Government would look kindly on a deal whereby they made some money on unwanted ordnance rather than spending money on its disposal."

"I see…" said Lord Cunningham, scratching his chin. "I think your brother is quite a smart man. While his idea – in principle, I dare say – is quite sound, I'm rather afraid that he has missed one vital point, however. Supposing he buys these boots and finds a certain quantity that can be used to fight in another war, would the British Government look kindly upon the transaction if they were sold to our enemy to fight against us?"

"A very good point," Morris readily agreed. He had not thought of this either, but he had an answer that might work. He wanted Lord Cunningham to suggest it, so worded his response carefully. "Certainly that simply would not do. I wonder how the Government could prevent him from doing that? Or rather, if they could at all? No, it seems I have wasted enough of your time already, and I thank you sincerely for entertaining my proposal. We had hoped we could turn a small profit on them, and at the same time divert taxpayers' money into something more worthy," Morris said as he made a half-hearted effort to rise.

"Well," Cunningham lifted a hand slightly, indicating Morris should hear him out, "I think your idea and way of thinking should be commended. I'm just thinking out loud how I could possibly make this work for both parties."

"You think you might?" Morris settled back in his chair with an expectant look.

Lord Cunningham scratched thoughtfully at his chin once more. "How many old boots do you say are on the wharf?"

"I personally haven't seen them, but my brother has. He tells me that pile might possibly fill your office twice over. Most of the boots are beyond repair or re-use. I assume you have not seen the pile yourself?"

"Heavens, no," Cunningham laughed. "I've never set foot in South Africa, and nor do I intend to do so. No, I have no idea whatsoever, but it is my responsibility, amongst other things, to move reusable ordnance to where it may be needed. I wonder…" Cunningham seemed to drift off in thought as he looked over Morris' head.

Morris held his tongue. He wanted to see where this conversation was going. Cunningham opened a drawer on his right side and extracted a file filled with pages of varying sizes and colours, a rather untidy folder altogether, Morris observed. Cunningham paged through some loose sheets, looking very concerned, before closing the file quickly, and placing a protective hand on top of it. He then turned an unctuous smile on Morris

"I have a proposition," he said blithely.

"Yes?" Morris smiled while feigning innocent expectation.

"How many pairs of boots do you think are on that wharf?"

"I honestly have no idea," Morris reiterated.

"Indeed, neither do I," Cunningham admitted. "It would, therefore, be difficult to ascertain any values, or savings if you will, unless one were there to physically count the boots. I might suggest that we agree on a price per boot and we could then agree to sell them all to you."

"If that's the case, I would only want re-sellable boots, wouldn't I? I would not want to purchase boots that I would have to throw away."

"Good point," Cunningham conceded, "but perhaps we might agree on a very nominal price, on condition that you take the lot and take your chances?"

It was Morris' turn to scratch his head. "I don't know …" he mused aloud. "I don't like taking chances." To be truthful, he wasn't too sure if he liked this deal any more. Morris always wanted to be in control of an agreement, and now Cunningham was taking command. Furthermore, the last few days of trying to get this far were sending signals that it was not to be, and he was concerned that he was wasting his time and effort.

"I do believe there are a large number of useable boots in that pile, and it is only for that reason I have orders to relocate them," Cunningham said.

"Where are they going?" Morris asked out of curiosity.

Cunningham smiled smugly. "That's confidential, Mr Langbourne."

"Oh, do forgive me," Morris apologised, "I didn't mean to enquire after military matters. Well, for me to take a chance on behalf of my brother, the cost would certainly have to be nominal, such as one penny a boot, and we take our chances."

"A penny a boot?" Cunningham laughed condescendingly. "They are worth a lot more than that."

"Perhaps," Morris rocked back in his seat, "But we are taking a large risk, are we not?"

"Regardless. A shilling would be more like it," Cunningham smirked.

Morris smiled inwardly, Cunningham had shown his hand and Morris knew a deal was imminent. What concerned him was why, if the boots were required at some secret location, the official would now be prepared to sell them off. Morris unsuccessfully wracked his brain to find a plausible reason.

"My brother was not very complimentary on the quality of boots in that pile. After all, they have endured a brutal war. I doubt he would agree that even tuppence a pair would be worth any value."

"That's still a penny per boot," Cunningham continued to smirk. "I tell you what, Mr Langbourne, say we agree one penny per boot, no matter what the condition, I would need to see some volume to make it worth the Crown's interest. I would insist you purchase everything that I have requisitioned to be moved to Cape Town."

"Everything?" Morris asked, a little doubt creeping into his soul. "What quantities are we talking about?"

"Oh, I don't know exactly. I think most of it is already there," Cunningham said nonchalantly. "There's a shipment on its way from a place called Kimberley, I believe. Have you heard of that town?"

"Yes, I know it. All right then," Morris said cautiously, "my conditions are that I must not pay for any expense prior to my taking possession of the boots. No storage or transport costs and no wages for your men to oversee the counting and verification of the goods. The final count must be agreed by both your staff and mine. If we cannot agree on the numbers, then the deal is off," Morris added, attempting to give himself an avenue to exit the deal if he felt it was going the wrong way.

"Fair enough, I will accept your conditions but for the last." Cunningham immediately saw through Morris' ploy. "If the numbers cannot be verified, the discrepancy will be settled by half the difference between the highest and lowest count."

"If your men count less than my men, I can assure you we will agree with your figures," Morris chuckled.

A look of annoyance crossed Cunningham's face, and Morris correctly ascertained that Cunningham did not like young men who thought they were smarter than he was. He, therefore, toned his negotiations down and allowed Cunningham to lead the conversation once more. Twenty minutes later, the men shook hands and agreed to meet the following day to formalise their agreement.

Although Morris left the building pleased with the way the meeting had gone and felt that he had achieved his objective and most of his terms, he was made uneasy by something in Cunningham's demeanour at the end. He couldn't put his finger on it, but something niggled at him.

The following day, right on schedule, Morris arrived at Cunningham's office and scrutinised the sale agreement. The document was neither lengthy nor complicated. Cunningham had added a clause which set the date for counting the goods at three months into the future, his explanation being that he needed time for the other requisitioned boots to get from their current locations to Cape Town. Morris argued that it would not take three months for old boots to find their way to Cape Town from elsewhere in the country, and furthermore, the longer the footwear stayed in the open air and was exposed to the elements, the more they would deteriorate and lose value.

Cunningham countered that the boots had seen worse wear on soldiers' feet during the war and that lying in a pile on a wharf would not harm them any further. Morris shrugged to indicate his reluctant acceptance at that clause but became increasingly wary of Cunningham's continuing excuses and explanations. At one point he almost withdrew from the deal entirely.

The other clause that concerned Morris was the one detailing the payment terms. Cunningham wanted a deposit and the final payment within one week of Morris' taking possession of the goods – the day both parties would have agreed and signed off on the quantity counted. Morris objected strongly, aware that he no longer cared if the deal fell through if he did not get his way on this point. Reluctantly, Cunningham agreed that no deposit would be required, and payment would occur three months after the signing off on the quantities.

Another clause in the agreement stated he was forbidden to sell either the usable or the unusable boots to an active enemy of England or her colonies. Initially, that bothered Morris, as it limited his potential customers, but he fully understood the reason why this was a requirement of the deal. Yet an addition to that clause did catch Morris by surprise, he was not permitted to sell the boots to any private citizen nor to any company, but only to a bona fide government. Cunningham explained that that clause protected the British Government from Morris' selling the goods to another entity, who would then not be bound to the agreement and would thereby be free to sell the boots to anyone, even someone undesirable to the British Government itself. Morris grudgingly accepted the clause, and both Cunningham and Morris signed the document.

Morris trudged back to Finsbury Pavement, all the while feeling he may have made a big mistake. In his mind, he continued to play the deal and the contract over and over again, but the only obstacle he could think of was that most of the boots were likely to be complete rubbish. He would be out of pocket, and even then he would probably have to pay someone to dispose of the boots before the harbour master, or the port authorities started to charge him rent on the wharf.

When he arrived home, Rose Bertha welcomed him with an affectionate kiss on the cheek, but she immediately sensed his tension and fussed over him, leading Morris to his favourite chair and pouring him a hot cup of tea. Knowing Morris' great weakness, a freshly baked slice of shortbread was served to him on a fine Wedgewood china plate.

"What bothers you, my husband?" Rose Bertha asked.

"Oh," Morris broke away from his thoughts, "I signed a deal today with the British Government, and although I firmly believe it is a good deal, it is the first time in my life I am not fully content with it."

"I am positive it will work out just fine, Morris. We all know how exceptionally perceptive you are when it comes to business."

"Usually I ensure I am totally confident of an outcome, but, for the first time, I most certainly am not. There are too many variables that I am not in control of. Some pompous civil servant is calling the shots this time, and it irks me."

"Oh dear," Rose Bertha tried to soothe him but wasn't too sure how to discuss business matters with her husband.

"I have agreed to buy a pile of second-hand, army boots," Morris continued, staring out the window as he spoke. It was as if he was talking to himself. Somewhat relieved, Rose Bertha gave him free rein. "David told me about the importance of footwear during the war," Morris continued, "so when an opportunity came up, I seized it."

Morris continued to ramble on about the deal, and his ambivalent feelings about Cunningham. He expanded on some disquieting thoughts between the ratio of usable and unusable boots, and whether or not the proportions would be in his favour.

Although Rose felt she had a reasonable suggestion to offer, she chose her words carefully so as not to increase Morris' distress. "From what you tell me, my dear, if most of the boots are no good you might be up for the added expense of paying rent for the rubbish while you dispose of them. That would be like rubbing salt in an open wound. Perhaps you might devise a plan where you separate the good from the bad during the count. If the bad are placed on a mode of transport for disposal as they are counted, and the good on another transport for storage right there and then, that would alleviate the threat of the port authorities charging you rent. That way you will not have to store the worthless goods while you sort through it yourself afterwards."

Morris stared at Rose Bertha in surprise, suitably impressed by her solid grasp of the situation, and her ability to offer a practical solution to a pressing problem.

"What an excellent idea, Rosie!" Morris exclaimed. "I do believe you are onto something. Yes, indeed, that would be the right thing to do. I must write to David at once and let him know what I expect of him."

"Wonderful," replied Rose Bertha, delighted that her husband had actually listened to her suggestion. She knew Morris was not an easy person to deal with in business, and she had just provided him with an acceptable solution to one of his more pressing problems. "While you do that I will make some dinner for you."

"Wait," Morris reached over and gave her hand a quick squeeze. "David's letter can wait another day. After all, we have three months reprieve. Allow me to take you out to your favourite restaurant tonight."

Rose Bertha beamed. This was proving to be a big day for her. "That would be delightful. I had already made Bubble and Squeak, but we can have that as leftovers tomorrow night."

"Perfect," Morris smiled, somewhat relieved.

Morris sat at his desk and stared out of the window. The building opposite had minuscule balconies attached to each flat, and an elderly lady was standing outside hanging her washing out to dry on a thin, fraying string. Although Morris seemed to be watching her intently, his mind was working on the precise instructions he needed to give David in his letter. Because what he had to say was imperative, and he didn't know exactly where David was, he decided he would send telegrams to Jack Shiel in Port Elizabeth and to Louis in Johannesburg to alert them as to his impending letter. Between them, Morris was sure, they would alert David to the message that would be waiting for him at the Standard Bank in Cape Town.

The old woman stared down at the street below for a few moments, before disappearing with a flurry inside and shutting the door. Morris dipped his pen in a bottle of ink and began writing.

Friday 12th December 1902
Finsbury Pavement
London

Dear David,

By the time you get this, I am hoping you would have returned to Cape Town from Port Elizabeth and East London. I write to inform you of an agreement I have entered into with the British Government.

I have agreed to purchase the boots you spoke about on the Cape Town wharf for B pence per boot, regardless of condition. I have assumed that a good 80% of them will be useless.

The terms of the agreement are that three months hence all boots on the wharf must be purchased. (There is still a small quantity joining the current pile from other areas of South Africa, and they will form part of the deal.) Until a count is undertaken, which will begin on the 14th March 1903, there will be no rent or storage expense to us. Immediately the quantity is agreed, we will be subject to storage, rental etc.

Based on that premise, I require that you attend the Cape Town harbour just before the count date and engage a small team to count and to sort the good from the bad, in production line formation. Boots unfit for use must be loaded onto a wagon for disposal immediately. Boots that can be repaired, cleaned and reused must be placed on another transport and loaded onto a rail wagon to be shipped to the Johannesburg warehouse, there to be stored by Louis. I will advise how to handle the goods once we know how many we can salvage.

You must avoid paying storage, demurrage or rentals for the stock. By nature their fees are ludicrous. My father-in-law, Mr Friedlander, will assist me in finding a market, but this will take some time.

I am confident you will work out an efficient and worthy system to deal with

this purchase.
   Your loving brother,
   Morris
   P.S. It is imperative you telegram your receipt of this letter.

Morris read through the letter once more, folded it in his precise way, placed the correspondence in an envelope and sealed it. Walking down to the Post Office, while braced against the icy chill of the London winter, he felt more comfortable with the deal and told himself not to think further on it until he heard back from David. He attached an overseas stamp on the envelope, slipped it into a scarlet-painted post-box and then walked down to the offices of Lloyds of London.

Presenting a familiar face, Morris was led courteously into the office of Yoni Goldberg, who greeted him warmly. Despite the wintery cold, Yoni's office was quite comfortable.

"How was your honeymoon? How was America?" Yoni asked enthusiastically, a big smile escaping his bushy, jet-black beard.

"Excellent. An education, in all honesty," Morris smiled broadly. "I have much I need to discuss with you, much news, and ideas I have that I would prefer to pass by you first."

"Wonderful! I would enjoy that very much."

"Perhaps we could talk over dinner? Tonight, if that is agreeable to you and Mrs Goldberg?"

"Absolutely, Morris. We have nothing planned for tonight."

"Lovely. Might I suggest you and Mrs Goldberg come to Finsbury Pavement? I would like Mrs Goldberg to see what Rose Bertha has done to the flat. Rose Bertha will make us one of her delicious meals," Morris beamed proudly.

"Seven o'clock? Would that be suitable?" Yoni asked.

"Indeed, perfect. I look forward to it," Morris stood and shook his mentor's hand firmly.

When he reached the street, Morris noticed a tea-room across the road and decided he would treat himself to a strong coffee and a sweet cake. With hands dug deep into the pockets of his woollen overcoat, Morris crossed the road with a determined step. On reaching the door, however, he stopped.

It crossed his mind that perhaps he should go home and let Rose Bertha know to expect company later that evening. Leftover Bubble and Squeak would certainly not do; a roast crossed his mind, instantly causing him to salivate slightly.

Looking up the street, he saw a swirl of dead leaves spinning aimlessly at the icy wind's mercy. Under these circumstances, it was not a terribly hard decision for Morris to decide that a little coffee and a slice of cake would not make much difference to Rose Bertha's dinner preparations; there must be plenty of time to prepare a roast, he thought. Morris, therefore, pushed open the door without any further qualms.

CHAPTER SIXTEEN

Africa - 1903

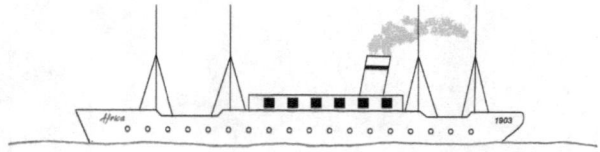

Stepping onto southern African soil once again, David took a brief moment to breathe in the warm air that drifted in from the Karoo. Before he turned to help his wife and child off the gangway, he smiled inwardly, feeling as if he had come home.

Cape Town harbour was bustling as always, the clear skies promising a sweltering summer's day. Having disembarked safely, David led his family to where the luggage would shortly be unloaded. He stopped once again to admire the majestic Table Mountain, its level summit draped in its customary summer "table-cloth" of cloud, whose wispy edges drifted ever so gently into the void below.

"I do wish they would hurry up with the baggage," Hanna complained, "I'm feeling positively queasy."

David was hauled back to reality. "Would you like to sit down, my darling? I can find you a bench."

"No," Hanna sighed, "I'll be alright. I'm simply not accustomed to sea travel."

"Perhaps it is the heat," David suggested. "After the ice cold of England, the contrast here is quite significant."

"I don't know…" Hanna sighed again. "The last time I felt queasy when I got off a ship was because I was bearing a child."

David looked at her with a mixture of surprise and delight. "Do you think…?"

"I don't know," she shrugged. "I just wish they would hurry up."

"Yes, we should soon be on our way. Would you mind waiting here for a moment while I look for a coach to take us to our hotel? It's not far off."

Hanna smiled in relief. "An excellent idea."

David hurried off to where a line of horse-drawn coaches were waiting and secured a ride to the Mount Nelson Hotel, a very prestigious establishment on the edge of the city, above the original Company Gardens. Highly recommended by many notable people, the Mount Nelson had been commandeered as the headquarters of the war office during the recent Boer War. Now that the war was over, the hotel had reverted to its original function – offering hospitality of the first order.

Walking back to where Hanna stood with Ettie, David noted the pile of old boots – a little bigger than he remembered – still lying unattended on the wharf. The unmistakable growing pile was attended by a British Army private, followed by two African men in Western clothing, each pushing a wheelbarrow further laden with more old boots.

Casting a quick look at Hanna, who hadn't moved from her position, David changed direction and cut off the soldier.

"Excuse me, sir," David said, as he caught up to the man and walked alongside him, "I'm most curious as to why you are piling up old army boots here. May I ask the reason?"

"Yes, you may," the man smiled, pleased to engage in some conversation. "These are all old boots that soldiers who are returning home have handed in. They can't be used again, so they are required to be destroyed."

"So why dump them here on the wharf?"

"There is a rail track just over there," he pointed to some iron tracks just twenty yards away. "They will be loaded onto a rail wagon and carted to the dump just inland from here. Some old boots have already found their way there."

"That sounds logical," David agreed. "May I take a look at some of them?"

"Certainly," the soldier stopped and motioned his workers to do likewise.

David picked up a couple of the boots and turned them over in his hands. The private was right; they were well-worn and entirely unusable. One of the boots had a hole that had clearly been caused by a bullet which had entered one side and exited the other, splattering the inside with what was now so much dried blood. As if the boot had developed an electric shock, David dropped it the moment he realised what he was holding.

"Oh my Lord," David groaned as he wiped his fingers unconsciously on his trousers. "What a brutal war!"

"Yes sir, it was. Last week we found a boot that had three toes still inside."

"Oh heavens," David grimaced. "Well, thank you for your time. By the way, do you ever find any boots that can be used again?"

"Yes," the man smiled, "they get sorted into another pile and placed in that warehouse over there," he pointed to a corrugated-iron shed slightly past Hanna's location. "We don't find many, though."

As David looked at the shed, he noticed Hanna wobble unsteadily on her feet, so he thanked the army soldier and immediately trotted over to her side.

"Oh David," Hanna complained when he reached her, "I feel awful. I do believe I am with child again."

"Come on," David smiled affectionately, "I'm taking you to the Mount Nelson right away. I will come back for our luggage."

The thought of an addition to their family filled David with joy. The plans of opening a business in Port Elizabeth, East London, and Cape Town were given little more than a fleeting thought. As far as he was concerned, he had more than enough time to work out the logistics. Right now, though, Hanna had to take centre-stage in his life.

When Louis and Harry disembarked in Cape Town ten days after David, they were surprised to find him waiting for them at the bottom of the gangway. Quite predictably, the reunion was very warm, punctuated by much laughter and quick-witted banter. As he loaded his brothers into a buggy and headed to the Mount Nelson Hotel, David broke the news about Hanna and explained that, although he had planned to proceed to Port Elizabeth within a day of their arrival, Hanna's circumstances had altered that somewhat.

David had immediately concentrated his business attention instead on Cape Town and had secured some premises in Commercial Street, where he planned to set up a wholesale store for Morris. The lease would begin in May 1903, about five months' hence, a date which had been arranged by David to give him time to travel to Port Elizabeth and East London where he needed to set up stores there, too. David asked Louis if he would stay in Cape Town an extra week and recruit staff for the venture, while he went to Port Elizabeth and East London. He would thereafter proceed to Bulawayo, where he would settle Hanna into their home and leave her close to her parents.

Louis would then be required to go to Kimberley as agreed, while Harry's plans would stay the same. He would proceed directly to Rhodesia; first to Bulawayo and then to Salisbury. Because David and Hanna anticipated that she would give birth in July, David suggested that the three brothers regroup in Bulawayo for the event, where they could have an indaba to discuss how the company might stand at that time.

"*You* are calling an Indaba?" Harry winked at Louis.

"Well, Morris is the head of our brotherly family," David returned the wink, "but in Africa, I would assume I am head of the business."

"I think that goes without saying," Louis smiled. "Agreed, an Indaba is called for in Bulawayo immediately after the birth of your next child."

"What do you think it will be," Harry asked, "a boy or a girl?"

"I think a girl, but Hanna thinks a boy."

"I'd go with a boy," Louis said. "Harry?"

"Hmm… I think it will be twins, a girl first then a boy."

David laughed hard, he was enjoying having his brothers around him.

"Tell me," Louis suddenly became serious, "that pile of boots? Is Morris serious?"

"I hope not," David frowned. "I made some enquiries and even physically checked some of the boots myself. They are all total rejects. Absolutely useless."

"Perhaps you should send Morris a telegram and tell him not to bother," Harry suggested.

"I already have. I told him the boots had already been sorted and destined for the rubbish dump. Do you know there are sometimes body parts in some of those boots?"

"Heaven forbid!" Louis exclaimed. "You know, Morris is brilliant, but sometimes I have to question his thinking."

"Take nothing away from him, though," David defended his elder brother. "Some of the ideas he has come up with have been phenomenal. Just look at where we are today; this is all his doing, make no error. However, I must agree, some of his ideas are ridiculous, like buying a ship. Truly, sometimes I do wonder."

The boys were still laughing at Morris' expense when the buggy drove up the softly curving drive of the Mount Nelson Hotel. After checking in they all met Hanna and Ettie in the tea garden, and the banter and joy continued till well after dark.

David was having the time of his life. Everything was falling into place very nicely, thanks to the dependable people around him.

David took his two brothers to the new premises on Commercial Street the following day, before checking out of the Mount Nelson with his family later that afternoon. Early the next day, Harry left Cape Town for Rhodesia, while Louis stayed behind for a further week to recruit competent managers and staff for the impending business.

A few hours after his departure, Harry's train was delayed at a small town in the Karoo called Matjiesfontein. After a very dull one hour wait, the conductor walked through the carriages and invited everyone to disembark and to take a stroll about the settlement, since a problem had arisen with the engine, which might lead to an extensive delay. The conductor assured the passengers that three powerful blasts of the train's whistle would be given in order to summon the passengers back to the train, ten minutes before their departure.

Although Matjiesfontein was not a big railway siding, it did have two striking features; a well-kept cricket oval, and a magnificent hotel called the Hotel Milner. Not surprisingly, almost all the passengers on the train soon made their way to the hotel.

Although Harry very much admired the establishment, he rather thought it appeared out of place; too majestic for such a barren and remote part of the country. On the right-hand side of the late-Victorian building was a bar festooned with cricketing memorabilia. Apart from some signed, sepia-coloured photographs of former cricketers which, had been framed and hung on the walls, one could find the occasional autographed cricket bat, cap, or ball. Not only did Harry know very little of the sport, but the mob that was at the bar counter trying desperately to purchase some liquid refreshment also lessened his interest in the room even further.

Harry instead chose to amble into the dining-room, which had been lavishly adorned with crystal chandeliers, regal paintings, and heavy drapes that hung from ceiling to floor. The meal was a self-service affair at a row of bain-marie serving dishes, all of which were empty. Near the entrance to the dining-room was a man selling meal tickets. Hands in pockets, Harry casually sauntered over to him, intending to purchase a meal, before standing in the queue, patiently listening to the conversation between the ticket-seller and a fellow passenger in front of him.

"That's damn expensive if you ask me!" the customer complained, rummaging in his pockets for some cash.

"Well, we are very isolated, sir," the cashier said defensively. "Besides, the meal ticket includes a starter of soup, a main of steak, egg, and vegetables, including potatoes, and a choice of three puddings."

"Damned highway robbery!" the customer exclaimed. "All I want is a bowl of soup!"

"The meal ticket is for the entire meal, sir."

"There!" the customer roughly handed the cashier a fist-full of coins. "I'll have you know that I could buy a delightful meal for both my wife and myself for the same price in Cape Town."

"Thank you, sir," the cashier murmured without batting an eyelid and gave the man a ticket with a number written on it. "As I said, we are very isolated..."

"I know, I know" the customer grumbled. He snatched his ticket and turned on his heel so abruptly that he stumbled into Harry and was forced to apologise.

"Would you like a meal ticket, sir?" the cashier asked Harry kindly.

Harry glanced at the throng near the food counter, muttering amongst themselves, and noticed that even those patrons already seated were not yet eating.

Harry smiled at the man. "I'll pass, thank you." With his hands still in his pockets, he slowly walked over to one of the walls and studied the paintings.

Barely a minute later, the mumbling at the food counter intensified to a cheer and a "Hoorah!" as a waiter in a spotless, white uniform staggered through a set of swing doors, carrying a heavy, metal urn which contained the first course of soup. As he removed the lid, copious billows of steam sent tendrils of moisture towards the ceiling. Patrons quickly formed a line, as the waiter began ladling the boiling liquid into their bowls.

Harry had some regrets that he had not purchased a ticket after all, but the idea of queuing for a meal did not really appeal to him. Instead, he chose to leave the dining-room and to explore the magnificent hotel further. As he walked out, however, he noticed that the cashier had packed up and disappeared, together with his table and cash box.

"Well, that puts paid to any idea I had of enjoying a meal here," Harry said to himself. Walking through the reception area, he noticed that it was likewise unattended. Deciding he might just settle for a beer, after all, Harry discovered that the two barmen serving behind the bar counter had also vanished, leaving some very frustrated potential customers standing around waiting to be served.

Suddenly three short blasts from the train's whistle ricocheted off the building walls and reverberated around the settlement. All the patrons inside the Milner Hotel went deathly quiet.

"You have got to be joking!" a lone, male voice boomed from the dining-room. Angry chatter erupted immediately after that.

Harry left the commotion behind him and strolled back to the train without taking his hands out of his pockets. On clambering aboard, Harry saw the conductor checking passengers' tickets. He pulled his out of his jacket pocket and presented it.

"Thank you, sir, my apologies for the delay. I hope you enjoy the rest of your journey," the conductor beamed.

"Thank you, I am sure I shall. That's a magnificent hotel. Most impressive. Do you know who owns it?"

"Indeed I do," the conductor puffed out his chest proudly. "Mr Logan. Came from Scotland a while back with his family."

"He must be a good businessman," Harry commented, with barely disguised sarcasm.

"Indeed he is; owns almost all the refreshment stations along the railway line in the Cape Province. Many hotels, too. I should think the

Milner Hotel is his flagship."

"I see," Harry smirked. "A bit of a cricketer too?"

"Indeed, indeed. Mr Cricket they call him. Please forgive me, sir…" the conductor politely excused himself to check other passenger tickets as they boarded the train.

Harry made his way to his compartment and settled in. His fellow passengers were decidedly upset and angry as they walked past. His travelling companion was not exempt from the pervasive ill-will, sitting across from Harry in their compartment and glaring at him angrily.

"Did you get any food?" the man grumbled.

"No," Harry said calmly. "There were too many people in the queue, so I gave it a miss."

"You're lucky. I was forced to pay good money for a three-course meal and all I got was a bowl of insipid soup that was so damn hot I couldn't eat it in time."

"Did you ask for your money back?" Harry goaded, knowing the answer but feeling that a little amusement on this tiresome journey might go a long way to relieve the boredom.

"Get my money back? Are you joking? As soon as the train whistle blew, there was no staff to be seen anywhere! Ten minutes they give you to get back on the train, can you believe that? Ten minutes! I shall be writing to the owner of the hotel when I get to Kimberley."

"Good luck with that," Harry said as the train began to shunt, before pulling away gently. He stood up suddenly. "If you will excuse me, I think I might make my way to the dining car. I'm sure there will be something to eat there. Are you coming?"

"No, thank you," he muttered, "I think I've lost my appetite, and besides, I have burnt my tongue on that blasted soup."

Arriving in Bulawayo without further incident, Harry immediately had Mr Loxton and Mr Johnson brief him on what had happened during his absence. After a lengthy meeting with Ivy Collier, going through all the books of accounts, Harry was satisfied that, during his absence, Loxton and Johnson had run the business to his satisfaction. With his mind at ease, Harry booked a ticket to Salisbury barely three days after returning to Bulawayo.

Although his last visit to Salisbury had not been that long before, Harry noticed some subtle changes, a new building here and there, a dirt road where one hadn't been before. Checking into simple accommodation on the outskirts of the settlement, Harry set about looking for suitable premises for a warehouse.

He found a property to rent just two roads behind the main street of the town; a quarter block on the corner of Speke Avenue and a street called Inez Terrace. Speke Avenue had been named after a famous British explorer, John Speke, who claimed to have discovered the elusive source of the River Nile along with the explorer Richard Burton. This had caused a massive controversy throughout geographical societies worldwide, prompting several independent explorations to prove (or disprove) the claim.

Harry noted that on the opposite corner stood a property housing a wholesaler's business, Kaufman and Sons. He wondered if that Kaufman might be related to David's friend, Abe Kaufman. As the population in Salisbury was reasonably intimate, Harry assumed that this was quite possible. Taking that as a favourable sign, Harry found his way to the agent's offices and began the formalities of putting in an offer for the premises he wanted.

The rental process would take at least another fortnight, because the owner, existing tenant, and agent were either in Bulawayo, taking a holiday, or (in the case of the previous tenant), deceased, which Harry found somewhat irksome. He was undecided whether it would be a better use of his time to travel back to Bulawayo and return in two weeks, or spend the time in Salisbury, exploring opportunities for the family business. A visit to the Chamber of Commerce seemed a likely place to start and would perhaps give him some direction. Arriving at the building, he was not disappointed. He met a young fellow aged about nineteen, just one year younger than himself.

A slight man, Robert Shepherd, appeared fit and energetic with a friendly and open face, sandy hair and hazel eyes. Robert was filled with confidence, and this did not go unnoticed by Harry. Robert was equally quick to introduce himself and strike up a friendly rapport almost as soon as the two met. Robert told Harry that he worked for an agricultural supplies company and that his job was to sell seed and farming implements. He would go out into the farmlands with a list of what he had on offer, the quantities and prices, and secure orders. When Robert returned to Salisbury, he would hand his purchase orders over to another department where the orders would be filled. After a couple of days' break, he would repeat the process.

Harry chose not to divulge too much about himself, however, preferring merely to state that he was from Bulawayo and worked for his brothers, who owned a wholesale company and retail business. He deliberately neglected to tell Robert that he had an equal share in the company.

Robert had three main agricultural areas under his responsibility, a small citrus zone to the north, not far away, a tobacco area to the east, called "Marandellas", and another to the west called "Sinoia". What fascinated Harry was that Robert Shepherd's primary mode of transport was a bicycle.

"How long does it take you to get out there, for heaven's sake?" Harry asked in amazement.

"About two weeks round trip," Shepherd grinned. "About five days to my furthest point, which is Sinoia, a few days visiting farmers, and about five days back."

"Fascinating," Harry shook his head in awe. "And where do you sleep? You must be miles from civilisation during your travels."

"Farmers," Robert grinned. "I stay with farmers along the way. The Rhodesian farmers are most hospitable. It also suits my type of business, being a salesman. Why don't you join me? I'm heading out to Sinoia tomorrow. Back in a fortnight. You never know, you might pick up some business along the way."

"Oh no, I couldn't possibly do that. At any rate, I don't own a bicycle."

"That's no problem, the shop has several of them at my disposal. I hear that there is a cave out that way. Apparently, it is absolutely magnificent. I am told the water at the bottom of the cave is the most superb blue, more beautiful than the sky on a clear day.

"Really?" Harry's interest was piqued.

"On this trip, I intend to visit them. Some of the locals talk about the caves."

"Well…" Harry pondered the idea. He had two weeks at his disposal.

"Go on, be a sport," Shepherd nudged Harry jokingly. "At any rate, I could use the company."

"Alright," Harry smiled and straightened himself. "Why not?"

They met the next day at the agricultural supply store, which was nothing more than a timber and wrought-iron shed on the far side of town. Harry carried a small leather tote bag with just a change of clothing and his razor to keep himself presentable. Robert Shepard carried much the same in his own canvas tote bag. Harry was assigned a spare bicycle, and a quick inspection of the contraption made him chuckle.

"What's so funny?" Shepherd asked, smiling in amusement.

"Raleigh Bicycles. My family business imports these into Rhodesia from England. I'll bet you my new shoes we sold this cycle to your boss."

Robert grinned. "Well, you had better hope it doesn't break down on the journey. That could be embarrassing for you."

Harry found the first day of cycling difficult. The road to Sinoia was a bumpy one, composed mostly of hardened ruts in the ground from wagons that had passed by during the wet seasons. Often Harry would have to stand on the pedals because his rear-end had become increasingly uncomfortable, and – as the first day neared its end – his discomfort intensified into something of a pain.

Harry persevered nevertheless, while the subsequent days passed by in jovial conversation. Harry found Robert to be both a pleasurable companion and a source of intriguing information. Dotted here and there with thorny acacia trees, the passing landscape was pleasing to the eye, filled with the orchestra of a myriad of insects and wild birds. Harry was swiftly coming to understand why his brother David loved the bush so much.

Since Robert's family were Irish Canadians by origin, Harry found the twang in his friend's accent quite captivating. Being out in the African bush with such a pleasant companion pushed his physical discomfort to the back of his mind. A good two hours before dark each evening they would arrive at a farmstead where Robert would greet the owners like old friends before introducing Harry, who was equally accepted as a friend at once.

Depending on when the two boys arrived at the farmsteads, they were offered very welcome hospitality in the form of delightful teas or wholesome meals. Harry was enjoying his escape from the rigours of business, almost forgetting at times about his family's commercial interests. He could see why Robert enjoyed his job, and, more specifically, why he was so successful at what he did. As the days passed, Harry's tough facade began to soften. He was out in the bush, incommunicado, and – for the first time in his life – his responsibilities were not uppermost in his mind.

After a week of carefree riding, they arrived in the small settlement of Sinoia. There wasn't much to it, a few general stores, a lodging, some stables for horses, and pens for the cattle. There was a bar which the two young men made a bee-line for, to slake their thirst with a warm beer. Robert advised that they could check into the lodging, but he didn't recommend it. He preferred to cycle another hour further out of town to stay on a nearby farm owned by a Mr and Mrs Joubert. It would definitely be more comfortable in Robert's opinion, especially as he had an excellent rapport with the farmer. Harry agreed to the suggestion without hesitation.

Lying just to the north of the settlement, Leon and Gail Joubert had built a sturdy farmhouse with bricks made from clay that had been found on the property. The homestead had three bedrooms, a lounge, dining room, and kitchen, but by far the most comfortable and frequented area was the outside patio which overlooked a splendid lawn. Their home had been thatched with straw, making the entire house (patio included) both cool in the summer and warm in the winter.

With a solid build and skin bronzed by years of sunshine and hard physical work, Leon was a dedicated farmer. Thanks to many years of experience and hard work, he had become very successful and was well regarded by the local farming community. Gail was very much a hands-on lady, preferring to concentrate on the livestock, goats, horses, and cattle. She kept her fair hair cropped short and had green thumbs, maintaining a flourishing garden at the front of the house, and a prolific vegetable and herb garden at the back.

Gail and Leon were exceptional hosts, welcoming the young men into their home and providing nutritious and tasty meals. As the day drew to a close, they would all gather on the patio and watch the sun go down, sharing jokes, stories, and anecdotes, while sipping on a beverage of sorts and nibbling on a snack, usually made of leftovers from the day before. The first night under the Joubert's roof left Harry with a warm feeling of well-being.

The following morning saw the young men part company, with Robert visiting three farms not too far apart, while Harry cycled back into the settlement of Sinoia to see if he could conduct some business. Harry concluded all the business he could muster within two hours, having secured an order for ten Raleigh bicycles, a hundred enamel pots and pans and twenty heavy-duty grey blankets. When he realised that no further business was possible in town, he rode back to the Joubert's farm and whiled away the day, waiting for Robert to return.

Since he had enjoyed yet another successful day, Robert came back in the early evening, covered in smiles. While relaxing on their host's veranda, sipping a very welcome cup of tea, Robert turned the conversation to the hidden caves he had heard about.

Leon cast a lazy glance off to the west. "They are not too far away, actually," he mulled.

"You've been there?" Robert asked with some notable excitement in his voice.

"We both have," Gail smiled, "I would recommend you take a visit, the caves are breathtaking."

"How do we find them?" Harry asked quickly.

"I'll draw you a map," Leon suggested. "It will take you about two hours to get there on your bicycles. The easiest way is to cycle back to town, turn right, and travel about an hour west. They're not difficult to find."

"Do you know who found them?" Robert's excitement was palpable.

"No," Leon laughed and picked up his heavy mug of tea, "not initially. There is a story behind the caves, though."

"Frederick Courtney Selous," Gail continued, "the big game hunter, is believed to have been the first European to come across the caves. It was in the late 1880s if I recall."

"Oh!" Harry exclaimed, "I've met him. I sold him a sheath knife when he came into our warehouse in Bulawayo. When I first arrived in Bulawayo, Mr Selous played a critical role in defending the settlement from the Matabele, after they had placed the town under siege."

"That's right," Gail smiled at Harry with a nod, "he formed the Bulawayo Field Force. I dare say without him Bulawayo might have been in big trouble."

"Anyway," Leon brought the subject back to the caves, "Selous was the first European to find them, but before Selous, long before him, there was a band of outlaws in the area who would rob their victims and then murder them by throwing them down the caves. At the bottom of the caves, surrounded by sheer rock cliffs and about one hundred and fifty feet down, there is a large pool, the water of which is the most beautiful blue. If the victims survived the fall, they would drown.

"Then a leader called Chinhoyi came to the area and killed the outlaws, so he was made a Mashona Chief, and used the caves to protect his people from the Matabele. One day they were caught off guard and were overthrown, literally thrown down into the caves."

"Good grief," Robert mused, "a bit of a violent history there."

"Sadly much of Africa's history is violent," Gail shook her head slowly in despair. "They call the caves 'Chirorodzva', which translates as 'Pool of the Fallen'. Legend has it that the bones of the victims whisper to each other at the bottom of the pool of blue water. It is very quiet down there, so it is also known as the 'Sleeping Pool'."

"You've been down to the bottom – to the water I mean? I thought you said the pools were at the bottom of a sheer cliff." Harry queried.

"Yes," Leon replied, "a little to the south of the main cave is a smaller cave that slopes down to the water. When you get down there, you can look up at the opening 150 feet above. You'll see clouds and sky. It's an easy walk down, but before you go, ask some of the villagers in the area for permission. They might even show you where the entrance to the access tunnel is so that you don't have to look for it."

"Fascinating," Robert grinned.

"Come on, boys," Gail stood suddenly, "let's go inside. The mozzies are coming out, and it's almost dinner time."

As the men obeyed, Harry stood slowly and stretched his back, casting a look at the setting sun. The sky had turned into streaks of orange, yellow, and mauve; a certain peace hung in the air. He had been welcomed into a community of farmers, a loving group of people who accepted strangers into their lives without reservation. Facing continual hardships, these were people of the earth, who brought no airs and graces, but took everyone as their own, and just loved their land, their crops, and their animals.

Since Leon and Gail embodied these beautiful people, Harry felt entirely whole and content, basking in their hospitality. Crickets chirped nearby, a lone frog croaked in the distance, and, for the first time in his life,

Mother Africa gently touched the heart of Harry Langbourne.

Accustomed by that time to long journeys in the bicycle saddle, Harry kept up easily with the brisk pace set by Rob. Armed with Leon's crude map, dawn was just breaking when the two young men set off to find the caves, the excitement of adventure burning furiously in their hearts.

Leon's sketchy map was simple to follow, and the salient points and landmarks were easy to find. About a quarter of a mile from the caves, the boys came across a village and sought out the chief, who, correctly interpreting Rob's limited knowledge of the local Shona language, happily granted them permission to visit the caves. In return, the chief received a gift from Rob of some sewing needles, cotton and thread, a length of cotton cloth and two small, hand-held mirrors. The members of the village were equally welcoming, while an enthusiastic young man was instructed to guide them directly to where the caves were located.

The three men thus set off promptly on foot, and in very short time they arrived at what seemed to be a massive hole in the earth. While the rock sides of the cavern were quite sheer, they managed to approach the edge by crawling on all fours and peered tentatively into its depths. What they saw was breathtaking.

After spending so much time in the bush, looking at the earthen colours of the ground and the stunted, pale-green, yellow, and beige hues of the bushveld, the view below them was quite striking in contrast. A deep, cobalt-blue pool of liquid – smooth as silk – lay silently far below, reflecting the sky with absolute clarity, and quite overwhelming them with its unearthly beauty. The fact that all this was hidden over a hundred feet underground was all the more astounding.

"Oh, my word!" Harry exclaimed. "It's incredible!"

"I actually cannot believe what I am looking at," Rob whispered to himself.

For a good few minutes, the young men stared into the spectacular water below. It reflected the clouds above them like a perfect mirror. Harry shuffled and lay on his stomach in a more comfortable position. Rob followed suit and took in the silence, beauty, and serenity. The only movement to be discerned was an occasional swallow that swooped down to its nest on the rock-face to feed its young, or to fly out of the cave at breakneck speed, and – in keeping with the ambience of the Sleeping Pool

– the movement of their wings was absolutely silent.

"Let's find our way down there and have a better look," Rob suggested in a whisper.

"Yes," Harry whispered back, "I want to feel that water. I've never seen water that colour before. I've never ever seen that colour either, come to think of it. What would you call it?"

"I haven't a clue," Rob replied, still whispering out of respect for the extraordinary power of the silence. "Royal blue?" Rob ventured.

Standing up cautiously and backing away from the lip of the massive cavity in the earth, Rob explained to their guide, through broken Shona and hand signals, that they wished to descend to the water. The man, having understood, strode off around the edge of the precipice with Harry and Rob following obediently, before arriving at a thicket of thorny, acacia bushes. They watched as their guide carefully picked his way through the foliage. When he indicated for them to follow him, they complied, and carefully stepped through, to be greeted by a cavernous opening in the ground.

This cave was more like a tunnel that sloped down into the bowels of the earth, or so it seemed. Rob and Harry thanked the Mashona man with a traditional handshake. He walked back a few paces past the acacia shrubbery and took a seat on a rock, while the boys excitedly walked a few yards into the cave's mouth, staring into the darkness and waiting for their eyes to adjust to the gloom below.

"You first," said Harry softly.

"I wonder if there are any dangerous animals down here," Rob almost whispered, suddenly a little nervous.

No clear path could be seen leading down among the large rocks that were strewn about, and they needed to make the traverse carefully. The sides of the cave were smooth and imposing, with the roof at least two or three times the height of an adult man above them. Nothing seemed to indicate that their journey down to the level of the water would be cramped in any way. As their eyes began to adjust, Harry noticed a little water oozing out of the walls in places, while random lines of white lime deposits left clues as to where water had once seeped away.

Harry picked up a small rock and threw it down the gullet of the cave. It clattered noisily, echoes bouncing off the solid walls, before falling silent. Suddenly about half a dozen creatures came flying out the cave and over the boys' heads, causing them to duck involuntarily.

"I didn't know birds lived in caves," Rob whispered urgently.

"I think those are called bats," Harry smiled. "My brother loves creatures, especially birds, and he told me that bats live in caves. If I recall, they hang upside down when they sleep."

"This place is so bizarre," Rob mused.

"Why do you say that?"

"Haven't you noticed? Everything is so quiet. Up top swallows were nesting in the cave, and in here, there are bats, and they all fly without a sound. Did you hear any wings flapping? Have you heard a bird chirp? Even we are whispering."

"I think we are safe." Harry tried to sound confident, but in reality, he was becoming increasingly uncomfortable, staring down the dark tunnel.

Both boys looked back at the opening for a thread of confidence from their guide, but they could not see him.

"What about snakes?" Rob said nervously.

In silence, they gazed down the dark cavernous hole again, trying to force their eyes to see if anything sinister was lurking.

Harry tried to sound knowledgeable. "I believe bats eat snakes," he attempted to say confidently, "so there won't be any down there."

"What about spiders? I hear there are some spiders in Rhodesia that can kill a horse."

A cold fear gripped Harry as his courage was finally tested to the limit. He did not like spiders one iota.

"Do you think bats eat spiders?" Harry asked nervously, a thin sheen of sweat starting to show on his forehead.

"I haven't come this far just to stare down this hole. I'm going in. Coming?" Rob asked as he took another tentative step downward.

"I suppose humans have been down there and came out all right," Harry shrugged and cautiously followed Rob.

At about the halfway point, the boys began to see the edge of the clear, unimaginably blue water. Light from above, where they had been a little earlier, streamed into the cavern, giving the lads copious light to navigate the uneven pathway. On reaching the water's edge, the boys stood in silence, staring into the fascinating liquid, their vision penetrating far into the depths of the crystal clear water.

"Unbelievable," Harry broke the silence, his voice echoing strongly off the far wall.

"I have never seen anything like this," Rob marvelled, looking up at the sky, and the ledge that they had only recently been peering over. "I'm going to have a swim. You coming?"

Rob started to remove his shoes as Harry looked tentatively at the far side of the cave.

"I can't swim," Harry admitted. "In any case, do you think it's wise?"

"Why not?" Rob paused as he was about to rip his shirt off over his head.

"We don't know if there are crocodiles or man-eating fish that live in there. Besides, there are the souls of all the bones lying at the bottom. What if they reach up and grab your foot and pull you down to join them?"

Rob stared at Harry, a look of uncertain horror etched across his face. Slowly, he pulled his shirt back down and stood silently for a moment, fear and doubt creeping into his mind.

"You think so?" Rob asked.

Harry shrugged. "I have no idea, but I'm not getting in. Besides, look how deep it is."

Rob stared at the water for a while, looking for movement, or the sign of a crocodile having exited the tranquil pond, perhaps a discarded skin that a snake may have shed. Finally, he began to unbutton his shirt.

"I'm going in. I'm sure it's safe," Rob said confidently. "I'm not coming this far just to look at it. I want to immerse myself in the water. This place is magical, that's the only word I can find for it."

"I agree," Harry said as he stepped over to a rock and sat upon it. "I'm surprised more people don't know about this place. My brother once found a place in the bush near Bulawayo with a friend of his, Abe Kaufman. It sounded a bit like this place, but on a much smaller scale. David never said that the water was as blue as this. And it certainly wasn't this deep underground."

"You must take me there one day," Rob said as he placed his folded shirt on a rock and began untying his shoes. "There is so much of this continent I want to see."

"Sadly, David keeps the location a secret. Even I have never been there."

"Maybe I'll find it myself," Rob chuckled as he continued to strip off his clothes. Once completely naked, he stepped over to the water's edge and tested the temperature with his foot, continually searching the depths for movement or danger.

"What's it like?" Harry asked, somewhat bemused at the sight of this pale, naked man, who seemed anxious to enter the water, but at the same time wired with fear, like the tightly wound spring of a clock. He watched the outgoing ripples start their circular exploration of the furthest reaches of the cave.

"Magnificent," Rob looked back at Harry briefly with a broad smile. "Just keep an eye out for crocodiles."

Rob lurched forward and pushed himself out into the serenity of the pool. His breaststroke was graceful and silent. When he was about ten yards out, he paused and turned to face Harry, treading water as he took in the wondrous spectacle of nature. He looked straight up above and watched a pure white fluffy cloud, high in the sky, drifting lazily past the opening of the cave. Then, taking a deep breath, Rob let himself drop silently below the surface.

Harry watched his new friend gracefully sink deeper and deeper, the clarity was exceptional, and he could see almost every detail of Rob's movements. Rob halted his downward trajectory and turned 180 degrees to look to the far side of the cave.

When he looked downward, he suddenly jerked violently. Rob began a frantic ascent to the surface, kicking wildly and reaching desperately with his arms. Harry leapt to his feet and watched in fear as bubbles streamed from Rob's mouth and nose, his sandy hair streaking back over his scalp as he thrust for the surface. Harry took a moment to look into the water behind and below his friend, dreading the sight of an aqueous monster speeding silently towards its prey but saw nothing.

Rob burst out of the water, eyes bulging in fear, gasping for air and thrashing madly as he forced his way to the edge, where Harry stood ankle-deep, shoes and all, ready to pull the hapless man to safety. Gripping an outstretched arm, Harry hauled Rob to the safety of solid earth.

"What happened? What did you see?" Harry asked, shaking, adrenaline tearing through his system.

"Nothing," Rob responded through a gasp of air.

Harry stared at his friend blankly. "Nothing?"

"Yes, nothing. It's bottomless. That's what gave me a fright. I could see for miles down there, and there is nothing, absolutely nothing."

"Nothing scared you senseless?"

"Yes, a horrid feeling. I suddenly realised how vulnerable I was. Suddenly I had the thought of crocodiles, or some undiscovered, prehistoric monster, that might appear from under me. Also, I realised I might have dived too far down and would run out of air before I made it back."

Harry looked at Rob, a mixture of confusion and disbelief etched over his face. "Good heavens, Rob. You scared the bejeebers out of me!"

"Sorry," Rob laughed suddenly. "I don't know what came over me. I tell you what, though, it's scary down there."

"Look at me!" Harry waved his arms wide, not amused at all, and looked at his feet, "my new brogues and socks are all wet, not to mention my trousers."

"Sorry, mate. But I really do appreciate your coming to my aid. I can tell you I will never go back in there, as beautiful as it looks. It's very scary swimming into the unknown."

"Maybe it was the souls of the dead that chased you out," Harry chuckled and then began to laugh. He could now see the funny side of it and went into fits of laughter, so much so that he had to sit down and hold his stomach. His laughter was so contagious that Rob eventually joined in, laughing at himself and at the spectacle he must have presented in his panicked effort to get out of the Sleeping Pool.

The boys stayed in and around the cave for about three hours, exploring and enjoying the beauty around them. Making their way back to the village, they extended their thanks and appreciation to the villagers and the chief, mounted their bicycles, and headed back to the warm hospitality of the Joubert's farm.

"You do have a story to tell the Jouberts, haven't you?" Rob chuckled.

"Oh yes," Harry grinned, "you can be sure of that." Then they began to laugh all over again.

Sitting on the Joubert's porch that evening as they watched the sun sinking in a blaze of African glory, Harry's rendition of the day's events had everyone in stitches. Even laughing at his own actions, Robert embellished the story significantly. When the mosquitoes became all-too active, however, Gail ushered the menfolk into the house in her usual style for a wholesome dinner. The banter continued to flow well after the meal, which was concluded with a pot of hot coffee and some traditional boerbeskuit made of dry bread, which Gail called "rusks", and which were required to be dunked into the coffee to soften.

Later on, the boys washed in an outdoor area before heading for bed, exhausted, and feeling exhilarated by the events of the day.

"It's been a great trip, thank you," Harry said as he blew the candle out next to his bed.

Rob spoke out of the dark on the far side of their bedroom. "Yes, it has," he replied.

"Next time I come to Salisbury I might join you again," Harry suggested.

"Indeed you must," Rob managed to say through a yawn.

"How would you like to work for my family's business?" Harry asked, his eyes starting to feel very heavy. "We might be looking for a manager of the Salisbury office when we establish it, and I think you would be just the ticket."

"I'd like that very much. When can I start?"

"Oh, I'm not sure, but probably within a month or so. We can chat about it tomorrow."

Nothing more was said because the young men had fallen sound asleep within a few moments.

For Harry, on the other hand, the trip to Sinoia had been a very welcome break from his family business, and – without him actually realising it – it had been the first time he had ever had a holiday without the company of another family member. It was the first time in his life, therefore, that he had experienced such freedom of spirit, such cheerful abandonment, and unrestricted laughter. He didn't have to worry about how his peers regarded him, and he felt free just to enjoy the people around him, the genuine hospitality offered, and to be considered merely as a young man called "Harry".

CHAPTER SEVENTEEN
The Dilemma

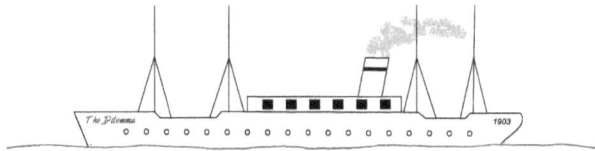

Because he felt that there might be pressing matters in Johannesburg, Louis decided to pass through Kimberley and return to that diamond-mining hub in a week or two. He was right.

Alighting from the train in Johannesburg, Louis made his way to Danie Coetzee first, hoping that their partner would fill him in on developments while he had been away in England. Louis was somewhat surprised to see Danie's reaction when they met in his office. It was more one of relief than a pleasant "welcome home".

Danie ushered Louis into his office, looking flustered. "Thank goodness you are back," he breathed.

Louis was suddenly very concerned. "What happened?" he asked.

"Everybody is looking for you. They all want to place orders urgently, but because they can't find you, these people are approaching me."

"Well, that's good, isn't it?" Louis asked apprehensively.

"Yes, it is, but I am now being – what would you call it?" Danie looked out of his window despairingly, "harassed."

"Harassed?"

"Yes, your customers are pursuing me here, in my accounting company; they are accosting me in public restaurants and Chamber meetings. I thought you would return a week ago, more than a week ago."

"Harry and I took a week out to visit Paris. I can only apologise, Danie. What do these people want?"

"Your goods, of course. They are in high demand. You need at least to leave some staff behind in your warehouse, Louis. You cannot just go away and close the door," Danie almost pleaded, throwing his arms in the air. "As a director of your company, I have taken the liberty of discussing this with your brother, Morris, and he has telegrammed me the authority to employ some staff for you."

"You have employed staff for me?" Louis was incredulous. "How would they know where to start? They don't understand..."

Danie held up a hand to cut Louis off. "No, I have not engaged them yet, I have merely interviewed potential employees, and have shortlisted three men whom I believe to be suitable. I need you to meet with them and make the final decision on the best one for the job since I do not fully understand the finer workings of your warehouse either."

"Oh," Louis sounded relieved, "well, from what you tell me, and the fact that I lean heavily on your judgement, I will take all three without a further interview. After all, I see no reason to repeat the process that you have already conducted."

"Very well," Danie looked pleased, and even allowed a smile to erase the crease from his brow, "I will send them to the warehouse this afternoon to meet with you."

"Excellent! Thank you, Mr Coetzee," Louis nodded. "This will actually work in perfectly as I have to go to Kimberley in a fortnight. I will have the time to instruct these new employees on how my systems work and what will be required of them."

"Why are you going to Kimberley so soon?" Danie asked. "There is enough work piling up to keep you busy for months. When you get to your warehouse, you will find many written orders have been pushed under the door."

"That is excellent news," Louis beamed. "Together with my new staff, we will get through the backlog in no time. I will also visit the various establishments and apologise to our customers for the delay in fulfilling their orders. Morris, however, wishes to open a warehouse in Kimberley, so I must attend to that with minimal delay."

"Morris wants to expand into Kimberley?" Danie raised his eyebrows in surprise. "Your brother is very unpredictable. I would not have suggested that myself, not yet anyhow."

"It gets worse," Louis sighed. "Morris also wants warehouses in Port Elizabeth, East London, Cape Town, and Salisbury. David is in Port Elizabeth right now, and Harry is in Salisbury as we speak."

"You are joking, of course," Danie rocked back in his chair and chuckled, but it was strained as he had a sinking feeling that Louis was being very serious.

"Sadly, this is his directive to the brothers."

"So tell me," Danie leant forward staring directly into Louis' eyes, "apart from the capital he will need to expand so rapidly, which he doesn't have, how does he expect to fill his warehouses?"

"Morris is thinking about buying a ship to transport our purchases," Louis said while trying to keep a straight face.

Danie said something as he pushed himself back into his chair. Louis wasn't sure what he said, but it sounded like a local Dutch expletive.

The weeks following Louis' return to Johannesburg were intensely busy. Having three competent employees who excelled in their positions enabled Louis to work on the back-orders, to fulfil new orders, to wine and dine with influential people, and increase his sales – all this in two separate towns.

Kimberley was hard. The residents were rough, business was tough, and the environment was harsh. Nevertheless, Louis refused to be hindered by any obstacle, making steady progress despite everything, and securing premises that could be used for the next branch of Langbourne Brothers. Just as Harry had done in the north and David had done in the south, Louis engaged a local Kimberley resident to manage and control the future business under his supervision. Meanwhile, the telegrams flowed almost daily between the brothers, keeping each other up to date with their respective progress.

David had a most enjoyable time in Port Elizabeth, insisting that the family stay at the Grand Hotel while showing Hanna where their informal "office" in the dining room was located. Shadreck, the head waiter, was still in the employ of The Grand, his wide smile clearly indicating his happiness at David's marriage and daughter. As Hanna was obviously with child once more, this pleased him even further.

Hanna was introduced to David's friends, and in particular to Jack Shiel, his mentor. Since Jack had also recently married, every opportunity to meet together for dinner was taken, Hanna and Margaret striking up a strong friendship. David also took Hanna to meet Sonja du Plessis at her home, taking the opportunity to show Hanna the back veranda, where their crude cigarette factory had begun their journey into the world of commerce and business. The veranda was smaller than David remembered, but the memories still flooded back, and he could still hear the harmonious isiXhosa work-songs their female workers would break into every day. The fond memories rippled his usually calm façade, and brought an unexpected lump to David's throat,

The highlight of his stay in Port Elizabeth, however, was a short journey he made with Hanna and Ettie to the village of Nguni and Daluxolo, where they were welcomed like royalty with a goat specially slaughtered for the occasion. Daluxolo's wife, Nkosazana, immediately took in Ettie as one of her very own children and promptly put her with her own offspring to play and have some fun with children of her own age. Hanna herself was welcomed amongst the women of the village, while the menfolk sat under a tree, talking and laughing endlessly in a language that Hanna could not understand.

From time to time she looked at David, surrounded by his amaXhosa friends, and saw a side to her husband that she had never known to have existed. It was as if he was at home, as if he belonged. David was relaxed, and when he laughed, it came from deep within, oblivious to who might be watching, devoid of any care in the world. David was at peace in the company of his oldest and dearest friends.

"Nkosazana," Hanna reached over and touched the regal amaXhosa lady on the arm.

Nkosazana responded with a smile. Since neither could speak each other's language, Hanna was at a loss as to how to express how grateful she was that her husband and Nguni had saved David's life on so many occasions. She wanted to thank her for the deep, unbreakable friendship and loyalty the men had shared, and for the special bond they had developed. Hanna knew deep down that David, to a large extent, had only become the man he was – a proper gentleman and an extraordinary person - because of the influence of Nguni and Daluxolo.

When yet another round of deep and raucous laughter boomed from under the tree. Hanna looked across at the men and smiled. When she turned back to face Nkosazana, that elegant lady was looking at her, her eyes speaking volumes. Nkosazana nodded with a gentle smile. Since she understood perfectly well what Hanna had wanted to say, no words were necessary.

Owing to the many contacts and acquaintances enjoyed by David, finding a warehouse for rent and employing a very competent manager proved to be simple tasks. The Port Elizabeth trip was thus declared a great success on so many levels.

David checked Hanna and Ettie into the Mount Nelson for the second time that month. He was pleased that all his planning and negotiations had gone well and that soon he would be on his way back to Bulawayo. Cape Town had been a necessary detour, although more than slightly out of the way, because some loose ends had needed to be tied up before his return to Rhodesia. With another child due, he was keen to get Hanna back home to be settled close to her parents.

Content that his family were comfortable, David strode down to Commercial Street to view their future premises. It would not be available to him for another three months, but he was satisfied with that period of time. He then walked down to The Standard Bank to cash a cheque, before moving on to the Post Office to see if any mail had come in for him.

After an annoying wait, the postal clerk confirmed that a letter had been received in his name, and retrieved the envelope from a crude concertina file under his desk. Long before the clerk had handed the correspondence over to him, David recognised Morris' handwriting. Walking casually out of the rather grand Post Office doors and into the blustery wind, David tore the envelope open and unfolded the letter contained within. After barely reading the first few lines, David stopped in his tracks, horror etched across his face. The wind buffeted the page relentlessly, causing David to grip it more firmly in order to understand every word, which he then read twice to be entirely sure.

"All the boots on the wharf…" David mumbled aloud, "all the boots …

for one penny per boot?"

Pocketing the letter in his jacket without folding it, he turned to walk back into the Post Office, only to halt in confusion, not sure of the best way forward. He was by this time in a mild state of shock, pausing for one moment to re-read the letter, putting it back in his pocket once again, then turning on his heel and walking down to the harbour at a very brisk pace.

"He thinks eighty per cent will be useless?" David continued to mutter under his breath, "more like a hundred per cent! All the boots on the wharf? Has he gone completely mad? Where's he going to put them? What's he going to do with them?"

When David entered the dockyards, he made a bee-line for the pile of old military boots. He could see them up ahead, but to his dismay, the collection of leather footwear looked a lot bigger than it had previously. When David reached the small mountain, he groaned aloud, because the heap of boots was not only higher, but thicker, and in his mind, had grown to twice the size. Immediately, he began trying to find the young soldier who was feeding this grotesque mountain of waste. David located him not far away.

"Excuse me, sir," David began.

"Oh, good day, sir," said the soldier. "We have met, haven't we?"

"Ahh, yes, about a month ago. I was curious about that pile of old boots."

"Yes, I remember. How can I help you?"

David looked over his shoulder at the imposing feature. "It seems to me that the pile has grown quite considerably,"

"Indeed, sir, and – sad to relate – I am led to believe it will grow a lot bigger very quickly."

David's heart skipped a beat. "No, surely not. How much bigger?"

"Well, that's the funny thing," the private scratched his head, looking somewhat confused. "I received orders to retrieve all the boots we discarded in the dump and put them back on this pile."

"Why, for heaven's sake?" David was starting to panic.

"Beats me, but then that's the army for you, isn't it? Do this, then undo it, then do it again. Dig a hole and fill it in, hurry up and wait, and all that nonsense."

"Are there more boots coming from the dump?" David queried, sweat starting to form on his brow, despite the chill.

"No, that's all, thankfully."

David sighed. "Well, that's a relief."

"Why do you ask? Why should it worry you?" the private asked out of curiosity.

"Oh, no real reason. I am just surprised. Well, thanks for your time, sir," David bid him a farewell with a friendly smile.

"Always a pleasure, sir, any time," he replied, apparently happy for the company.

David walked a few paces, then suddenly spun around to face the man again. "Excuse me, did you say that pile would be getting bigger?"

"Yes, sir," the young man frowned and stared at the chaotic pile of footwear, "That's the funny thing. I have orders to unload a ship loaded with old boots from India. It is scheduled to arrive before the end of the week."

"India?! W-what…?" David stammered. "What do you mean, India?"

"Strange, isn't it?" the man shrugged. "Then there are also ships coming from Australia, Canada, and Malaysia, all with boots. They need to be sorted, of course, the reusable ones to be put in that warehouse as usual," the private pointed to the same warehouse he had indicated before, "and the unusable ones on that pile."

David felt his blood drain to his legs, and he swayed slightly. A concrete bollard lay on its side near him, and David stepped over to it, sitting upon it unceremoniously.

"You all right, sir?" the soldier asked, looking concerned.

"Oh, Morris," David groaned quietly. "I fear you've been outsmarted this time. If only you knew."

When David walked into the bedroom and deposited himself heavily on an easy chair, Hanna was understandably concerned. "What's wrong, my darling?" she murmured.

David stared for a long time at the floor before answering. "I fear that this time Morris really has got us into trouble. Big trouble."

"Why, what happened?" Hanna asked, her voice tinged by anxiety.

"Remember that old pile of boots on the wharf, the ones you saw me looking at when we arrived?"

Hanna wrinkled her nose in disgust at the memory. "Oh yes," she exclaimed, "they exuded quite an awful odour."

"Yes…" David breathed out a sigh of resignation. "Well, my good brother has entered a deal with the British Government to buy all the second-hand boots on that wharf. Because he is paying a penny a boot, some clever toff in the British Government has decided to transfer all of their second-hand army boots from across the entire empire and deposit them onto that wharf."

"Oh dear," Hanna said quietly. "But didn't you tell him not to bother with the boots?"

"I did, but our letters must have crossed. I have to be back here in three weeks to count all those boots."

"In three weeks?" Hanna exclaimed.

"Three weeks, during which time shiploads of boots will be added to the pile." David first paused, before looking Hanna straight in the eye. "I'm afraid we'll need to leave for Rhodesia straight away. We don't have a moment to lose. I need to get you back home and then return before the fourteenth of next month. I'm going to need Louis and Harry to help me. Oh dear, what has Morris got us into this time?"

"It seems you need more than Louis and Harry, my dear. Might I suggest you consider Nguni and Daluxolo, and perhaps the entire population of their village?"

David smiled. Hanna was right, and he would consider this. "That sounds like a sterling idea."

"I'm not unduly worried," said Hanna in her attempt to soothe her distressed husband. "You've been in much worse situations before, and you have always found a plan that worked. If anyone can find a solution, you can."

David reached up and gave Hanna a tight hug. "You're right. I'll make it work. I have to."

Before boarding the train destined for Bulawayo, David called at the Post Office and sent Morris a telegram. He had spent a restless night formulating the message, using the least words possible. He needed to make sure that Morris knew precisely what the situation was, and in no uncertain terms.

CHAPTER EIGHTEEN

London - 1903

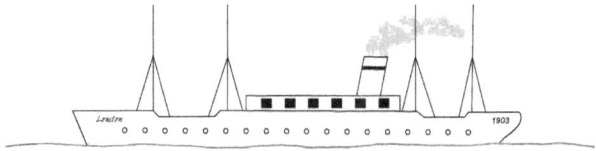

"Come on, darling," Rose Bertha sang out, as she draped an elegant coat over her shoulders, "we don't want to be late for dinner. Mother has been cooking all day."

Morris wasn't listening. He was sitting at his desk, three candles burning in a small candelabrum illuminating a telegram that he held gingerly in one hand.

Rose entered the living area and stared at her husband. "Morris?" she insisted. "Are you listening to me?" She suddenly became concerned when she saw the blank look on his face. "Are you alright?" she asked.

"Oh, sorry, I was lost in thought," said Morris, returning to the present. "Is it time to go?"

Dinner that evening was being hosted at the home of Rose Bertha's parents, who had also invited Morris' mentor and closest confidant, Yoni Goldberg, together with his lovely wife, Ruth. As much as it pained Morris to discuss his business with his father-in-law, he needed to explore possible solutions to his predicament with both Mr Friedlander and Yoni Goldberg. Morris knew he was in a tight situation, and as much as it meant that he would have to humble himself, he needed to tap the wisdom that lay with these experienced businessmen, being pretty much out of his depth. He knew he had been thoroughly outsmarted and needed some sage advice.

Although the evening started off well, with much hilarity and merriment, Morris struggled to pay attention. After an exceptional dinner, the men adjourned to the library, as Morris had anticipated, to partake in a brandy while Mr Friedlander also enjoyed a cigar.

Morris carefully picked the moment during which to begin the discussion. "Gentlemen," he murmured, "I wonder if I may prevail upon you for some learned advice? Unfortunately, I appear to have been taken advantage of, and I am not sure how to deal with this matter."

The two men nodded gravely, and each took a seat, prompting Morris to do likewise.

"What troubles you, Morris?" Yoni began.

"It all started with David and his capture towards the end of the Boer War. Many of his captors had no shoes and therefore struggled to fight effectively. When David made his escape, he also had no shoes and injured his feet badly on some sharp rocks in the process."

Morris paused to read the faces of his elders, who were both looking at him intently, so he continued.

"When my brothers left Africa to come to our wedding after the war, they noticed a pile of old army boots lying on the wharf at the Cape Town harbour. I thought that I might capitalise on this opportunity and, after exhaustive enquiries, I managed to strike a deal with a certain Lord Cunningham to purchase all the boots on the wharf for a mere one penny per boot."

"That sounds like a bargain if you ask me," Mr Friedlander said and took a long pull on his cigar.

"I thought so, too," Morris continued, "but the condition was that I was to take every boot on the wharf, and as there were still some boots in transit from around the South African region, the agreement was that I would give him three months to bring the rest in. Thereafter the count would happen on the 14th of March, and the agreed count would be purchased at the cost of one penny per boot."

"I can already see your problem, Morris," Yoni rumbled thoughtfully, "but it is not a major issue to postpone the date."

"I beg your pardon?" Morris cocked his head; Yoni had lost him.

"The 14th of March is a Saturday, our Sabbath. Ask this Cunningham gentleman to postpone the date to the Sunday on religious grounds."

Morris gritted his teeth in frustration. He had not even considered this aspect and was now beginning to realise that he might have spurned a monumental disaster for his company, and what's more, that this could signal the end of the enterprise entirely.

"I didn't realise that. My apologies, but that is just the tip of the iceberg. You see, David sent me a telegram after I signed the agreement. He had disembarked in Cape Town and physically inspected the boots. He reported that they were all totally useless. The good ones had already been separated from the pile and placed in a nearby warehouse."

"Oh dear," Friedlander began to understand the gravity of the situation. "Thank goodness the cost is just one penny a boot. How many boots are you looking at in monetary terms?"

"I estimated about £5000 worth," Morris said.

"You may have to take that on the chin, Morris. Are you also responsible for disposing of the stock?"

"Yes, and that would be an added loss."

"Oh dear," Friedlander repeated, "that's not good."

"It gets worse," Morris added, causing the men to raise their eyebrows in surprise. "This Cunningham character is using me to his utmost advantage. You see, he indicated that there were other old boots to come in from around the South African states, and therefore he needed the three months' grace. I accepted this, but because the agreement says 'all boots on the wharf', he is sending cargo ships with old boots from other British colonies. They are arriving in their tens of thousands.

"I realised something was wrong when David told me that the boots that had already been disposed of, had been recovered from the dump and returned to the pile."

The library descended into a deathly hush. Goldberg looked at Friedlander and then at Morris. The silence continued long enough for it to become uncomfortable, and Morris knew he was in big trouble.

"I don't know what to do." Morris resigned himself to the inevitable.

"I'm afraid neither do I," Yoni spoke lamely. "I don't know how you can get out of the contract."

"I'm afraid I don't think you can," Friedlander said without much confidence. "My experience tells me that if you fail to honour the contract, they will penalise you at least for the cost of freighting the goods, and that may sink you, if you will excuse the unintended pun."

Morris was in no mood for jokes. "I can't believe I didn't see this coming."

"Dealing with a government institution can be a hazardous exercise, Morris," Yoni commiserated with his young friend. "Sadly, this could end in court, or at worst, a prison sentence."

The evening thus ended on a very sombre note. Not since the time Morris had lost thirty wagons in the African bush had he felt so helpless, and once again, this impending disaster was all his fault. It was David who came to the rescue when he found the wagons one year later, but Morris very much doubted that even David could solve this monumental disaster.

Lord Cunningham smiled broadly at Morris, as he ushered him into his office. "Come in, Mr Langbourne," he gushed. "To what do I owe this pleasure?"

"Thank you for seeing me, sir," Morris smiled as he settled into his seat. "I have received communications from Cape Town that you are shipping in old boots from other colonies."

"Indeed," Cunningham said matter-of-factly.

"That wasn't the deal."

"Yes, it was, if I recall," Cunningham opened a drawer and extracted the contract they had signed.

"You indicated to me that there were other boots within the South African states. You did not mention other British colonies."

"Oh, but I did," Cunningham looked hurt. "Did you not keep a record of our conversation?"

Morris gritted his teeth. He could see he would not win against this man.

"Alright," Morris put on his sweetest smile again, "I do have another favour to ask, if I may? The 14th of March is a Saturday. I did not factor that into the discussions. May we amend the contract to the 15th for religious reasons? As you are no doubt aware, that will give you an extra day to add to the consignment."

Cunningham grinned. "For you, Mr Langbourne, and for this reason, I will certainly allow it. We can make the amendments to our existing copies. If you would kindly co-sign the alteration for me?" he slid his copy over to Morris. Morris made the correction and signed, then passed his copy to Cunningham who did likewise.

As the men stood to leave, Morris paused at Cunningham's office door.

"Lord Cunningham, just out of curiosity, would you have any idea how many boots might arrive on the Cape Town wharf by the 14th of March?"

"Hmm…" Cunningham scratched his chin thoughtfully, "I'm not too sure, but you might bank on a million pairs."

Morris wanted to grab the doorjamb for support as he felt his knees start to buckle, but he composed himself. He was sure his face echoed his bewilderment

"A million pairs? You mean two million boots?"

"Boots do come in pairs, don't they Mr Langbourne?" Cunningham laughed.

Morris didn't laugh with him.

CHAPTER NINETEEN
Cape Town - March 1903

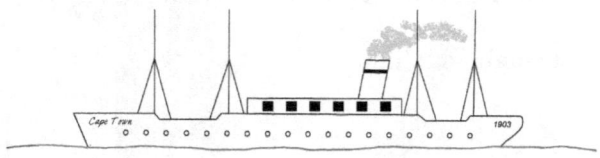

Having returned to Bulawayo and settling his family in their home, David had departed on the very next day with a surprised Harry to travel with him to Cape Town. Harry hadn't objected at all, because he had been keen to visit the beautiful city, as well as enjoying the opportunity to assist his family out of a very nasty situation. Louis had quickly reacted to the telegram that had been sent to him and had connected with his brothers in Kimberley. The remainder of the journey between Kimberley and Cape Town had been spent in many earnest discussions, devising plans to lessen the impact of their older brother's folly.

They had no reason to condemn Morris, nor criticise his mistake. On the contrary, they fully understood why he had entered the deal. It was evident to the brothers that someone had taken advantage of Morris and that their oldest brother had fallen victim to an unscrupulous bureaucrat.

"I asked Morris to send me the contract verbatim, by telegram," David said, as he smoothed out three sheets of Post-Office telegram paper on the countertop in their carriage.

Harry raised an eyebrow at the copious text. "May the Good Lord bless us," he murmured, "that must have cost him a pretty penny."

"Yes, but I don't care. I need to know precisely what the deal is. I need you all to know exactly what we are up against."

For a good half hour, the boys studied the telegram in depth, making little remarks, and working out how such an unprincipled official might have structured it for his own benefit.

"I would hazard a guess that we will be dealing with army officials in Cape Town. They aren't businessmen," Louis mused aloud.

"Exactly," David agreed. "However, some of them might be very astute. The gentleman Morris signed the deal with knew what he was doing, not so? He must have been very cunning and pretty smart to outwit Morris."

"I'll say!" Harry exclaimed.

"They will be following this contract to the letter, I'm sure of that," David sighed.

"Any idea what we are in for, all told?" Louis asked.

David shrugged and leant back in the plush carriage seat. He had no idea, but it was certainly not looking very encouraging. "All we can really do is extract the best out of a bad deal."

The train sounded its whistle, and the brothers felt the wagon jerk slightly as the driver applied the brakes.

"All right, chaps," David sat upright and folded the telegram into his pocket, "this is my stop. I'll see you in Cape Town. Good luck to you both."

The boys shook hands before David alighted at the De Aar railway station, where – four hours later – he would catch a connecting train to Port Elizabeth and would then head directly to Nguni and Daluxolo's village on the outskirts. In the meantime, Louis and Harry would continue straight on to Cape Town and begin putting David's plan into action.

When Louis and Harry disembarked, they checked into cheap lodgings, close to the harbour entrance. Harry then hired a bicycle and cycled out of town, following the railway line. His job was to find a farm that boarded the line or that had the line passing through it. It took him less than an hour to find one that was just perfect. Using his new-found experience with farmers and their ways, he quickly developed a good rapport with the owner, renting a small portion of his land against the rail line for a couple of months. Since the rent was very affordable, Harry offered to have a water-well dug on the site as a token of gratitude. The farmer was delighted, and Harry, feeling very proud of himself, cycled back into town.

In the meantime, Louis had located a company that would rent out some small carts with low sides, each pulled by two donkeys. He promptly hired a dozen of these, all but one to be collected a few days before the big count. Taking a quick lesson on how to drive the cart and control the mule, Louis flicked the reins and guided the donkeys to a hardware store that had been recommended to him. Although he did not make any purchases that day, he found exactly what David wanted; wooden slats, wire, nails, and some necessary tools, such as a hammer, spade, twine, shanks of rope, and a very rudimentary pair of pliers. The next item was more difficult to find, but eventually, a bookstore with a section for stationery supplied his final requirements - three cash books, and a large box of coloured chalk of the sort used by school teachers.

The younger brothers later met back at their lodgings and discussed the day's events, and what the next day would entail, before enjoying a healthy meal and turning in early for the night.

A good portion of the following morning saw Louis and Harry at the offices of the railways, booking a few goods-train carriages. The plans fell into place very nicely; deposits were paid, and confirmations were received. Content that David would be pleased with their negotiations, the boys made their way to the harbour with two missions, firstly to befriend the army soldier David had seen and who had been tasked with the receiving and sorting of the old boots, and secondly to quietly observe their behaviour.

It didn't take long for the brothers to work out which soldier was in charge, he even fitted the description David had given them. Confident that they had picked the right man, they both adopted broad smiles and proceeded to approach him.

"Good morning, sir," Louis greeted the man warmly.

"Good morning, Gentlemen. How may I be of assistance?"

"My name is Louis Langbourne," Louis began and extended his hand.

"Ahh…" the man exclaimed as he reciprocated the handshake, "you must be the man who bought this lot."

"No, not I," Louis chuckled, "my crazy brother in England did this, and we are here to clean up his mess. This is my other brother, Harry Langbourne."

"Pleased to meet you, sir," the man smiled broadly at Louis' response. "My name is Hopkins, Private Leslie Hopkins. I've been tasked to unload all these boots and sort the good from the bad, or should I say, the not so bad from the very bad," his eyes twinkling with laughter at his own joke, at which Louis and Harry laughed in response.

Leslie Hopkins was about 18 years' old, slight in build with strikingly sharp facial features. His fair hair had been combed neatly back over the top of his head, fixed in place by a trendy men's hair-cream. He proudly sported a neat moustache, which looked very much in its infancy.

"We are a little confused with why our brother bought these boots," Harry said. "Where are they all coming from?"

"Well, I must say that two of us – my captain and myself, that is – were both rather perplexed why anyone in their right mind would want these boots in the first place. Mind you, we have our orders. Most have come from the interior, but recently we have had shipments from India and Canada. That ship over there, for instance," Hopkins pointed to a vessel tied up at a particular quayside, "that one is from England."

"England?" Louis exclaimed in surprise. "I didn't expect England to send their second-hand boots here. Are the ships fully laden with boots?"

"Oh no, not at all. It seems that before the ship departs with its usual cargo, they fill the extra space with boots. But when I say fill it up, I mean every nook and cranny is jam-packed with smelly footwear."

"Well, that's a relief…" Harry laced his comment with sarcasm.

"It seems like we are under pressure to unload these ships for you gentlemen," Hopkins offered with a smile. "Apparently, there is a contract that says there's a cut off on the 14th of March, and whatever is on the wharf after that date is yours. Thereafter, we need to count everything and agree on the numbers. I'm not sure when you start paying the authorities, but I think it's from the 15th."

"Actually, from the date we agree on the numbers counted," Louis confirmed. "Perhaps we could meet with your captain in due course. I'd like to confirm the terms of the contract with him."

"He's not here right now but does inspect me and the proceedings twice a day. Why don't you call past here after lunch? If he's on the pier, I'll introduce him to you."

"Splendid!" Louis grinned. "But in the meantime, would you mind if we stood over there somewhere to watch our stock roll in? We have just over a week to go, and my brother wants regular updates. We won't get in the way."

Hopkins happily agreed, and the men parted company. Louis and Harry found a concrete step a short distance off and settled in to watch the team who were unloading. Pretending to be merely watching and whiling the day away, the boys were actually planning, plotting, and devising battle tactics, a critical aspect of David's plan.

When Captain Cloete arrived for his afternoon inspection, the Langbourne boys cautiously and respectfully made their way towards him, then waited to be summoned by Private Hopkins. Their courtesy didn't go unnoticed, and a curt nod at Hopkins caused him to double over to Louis and Harry, inviting them to meet his boss.

Captain Cloete was a formidable man, quite large and round with a broad face. In his late thirties, he was clean-shaven with rosy cheeks.

The formalities done, Louis judged the captain to be very officious and so was careful not to make a joke of the affair as they had done with Hopkins. He kept the introduction, and their intentions, succinct. As intimidating as he looked, Cloete was very approachable and confirmed the terms of the contract exactly as the young men had understood it. Satisfied that all parties had agreed with the deal uniformly, Louis thanked Captain Cloete for his time and assured him that they would not interfere with his staff. The captain appeared comfortable with the boys and understood their interest in the arrival of their future stock.

Moving back to their shady spot, Louis and Harry stood about, discussing the growing mountain of boots, while surreptitiously watching the entire process of sorting, stacking, and transferring their unwelcome stock.

After six days of loitering about the Cape Town docks, the Langbourne brothers approached Private Hopkins and told him that they were expecting their elder brother to arrive and that they would not be around for the remainder of the day. Although the boys had kept a respectful distance throughout, they would often be approached by the private who had suggested that they revert to his first name, "Leslie, when the brass was not about", and they happily befriended the young man further.

Since they all appreciated the same sort of humour, Leslie enjoyed taking a few breaks from his otherwise monotonous task. Louis and Harry noted that his unofficial tea breaks became longer and longer each day. Given that they were as equally bored as he was, they didn't mind at all, since it also gave them the opportunity to ask some casual questions which would sometimes yield a few, rather interesting facts.

Promising to introduce David to Leslie the next day, Louis and Harry turned their backs on the harbour and the then three mountains of old army-issue boots. Mounting their hired cycles, they pedalled along the tracks until they reached the plot of farmland that Harry had temporarily rented.

The plot was nothing but a flat acre of earth, blanketed by thick knee-high shrubs and other vegetation that the locals referred to collectively as "fynbos". No structure of any sort could be seen, and no clearing, only a stretch of undisturbed scrub. Some ten yards away from the rail track, however, stood a circular hole that the boys had dug into the ground. At about three o'clock each afternoon, Harry and Louis would leave their quayside vigil and collect the hired cart and donkeys, before loading the cart with planks, iron sheeting, and other supplies. Then, sitting atop the wagon in a most undignified manner, they would head for the plot. It usually involved much more laughter than giggling.

Once at the plot, the equipment would be laid amongst the shrubbery, out of sight of anyone walking along the railway tracks, and then the lads would spend about two hours, digging the promised well. At about five feet down, the stony soil became quite damp, and that's where they stopped. Thanks to the dense fynbos, not even a passenger on a passing train would have noticed any activity.

Surprisingly, David's train was on time that day. Harry had walked one mile up the tracks with a yellow piece of material which he used as a flag to wave at the oncoming train driver; a signal that had already been agreed between David and the conductor and telegraphed to Harry. Applying the brakes, the train driver began to slow the train down until he reached Louis waving a red flag, where he halted, the engine hissing and gushing copious billows of steam. From the rear wagon, two large sliding doors were clumsily pushed open, and a large gathering of amaXhosa men and some women quickly alighted, forming a human chain as they unloaded their meagre belongings onto the earth.

Last to leap out of the rear carriage was David. He landed on uneven soil, staggered a few steps before regaining his balance, then trotted over to the noisy engine. A quick scramble up the short, iron ladder, a thankful shake of the train driver's hand, and David joined Louis at ground level. The driver gave the whistle two short blasts and then began shunting the train forward, the big steel wheels slipping momentarily on the tracks while steam and pistons powerfully forced them to move. The total time of stoppage having amounted to less than two minutes, the train soon picked up speed and continued on its way, almost ghost-like in the late-afternoon glow. An eerie silence descended on the group.

"Perfect timing," Louis beamed, "we were about to light a fire so that the driver could see us."

"A good omen, perhaps," David smiled and shook his brother's hand. "Come and greet Nguni, Daluxolo, and the rest of the team."

The amaXhosa brothers were delighted to see Louis again, while Harry joined them a little later after a brisk jog back from further up the line. Once again, the reunion was joyful, and much banter was shared before the other members of the village were introduced. David quickly became serious and took control of the situation, issuing instructions and directions. A makeshift camp was rapidly set up, a cooking-fire established, and the womenfolk took command of the food preparation. The women spoke little, but worked quickly and efficiently, each knowing exactly what to do. The menfolk worked like a well-rehearsed team, if a bit more vocal than their womenfolk, and rapidly constructed sleeping areas using the supplies Louis and Harry had deposited amongst the fynbos shrubbery.

Just before dark, Harry and Louis took their leave and headed back to their lodgings in town, but David elected to stay with his group. He had decided to walk into Cape Town at first light with Nguni and Daluxolo and a small selection of the men. David would be showing them the way and pointing out where they would be working. He planned to ensure Nguni and Daluxolo operated as independent teams because he knew the "big count" would be all-consuming for him and his two brothers.

Since he was well-accustomed to sleeping rough, David slept comfortably under the stars. His only interruption was a giant rain spider that ran across his face in the dark, and which had him nervously beating himself about the cheeks, although he soon fell back to sleep again. At the crack of dawn, he and the two amaXhosa brothers, together with a team of six men, began to walk towards Cape Town, following the railway tracks.

Arriving at the harbour, David was horrified by the massive increase in the mountain of boots. Louis and Harry stood nearby, signalling him to join them.

"Look at it!" David exclaimed in a half-whisper, pointing to the offending pile. "Where in heaven's name…? What is…? Where did they come from? I can't believe what I am looking at," David was overcome with horror; a knot forming in his stomach at the sudden realisation of the enormous escalation of the problem.

"Bad, huh?" Louis agreed.

"If only Morris were here," David mumbled, awestruck. "I don't think he has any idea what a predicament he has put us in. I could see this pile from miles away! This will utterly ruin us."

"Here comes Leslie Hopkins," Harry said, almost snapping David out of his trance, "Private Leslie Hopkins, he's in charge of sorting and unloading. A good man."

David was introduced to Private Hopkins, who recognised David from their earlier meetings. David quickly took to the man, successfully disguising his horror at the realisation of the scale of the operation, and convincingly making it seem as if he had quite expected the size of the second-hand boot pile. David confirmed that he and his team of amaXhosa helpers would stand on the perimeter of the pier and not interfere with the army's task.

"No problem there whatsoever," Leslie agreed with a smile, then looked over at the little huddle of amaXhosa men. "You will need a larger contingent than that on the big day."

"I have seventy-five men in total. We are camped a few miles out of town. These men will be the team supervisors. I hope you don't mind if I bring them down here every so often to plan how we will relocate our boots?"

"Of course not," Leslie readily agreed, "after all, I'm sure you will want to escape the Harbour Administration's exorbitant rent as soon as possible, especially as I can't see much value in that junk."

"Well, exactly," David sighed, causing Louis and Harry to toss their hands in sympathetic resignation and wipe their brow in objection to the predicament their eldest brother had created. "Which reminds me, would you please introduce me to the harbour master?"

"Certainly," Leslie smiled, "but he doesn't seem to be around at the moment. I'll come back for you in an hour. If you will excuse me, though, a ship from Australia arrived last night, and I need to get cracking. Don't worry, I believe their consignment of old boots is not significant."

"That's a relief..." Harry once more laced his voice in sarcasm.

"And may I also ask you to introduce me to your superior?" David enquired.

"Captain John Cloete, or Jimmy as his friends call him," Leslie winked, "is my superior and the overall man in charge of the operation. He will be down here later. I will introduce you to him with pleasure."

"That would be splendid," David beamed.

As the men parted company, Louis and Harry took David aside and, although seeming to have a casual conversation, dropped their voices to a hoarse whisper.

"That pile of boots there," Louis gave a slight nod in its direction, "has not only grown to twice its size since you first saw it, but there are two new piles behind it, each half the size."

"You mean there are three of those mountains now?" David's eyes shot angry daggers at Louis.

"Sadly, yes," Harry continued, "but there is some good news."

"Please," David said through a loud sigh, "please give me some good news."

"With all the boots suddenly arriving on those ships," Harry nodded at the waterfront with his hands firmly in his pockets, "Leslie couldn't keep up with the sorting, so Captain Cloete instructed him just to pile them up, and only the obviously good boots that they happen to come across, those hardly worn, to be moved to that warehouse. As it is, their warehouse is almost packed to capacity anyhow."

"So what you are saying is that those two smaller piles behind this one have not been properly sorted?" David frowned.

"Exactly," Louis hissed.

"So..." David smiled slightly.

"Exactly!" Louis repeated, grinning profusely. "We can safely consider the first pile to be total junk, which we can transfer directly to the disposal area. We need only to concentrate on the two smaller piles."

"Right," David said as his mind turned over like a boulder rolling down a mountainside. "We still have to count the junk, though, because Morris has agreed to pay for every boot, regardless of the condition."

"Sadly," Harry's sarcasm was again evident.

"All right, all right…" David repeated, staring into space. He gradually came back to reality with a broad smile. "We need to talk to Cloete. It's imperative we get him to agree to our suggestions. I thought we could move these boots in a day or two, but I can see now that it will take us about a month or more to move this rubbish. But, because we now know we can salvage some reusable boots, it takes the pressure off a bit."

"My thoughts exactly," Harry concurred.

The boys walked back to Nguni and his team, and they all squatted in a tight huddle. David dusted the earth at his feet with his hand and drew a squiggly line with his finger in the dirt, followed by three oval circles.

"This is the water," David pointed to a wavy line, "and these are the mountains of boots," he looked at Nguni and Daluxolo to see if they understood.

A curt nod answered his question. He then went on to explain the situation and pointed out various aspects of the harbour, the wharf, the railway lines, the roads to be used for the carts, and where he expected the trains to park for loading. He also explained that the boots could only be moved after they had counted them. Then, with nothing further to discuss, David dismissed his amaXhosa team, sending them back to camp to get some breakfast in their bellies with a promise to discuss more plans later that afternoon.

"Boss Morris has given you a big job once more," Nguni scowled, then let a low chuckle escape.

"Yes," David sighed in resignation, but smiled sheepishly.

"We understand your brother. He is a big chief in your family. We fix your problem."

"You always do, Nguni. You always do," David stood, clasping his friend's forearm in manly thanks. "You are a good friend."

Nguni simply laughed. "Masihambe!" he barked at his men. They turned and walked in the direction of the farm, leaving the Langbourne boys watching them with deep respect.

It was Harry who broke the silence. "You know we'd be lost without them,"

"You can say that again," David sighed, before perking up once more.

"Come on, we have work to do."

After Captain Cloete had arrived at the harbour, close to ten o'clock that morning, and had conducted his brief inspection, Leslie signalled the three Langbourne boys to come over to him.

Leslie introduced David. "This is Mr David Langbourne, sir. He is in charge of the Langbourne party."

"I understand that you have purchased this inventory, Mr Langbourne," Captain Cloete frowned as he shook David by the hand.

"Not me, sir, it was my brother in England."

"Oh, really?" Cloete raised an eyebrow. "So there are four of you, are there?"

"Indeed," David grinned. "I believe you have met my two younger brothers, Louis and Harry. Our eldest brother, in England, is Morris."

"So, let's get down to business," Captain Cloete suddenly moved the formalities onto the matter at hand. He didn't have much time for pleasantries or business, he was a military man first and foremost. "I have a copy of the contract your brother signed with the government. Do you need to have sight of it?"

"No thank you, sir," David declined the offer. "I already have a copy. I believe we begin the count on Sunday?"

"Yes," Cloete confirmed, "shall we agree to start at six o'clock on the hour? And then stop at the first sign of poor light?"

"That is acceptable to us, thank you, sir."

Cloete appreciated the manner in which David respected the captain's rank and the older brother's conduct. In fact, he found the entire Langbourne family to be altogether extremely polite, well-mannered, and respectful.

"Splendid," Cloete smiled. "I dare say it will be somewhat of a formidable job in counting this lot. Do you have any help, perchance?"

"We have help with the more manual tasks, sir, such as loading and packing and if we need any more, we will contract out the extra work locally. The three of us will verify the counts with you."

"Excellent," Cloete was finding the meeting to be proceeding rather to his liking. "I have a team of men to count and verify, and I had planned to have 20 tables spaced along that area there," he said, pointing off to his left.

David looked over his shoulder at where the captain was indicating. "Perfect, we would be happy with that. May I ask a question?"

"Please do," Cloete puffed his chest out to affirm his authority before the question was even asked.

"How do you envisage doing the count? One boot at a time, or by weight?"

Cloete hadn't thought of counting by weight. A momentary blank look was not missed by David, who smiled inwardly; he knew he had the upper hand.

"One boot at a time, of course. Accuracy is paramount," Cloete frowned.

"That is what I had understood," David agreed with a smile. "I must say, though, I did not realise how many boots were involved. There must be hundreds of thousands of them. I fear the count could take a good two months or more. What would your estimation be?"

"About that, perhaps even three months."

"I'm sorry my brother agreed to the boots being counted individually. It really has created such a mountain of work for all of us and tied up so many resources for so long for such little value. I personally must apologise for this folly of his. I cannot imagine the inconvenience this must put you and your men to."

"Yes, it really is a futile exercise in my personal opinion," Cloete smirked, but he wore a frown as his mind was elsewhere. "You say your brother insisted they be counted individually?"

"Yes," David sighed theatrically, "that's what he told me."

"I don't recall anything in the contract that said he insisted on that."

"Really?" David responded with exaggerated surprise. "That does open up other options then, doesn't it?"

"I would assume so," Cloete went blank for a split second as he wracked his brain over the contract in his office. "If we were to count the boots by weight, you would accept that on behalf of your brother?"

"Of course," David smiled, "my brothers and I are equal shareholders in our family business, and if three of us agree to that, we will out-vote a dissenting brother. We would accept that, wouldn't we?" David turned to face his brothers, who nodded eagerly.

The frown on Captain Cloete's brow deepened. "Well, it would be logical to count the boots that way, and I would be happy to authorise that on our side, the problem is we have no access to measures or scales to ascertain the weight."

"Oh dear," David feigned disappointment, "the idea was good while it lasted. I had hoped to make both our lives easier, and lessen the rent the army must be paying to the harbour authorities."

"Indeed, I had hoped to conclude our side of the deal as quickly as possible for that very reason," Cloete grumbled.

"There is another idea," David stared into the distance, pretending to think deeply. Cloete almost held his breath in anticipation.

"Go on," the captain encouraged.

"We have hired some carts and donkeys to move the boots from the counting tables into train carriages for disposal and storage. What if we, at the very beginning, count individual boots into a cart, until maximum capacity and record the number, then do the same with another three, or even five carts or ten, and take an average. We would just have to agree between us what the average number is per cart, then simply count carts. The process would work much faster that way and need less staff. Would you agree to that, chaps?" David cast a glance at his brothers, who nodded their agreement even more vigorously. Before Cloete could say anything, David continued. "You would be able to sign off your responsibility much sooner, possibly in one month, saving your Government quite a lot of money in the process."

"I think that would work," Captain Cloete scratched his chin in thought. "Indeed, I would be agreeable to that. It makes sense."

"Excellent," David smiled and extended his hand. "Agreed?"

Pleased with the suggestion, Cloete extended his hand and sealed the agreement. "Done!"

On the Friday before the big count, six rail carriages were shunted alongside the wharf and uncoupled before the engine steamed off without so much as a courteous farewell. The brothers opened the sliding doors to each wagon and inspected the inside of each one to find them empty and cavernous. Harry stood outside each of the doors and inscribed large numbers on the concrete slab with a piece of coloured chalk – blue, yellow, green, and white – and each doorway with its own number and colour.

Because David knew that many of the amaXhosa villagers had little use for numbers, colour-coding was the best alternative. He understood that, when it came time to move the boots from the piles into the trains, they could easily ask the driver of a cart to follow a specific coloured line on the ground. Chalk was a perfect solution, because – should a wagon be placed in a different location, or a route needed to be altered – a bucket of water and an old rag would soon fix the problem.

The twelve hired carts had been parked alongside the rail wagons, and the donkeys were stabled nearby. The past two days had seen the wagons undergoing minor alterations while they had been parked at the campsite at the farm. These modifications involved attaching crude side rails on three sides to enable more boots to be loaded onto the tray without their falling off with the movement of the cart. They looked awkward and somewhat clumsy, but the Heath-Robinson contraptions would serve their purpose well.

The Cape Town administration had already allocated a dumping area to the military, which Harry and Louis negotiated to take over from them. They were levied a small fee for the use of the dump, which they happily paid, and spent a couple of hours at the site working out the logistics of disposing of the unwanted goods. The brothers were thrilled to discover that the piece of land, long established as a well-used dumping ground in a natural depression in the earth, was only about two hundred yards off to the north of an existing rail track.

Further negotiations with the railway officials resulted in an agreement for the brothers to halt their loaded wagons near the dump, offload the boots onto the ground beside the track, and return the carriages to the harbour to continue the clearing process. The railways agreed on a price for each journey to the dump, which the brothers accepted without complaint since they deemed it quite reasonable. The brothers further decided that they would employ a team of local men to move the boots from the tracks to the dump site.

David stood back and looked at the row of rail wagons and neatly parked donkey carts. It was late afternoon and all plans, as far as he could see, were in place.

"I think we are there, Chaps," David congratulated his team. "Nguni, please take your men back to the camp. Tomorrow we rest, and then the hard work begins."

"It is good," Nguni's low voice rumbled. "We are ready."

"Thank you, Nguni, and thanks to your people. I must talk to the army boss now. We will meet tonight."

As the brothers parted company, David led Louis and Harry to the pier, passing the ever-present jumble of boots staring down at them. Each time they walked past the offending mounds they would involuntarily stare at this monument to great suffering.

"Time to put my plan into action," David spoke to his siblings, "Let's hope it works."

"Good luck, brother," Louis replied, a hint of apprehension in his voice.

After they had walked into the harbour administration office and asked to see the manager, they were ushered into the office of a tall man in his fifties who greeted the brothers in a relaxed and friendly way.

"I had expected to see you a long time ago, Mr Langbourne," the manager said, "the entire town is talking about you. I assume you have come to negotiate our fees."

"Indeed," David confirmed, "we take possession of the boots the day the count is complete. We estimate that it will take about a month, so we were hoping to put all the formalities in place now."

"Splendid idea," the manager agreed, "perhaps we can conclude everything apart from the handover date."

"That's rather what I was hoping," David responded with a smile, "one less matter to concern ourselves with. Shall we begin?"

Just as Captain Cloete had instructed, the counting began on Sunday morning at six o'clock, but not before some necessary logistics had been discussed and specific plans put in place. Captain Cloete and Private Hopkins had organised for six desks to be placed on the wharf in a straight line, each manned by two men in army uniform. Behind each desk stood David, Louis, and Harry alongside six carts, each hitched to two donkeys. Another six carts and donkeys stood obediently with Nguni by the train wagons, all waiting for their turn to replace the carts at the desks as they moved off. Behind them stood a large team of amaXhosa men, ready to unload the donkey carts and pack the rail wagons. They were under the instruction of Daluxolo.

Another team of local amaXhosa men stood near the boots, supervised by Private Leslie Hopkins and a fellow soldier. Their job was to carry the boots from the piles, past the desks, and onto the carts. It had been mutually agreed that this method was in keeping with the contract, where the boots passed in ownership from the military to the civilian once they had crossed the line of desks, pending agreement on the final figure, of course.

Much to the barely-concealed amusement of the soldiers, Harry drew a white chalk-line from the first desk across to the first rail wagon, crouched and walking, almost crab-like, as he progressed at a half-run, half-walk. He then trotted back to repeat the process with the other colours, commencing at different desks, and ending at corresponding wagons.

"Where would you like to start?" Captain Cloete asked David.

"This one here, the big pile, if you don't mind, sir," David said respectfully, pointing at the offending mountain of boots, and pleased that he hadn't had to ask first.

"As you wish," the captain smiled. "Shall we begin?"

"Let's," David nodded and returned the smile.

The men agreed to start with six wagons to ascertain the average number of boots per cart, and so, methodically, one by one, the vehicles were loaded with a variety of boots from the first pile. When loaded, the numbers on each cart were not too far different, and so an average was readily agreed upon, enabling the counting to revert from individual boots to individual carts, thereby speeding the process up considerably.

The system of relays David had put in place was working well, and the process was moving at a cracking pace. Harry's role was to concentrate on the count, walking with delegated soldiers between the tables, checking off numbers of loaded carts in the cash books purchased for the occasion. David and Louis split their time between the transfer and loading teams and liaising with Leslie.

It was barely past midday when David called his brother to his side. "Louis," he said quietly, "how long do you think before all six train wagons will be full?"

"At the current rate, probably this time tomorrow."

"That's what I thought. I think Leslie needs more staff; they can't keep up with us. I'll have a chat with him. I'd like to see six wagons loaded in one day."

"Shall I book a locomotive to move the wagons tomorrow afternoon then?" Louis asked.

"No, let's take a chance and book it for tomorrow morning, say ten o'clock."

"Right-oh," Louis agreed and leapt onto his cycle, pushing off urgently for the railway office.

David strode over to where Leslie stood, directing his crew as they gingerly picked through the boots. A significant part of the pile had been removed, but from a distance, nothing seemed to have changed much.

"Leslie," David edged up to his young friend, "I'm a bit concerned you don't have enough staff. It seems we are ahead of you."

"All is well," Leslie assured David. "Captain Cloete is mightily impressed with what you are doing over there; he told me so," Leslie quickly placed a finger to his lips to indicate it was a secret. "He has assigned one of his staff to send me more men, because he wants to double the size of my team. We can't have civilians outperforming the military, can we?" he winked.

"Excellent," David beamed, "thank you. It's going well, don't you think?"

"Very well," Leslie agreed wholeheartedly, "a lot better than any of us expected."

"Good show. Well, let's see how we progress after your team increases. We might struggle to keep up once your extra men arrive."

It took almost three weeks to level the mountain of offensive leather and rubber footwear. The relays were working admirably, and when the first mountain of boots was nearly depleted, Harry took a bucket of water and a broom and washed some of his coloured chalk lines away, only to apply others towards a second train of carriages waiting behind the first lot.

When he saw that one of Leslie's teams had begun to tackle the second pile, he guided them to specific desks to ensure that the correct pile might be directed to the proper wagons. These smaller piles, they had correctly noticed, had not been previously sorted, and some good boots were among them. The entire first mountain had been moved to the disposal area and dumped, but now they had arrived at a point where they might salvage some of their losses.

These carts were directed to the second lot of carriages that were being sent to the farm, just ten minutes north, where they were hurriedly and unceremoniously dumped on the side of the tracks. This part of the exercise was messy and uncoordinated. There was no format or system involved in emptying the carriages, the aim was just to throw the footwear out onto the ground as quickly as possible to allow the train to be taken back to the harbour with as little delay as possible.

After a load of boots had been sent to the farm, David, Louis, and Nguni went along with a small team of men and immersed themselves in the haphazard and frantic exercise, returning to the harbour puffed and exhausted, but still managing a smile and a laugh between them. Back at the farm, the womenfolk would begin hunting for good pairs of boots amongst the mess.

"It's like panning for gold," Harry whispered to David one afternoon.

"How so?" David asked, curiously.

"Well, you scrape away the earth at the top until you get to where you think there may be flecks of gold, and then you start panning. That first pile of boots resembled the dirt at the top, now we are into the gold-rich soil. We have no idea what we will find, but we do know there is gold in there somewhere."

David laughed aloud, "Abe Kaufman would enjoy that analogy. Yes, you are right, that pile there is our gold-bearing pile. Let's just hope we find enough gold to pay the price of all this soil."

Harry laughed at his brother. "Any idea how many usable boots we need to break even?"

"It's complicated to work that out," David replied, some concern in his voice. "You see, it depends not only upon how many good boots we get but also what someone might pay for them. That is, of course, if there is a market for them at all."

Harry scratched his head, "I think there will be," he said, "and I think that Morris might have done the right thing, but was played false."

"Well, that's a good lesson for us all; don't deal with government contracts, too much can go wrong," David remarked. "Now it's up to us to find a way to make it work. We will, I am sure of that. Don't forget, we still have our secret plan to initiate."

"If it will work," Harry said, doubt etched in his voice. "When will you trigger your plan?"

David cast his eye over the remaining mess of scattered boots and then looked over at the trains where Nguni was sharing a joke with one of his men. "Tomorrow afternoon, that should do it."

"I want to be here when you make your announcement," Harry grinned mischievously.

"Sure thing," David flashed a broad smile. "When you see me untuck the back of my shirt, you get busy with that red chalk you've been saving. Then you and Louis come over and join me. Let Louis know. Then let's hold thumbs."

"Right-oh," Harry smiled and pulled a stick of red chalk from his pocket, flashing it at David, before replacing it. "I'm ready."

The following day, a refreshingly cool Wednesday afternoon, the last of the boots were being gathered by Leslie's men. David estimated that barely ten donkey carts worth of boots remained in the dwindling pile. While off to his left, Captain Cloete was busy talking to Private Hopkins and going through some paperwork on a clipboard, David reached behind and untucked his shirt to hang creased and crumpled below the seat of his trousers.

Having waited for this signal, Harry edged closer to the counting tables. Reaching down, he placed the tip of his red chalk stick on the cement platform and started drawing a long line to three coaches that had been coupled together. They had been standing separately from the others for the entire morning, unnoticed, and of no interest to anyone.

As Harry ambled back to David, Louis, who had also been watching eagerly for David's signal, strolled over to the harbour master, who was milling about near a ship that had arrived earlier that morning.

"Good afternoon, sir," Louis greeted the harbour master, "looks like you will be well rid of us soon and you will have your harbour back."

"Yes, indeed," the man replied. "I have been watching you lads, and you have done a sterling job. Heaven knows what you are going to do with that lot," he thrust a dismissive wave in the direction of what was left of the once objectionable piles.

Louis feigned a sigh. "I have no idea either," he replied, "but we will make of it what we must. I do thank you for your understanding and support while we have been here."

"No problem at all." The harbour man lowered his voice, and half covered his mouth with the back of his hand, "I must say, I'd rather have you lads as tenants than the military. They can be a difficult bunch to deal with."

Louis chuckled. "Well, we hope not to be in your hair for too much longer."

While Louis was talking to the harbour master, David and Harry strode over towards Cloete and Hopkins.

"All set?" David murmured to Harry.

"Yup," Harry said casually. "Good luck, Brother."

The two Langbournes approached Captain Cloete with a warm smile.

"Greetings, Messrs Langbourne," the captain welcomed David and Harry. "It appears to have been a very successful exercise. I thought we would be here at least another week or two."

"Indeed," David smiled broadly, "and I must thank you for your help, what with doubling your workforce to help Private Hopkins."

"Well, to be frank, I didn't expect you to be so organised and to work at such a brisk pace."

"Thank you, sir," David accepted the compliment.

"It could be all done by this evening, then we just have to agree on the numbers…"

"Oh," David, cut the captain off, "I am sure we will need another two days at least. Friday, I believe, on Friday we should all be done." He quickly tucked the back of his shirt into his trousers, the signal for Louis to bring the harbour master over to them.

"But there are barely scraps remaining," the captain gazed over David's shoulder at the remnants of old boots.

"With respect, Captain Cloete," David said, "we still need to empty that warehouse over there. I estimate another two days at least."

"What?" the captain exclaimed and looked back at the warehouse with all the reusable boots. "Oh no, those are ours."

"My understanding is that they are part of the agreement."

"That's what I thought," Harry quickly backed up his brother, looking somewhat surprised.

"No, that's … uhh…" Cloete quickly flipped through his clipboard.

"It's in the contract," David continued, keeping up the momentum. "It says all second-hand boots on the wharf are for our account. I'm sure it says that."

"Well, yes, it does, but…" Cloete stammered, still flipping through his paperwork.

Just then Louis and the harbour master arrived with the group.

"Afternoon, Gentlemen," the harbour master's loud voice caught everyone by surprise.

"Afternoon, sir," David shifted his attention away from the captain.

"Lovely day today, isn't it?"

"Yes, absolutely. You have given me my harbour back," he laughed from the pit of his stomach, "and removed that awful stench!"

Captain Cloete grimaced at the official, then returned to his paperwork. He found the elusive contract and ran his fingers through the text.

Cloete turned to David. "It says that all second-hand boots on the wharf are for your account, I must agree, but those boots are in a warehouse, not on the wharf."

"My understanding is that the warehouse is on the wharf," David looked at the captain, then quickly looked the harbour master in the eye. "In your opinion, is that warehouse part of the wharf?"

"Of course. Absolutely!" the harbour master boomed. "The lease for the building is held by the Authority."

"Yes, that is correct," Cloete sounded a little uncertain and returned to the contract to buy some time while he tried to make sense of it all.

"In fact," the harbour master puffed his chest out authoritatively, "the moment you leave this wharf, your lease expires. These gentlemen have signed the next lease, which includes that building, and they have paid a month's deposit for it already."

Captain Cloete looked at the harbour master with a perplexed frown. "We have just sorted the better quality boots into that warehouse."

"It was very kind of you to do that," David smiled. "We are very grateful, but our understanding is that everything on the wharf is for us."

Just then Private Hopkins reached over and tilted the clipboard slightly to read the relevant clause. "It does say that," he agreed, and looked at his superior.

"I cannot deny that," Cloete said weakly as he began to realise he had been outmanoeuvred on a technicality. He suddenly realised that very possibly the boots did, in fact, belong to the Langbournes. Even the harbour master concurred.

The group of people stared at Captain Cloete expectantly, as David pushed the point home. "To be honest," David frowned, "so convinced were we that the boots in the warehouse were part of the contract that we ordered three extra train carriages, over there," he pointed to the waiting wagons, "and you will note we have already drawn red route markings to them."

Everyone in the gathering silently tracked the red chalk lines all the way from the carriages to the warehouse.

"Perhaps I..." Cloete began.

"An elementary misunderstanding," David cut him off, almost apologetically. "I've made worse mistakes in my life."

"What about the time you...?" Louis said suddenly.

"Oh, don't remind me ... what a mess!" David chuckled and waved his hands in the air.

"Or my disaster with Miss Ablett," Harry added.

The brothers made fun of themselves, taking the spotlight off Captain Cloete. It worked, and the moment the subject returned to the warehouse, Cloete admitted that he may have misunderstood the agreement. It all seemed in order, and the boots in the warehouse technically belonged to the Langbournes. He was a little frustrated that they had wasted so much time sorting the boots out when it had not been necessary, but David's very grateful thanks for what he had done eased his mind. David made it known that Cloete's error would never be spoken of. In any case, it was not for nought.

He thanked the captain and Private Hopkins profusely for all their help, although perhaps mistakenly, in assisting them in their ridiculous folly. The handshakes that followed all round left David in no doubt that all parties concerned would conclude the deal on excellent terms. He felt good inside.

Two days later, on a quiet Friday afternoon, a large black steam locomotive reversed up to three wagons and shunted noisily against the couplings. Three squiggly red chalk lines ran off from the wagon's sliding doors into the wharf area, seemingly leading nowhere. A lone young man stood beside the carriages, thumbs hooked in his suspenders.

"Good afternoon, sir," the train driver called down to Harry.

"Good afternoon to you, sir," Harry returned the greeting.

"These are yours?" he questioned.

"Correct," Harry shouted through the hiss of the steam.

"Essexvale, in Rhodesia?"

"Yes, thank you, about twenty miles before you get to Bulawayo. You can't miss it," Harry added, somewhat sarcastically.

The driver laughed. "I know the place."

"There'll be a tall, lanky man at the siding waiting for you. Kaufman is his name. Scruffy looking bloke."

"Right-oh," the driver chuckled and waved a pseudo salute at Harry in acknowledgement.

Ducking his head back into the cabin of the massive steam engine, the driver pulled some levers, twisted some dials, and the locomotive gushed steam angrily from many hidden orifices. The wheels spun momentarily, creating some forward motion, and then just as suddenly, the deafening noise abated.

The driver's head popped out of the engine window as he smiled down at Harry. "Cheerio!" he waved.

CHAPTER TWENTY

London – September 1903

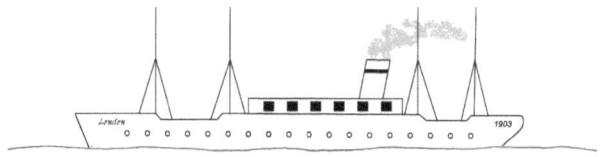

Morris was enjoying his steak, the gravy was rich and full of flavour – just the way he liked it. At the London Chamber of Commerce that day, the room was filled with the loud chatter of businessmen, exchanging views, or just enjoying the company of like-minded gentlemen. The cutlery sparkled on the pure white tablecloths, while the atmosphere was fast becoming thick from the smoke of fine cigars.

His thoughts were interrupted by his friend and mentor, Yoni Goldberg. "Morris?" he demanded, "You are not listening to me."

"I beg your pardon, I was lost in thought," Morris murmured.

Sitting across from him next to Yoni Goldberg was his father-in-law, Lionel Friedlander. The three were in the habit of meeting once a fortnight to exchange news, to discuss business and political trends, and to consider opportunities that might have arisen since their previous meeting.

"I asked if all was well with David," Yoni repeated.

"Oh, yes, perfect thank you. David and Hanna had a son two weeks ago in Bulawayo. A healthy boy, Ernest, they have decided to call him."

"Mazel tov!" Lionel exclaimed. "The Langbourne family is growing, and you too, Morris, will be a father in a few months."

"And you a grandfather," Morris was quick to wink at Lionel in jest.

"And your other brothers, Morris, how are they?" Yoni continued, his natural concern lacing his question.

"Very well, thank you," Morris replied amiably. "Louis is managing the South African branches – Cape Town, Port Elizabeth, East London, and Kimberley, not forgetting Johannesburg, of course – and sales are increasing continually. Harry has comfortably established the business in Bulawayo and is currently developing the business in Salisbury, a very progressive town. Unfortunately, David's movements are somewhat curtailed because of the birth of his son. He has also been very involved in sorting out the military boots that I bought. That debacle cost me £25,000 before expenses and almost crippled my family and me. Do you know that Lord Cunningham ordered boots to be retrieved from a dump and then added to my lot? The nerve of it!"

Yoni and Lionel exchanged knowing glances. They had heard through Rose Bertha, who was corresponding regularly with Hanna, that David's life had become entirely consumed with dampening the after-effects of Morris' folly with the boot saga. To top it off, local Bulawayo business and social circles were laughing heartily at the Langbourne brothers' latest venture. The Boer War had just ended, and there was not a hint of another war on the horizon. It seemed, to the Bulawayo business community at least, that the Langbournes were stuck with a lot of useless goods and no market.

"It's been a mammoth job for David," Morris continued. "He has had to sort the good boots into sizes, of which there obviously are several, and then by colour, since there were various shades of brown and black in the mix. After that, they needed to be paired into matching left and right boots. If that wasn't bad enough, David then had to lace them and tie the shoelaces together. Some didn't have shoelaces, so they needed laces which were cannibalised from reject boots.

"We had to employ a team of Matabele men, and that added to the cost. Nevertheless, after a quick wash to get any mud off – hey presto! David completed the job last week. My brothers, bless their hearts, salvaged a terrible situation into something we can deal with. Of the six million boots

I had to pay for, we have half a million pairs I can sell."

"You have half a million pairs of army boots hidden in the Rhodesian bush somewhere?" Yoni was not sure whether he should be bemused or horrified.

"On a friend's farm. A very good friend. We are not paying any storage fees, thank heavens."

"Who on earth are you going to sell them to, Morris?" Friedlander asked in amazement,

"There'll be another war one day."

Lionel stole a critical eye at Yoni. "A war that may not include the British. Your options are limited, Morris. I must be candid; many of us think you have been taken for a complete fool by this… this Lord Cunningham."

Morris smiled sweetly in a reaction that surprised his companions. "Perhaps I have, but when I find my buyer, we will see who gets the last laugh."

Just before Rose Bertha was due to give birth, Morris invited David and his family to England, so that Rose Bertha would have a special friend with whom she could share the exciting occasion. Hanna having jumped at the opportunity to visit, the voyage was hastily planned. Morris, of course, had ulterior reasons for inviting David; he wanted David to travel to a country called Romania, where he had heard of many exciting buying opportunities for their type of business.

"What's amusing you, my love?" Hanna asked David as they docked in Southampton.

"Nothing," he said innocently. "How are you feeling?"

"Oh, all right, I suppose. Perhaps a little tired and slightly queasy from the waves last night."

David's grin turned to a chuckle.

"What is it with you?" Hanna demanded, starting to chuckle with him, then waved a warning finger at David. "No!" she exclaimed.

David began laughing. "Every time, without fail, when you get off a ship you are pregnant."

"Not this time!" Hanna scolded David, but she was laughing just as hard as he.

She already knew that David was right.

CHAPTER TWENTY-ONE
Johannesburg - March 1904

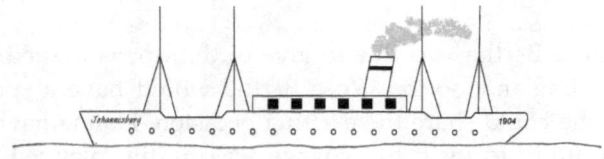

David and Hanna, along with their two children, arrived back in Africa after five months abroad. While in England Hanna had immersed herself in matrimonial duties with Rose Bertha, who had given birth to a bouncing baby boy they named Cecil. Hanna's time with Rose Bertha strengthened their sister-like bond, so much so that the parting after the extended stay in England was particularly painful for the two women.

David had spent much of his time in Romania and Paris, forging new contacts for the family business, signing business deals, negotiating prices, and expanding the geographic range of suppliers for their company. For David, boarding the ship home had come as something of a relief. He couldn't wait for the peace and quiet of the cruise and the return to a simpler African lifestyle and the familiar surrounds that were now so much a part of him. He had received the distinct impression that – because he had been so successful – Morris wanted him to continue with his international ventures. David's suggestion of sending Harry or Louis on such buying trips had not seemed to have been welcomed by Morris, who had felt that they were a steadying influence in their current spheres of operation. Morris had finally agreed that the two younger brothers could begin travelling once their businesses had stabilised.

David didn't mind the travel or the challenges of new countries, cultures, and languages, but he missed Hanna on these excursions, and had therefore decided to ask Morris if she could accompany him on the next mission. All indications were that David would have to return to London before their third child was born, which meant a very short visit to Rhodesia. It became clear to both Hanna and himself that his responsibilities in the family business were evolving into that of an international buyer, and therefore the international face of the rapidly expanding Langbourne Brothers.

Checking into a new and rather prestigious hotel in the heart of Johannesburg, David sent a messenger with a letter to Louis, and another to Danie Coetzee, inviting them to dine at seven o'clock that evening. Hanna was not feeling well so had excused herself from the reunion.

Louis arrived punctually at seven and Danie barely one minute later. David was welcomed back by the men, and the usual, pleasant exchanges about health and well-being ensued.

"Harry got in from Bulawayo this afternoon," Louis quickly updated his brother. "I have sent him a message to meet us here, but he will be running about half an hour late."

"Excellent," David enthused, "perfect timing. So that I don't repeat myself, I won't tell you about my news until he arrives."

"I can tell you," Danie said, as they took a seat at a table for four, "that your accounts are looking very strong. Louis is doing a tremendous job here."

"That is wonderful news. Good work, Brother," David congratulated his sibling before hailing a waiter. "What would you like to drink?"

The conversation then ebbed and flowed until Harry arrived in a very smart pin-striped evening suit. The reunions were again felicitous, and David could see a distinct change in Harry's features. He had lost some weight, and his facial lines were sharper.

"Tell me about Bulawayo and Salisbury," David invited Harry. "How's business?"

"It's all right. Our man in Salisbury, Robert Shepherd, is doing a marvellous job. He is really getting out into the farmlands and making the sales. Bulawayo is a little tougher; we are still somewhat regarded as the laughing stock of the community. I doubt we will ever get over this boot thing. How was Romania?"

"Romania was interesting, that I cannot deny. I have made some unusual purchases which you should see in about four months from now. Morris sends his best, by the way."

"That reminds me," Harry reached for his inside jacket pocket and passed David a sealed telegram. "This arrived yesterday at the Bulawayo office. It's for you."

David took the envelope and could immediately tell it was from Morris. "Why didn't you open it?" David asked as he tore at the envelope.

"It's for you," Harry repeated, "and I knew I would be seeing you today so I brought it along with me."

"Thanks," David frowned as he read the small folded telegram. His eyebrows suddenly arched high on his brow.

Louis looked at Harry, who merely shrugged back.

"What is it?" Louis asked impatiently.

David placed the telegram on the table face down and looked at the three men around the table, confusion written all over his face.

"What?" Harry was now very curious.

David lifted the telegram and re-read it, then peered at his brothers over the discoloured paper.

"Well, I never ..." David smiled. "You won't believe this. Morris says the Empire of Japan has declared war on the Russian Empire."

"Yes, I heard that," Danie said. "They say the Japanese attacked just hours before they declared war. The commentary is that it was unfair to do it that way. It is accepted, and expected, that one declares war first, then attacks. I believe they are calling it the Russo-Japanese War; there was an article in the paper about it earlier this week."

A sudden hush descended upon the Langbourne table as Louis, Harry and David exchanged glances.

Danie shrugged. "What am I missing?"

"I think I will read this message to you," David looked at the telegram again and took a deep breath. "Japan attacked Russia Stop. All our footwear purchased by Russian Government Stop. Sale price L pounds R shillings per pair Stop. Shipping instructions to follow Stop. Get cracking

Stop. Lion"."

Another deathly hush ensued.

"L pounds R shillings per pair?" Louis hissed, he could barely find his voice.

"You are joking," Harry said slowly and deliberately. "You are joking, aren't you?"

"What does that mean? Tell me!" Danie's eyes were dancing between the three brothers who looked somewhat stunned.

"Morris sold half a million pairs of second-hand boots to the Russian army for two pounds, six shillings a pair," David said as he re-read the telegram.

Harry leant forward and lowered his voice. "Correct me if I'm wrong, but I believe that should equate to over one million pounds sterling. Could that be right?"

"You tell us, Danie," David glanced at his accountant, who was now looking just as stunned as the brothers. "Kindly multiply that by half a million for us."

"I have to work this out," Danie sounded vague for a moment, as he pulled a fountain pen and notepad from his jacket pocket. He scribbled a bit, crossed some numbers out, added more, and then leant back in his chair, pausing before answering. "Yes," Danie frowned, "it is over one million pounds. One million, one hundred and fifty thousand pounds, to be exact."

A silent pause descended once again as all eyes were transfixed on Danie.

Louis broke the silence to state the obvious. "That's a lot of money," he breathed.

"I'll put that in perspective for you, Gentlemen," Danie said as he returned his notepad and pen to his pocket. "Yesterday, Louis complained to me that he had had to postpone the building of his home in Bulawayo because he didn't have the funds to pay for it. How much did you say it would cost to build your home?" Danie looked over at Louis.

"Just over £2,000," Louis said, still appearing in a state of mild shock.

"I dare say you could build a small suburb with this amount of money," Danie frowned. "Or maybe even a couple of ships," he added.

Everyone at the table fell quiet once again, as the enormity of the deal descended on the young men.

David suddenly broke the silence. "We have to deal with this immediately," he declared. "When can we depart for Bulawayo?"

"I only arrived this afternoon, but I will go back on the morning train," Harry said.

"Good. You need to organise rail wagons and attend to the usual paperwork to ship the goods out of Rhodesia."

"I am available immediately," Louis confirmed.

"Excellent," David nodded his thanks at Louis. "I need you to go to Cape Town right away and start negotiations with a shipping company. I'll telegram the details to you as soon as Morris sends them."

"I'll leave in the morning," Louis readily agreed, "What about you?"

"Hanna and I will join Harry. I must stop in Essexvale and ask Abe Kaufman to help with gathering a team of men to load a train. I know he would relish helping out."

Danie broke into the intense discussion. "You do know that you will have to tell your good wife that her week-long shopping holiday in Johannesburg will suddenly be reduced to a one-night stopover?"

David frowned mischievously. "That," he stated, "is not going to be well received," he grinned but made a mental note to excuse himself before the meal arrived to tell Hanna not to unpack her bags.

"So much for what the Bulawayo business community thinks now," Harry smirked.

"They don't need to know anything," David suggested. "Let it pass, and the saga will be forgotten in time."

"I agree," Danie said after a brief pause. "I must add, however, that – despite the pressures and demands that your brother creates for you – I have never seen such loyalty and teamwork within a family. I believe that these are the attributes that have made you all so successful."

David had to smile at Danie's comment. While he knew that the loyalty given to the family by his brothers was absolute, he also spared a thought for Nguni and Daluxolo. The dedication and friendship that these amaXhosa brothers had willingly given to his family in tough times had, without doubt, enabled them to reach the position they had achieved to this day. David waved to the Maître d', who swiftly bustled over towards him.

"How may I help you, sir?"

"Please provide us with a bottle of your finest Bordeaux."

The Maître d' smiled broadly, hurried off, and returned moments later with a large bottle of red. The table sat in silence as David nodded his approval, and the man opened the bottle with a small pop, signalling the releasing of the cork.

A little sample of red splashed the bottom of David's glass, and, after savouring the colour, aroma, and flavour, he gave the internationally recognised signal of approval; an intense frown, a curt nod, followed by a pleased smile. The other glasses were filled, then David's was finally topped up to a point, two-thirds above the base.

David raised his glass, the others followed suit, and he cleared his throat.

"I want to recognise Nguni and Daluxolo, for without them we would not be here today. And of course, I acknowledge our brother. Morris can be a hard taskmaster, but we cannot deny that he is a visionary," David beamed. "Gentlemen, I salute Nguni and Daluxolo, and our brother, Morris Langbourne."

TO BE CONCLUDED...

ACKNOWLEDGEMENTS

I am deeply grateful to Robert Landau (Switzerland) for his generosity and encouragement in the publication of this book, and for his recollections and information of his grandfather that have been integral to my research.

My sincere thanks, as always, to my mentor and first editor, Cindy Kramer, whose guidance I find invaluable. Of course, Mike Kantey, my final editor, whose experience in the literary world, and of southern African war, politics and culture, is a source of much-needed reassurance.

I give special recognition and thanks to my Audiobook team, Adrian Galley, who's magical voice narrated the series, and Devon Martindale of AudioShelf, who brought this production to life. I would be totally lost without these two remarkable gentlemen.

I extend my grateful thanks to my global proofreading team, Snow Tunks (Aus), Martin Robinson (Aus), Ashley Wilkinson (SA) Melissa Muller (SA), and Sue Arkell (Zim), and my book designers, Scarlet Rugers and Charlene Berzuela at The Book Design House.

Sadly, Barbara Harmel, a fascinating and kindly lady, who helped me 'join the dots' on some of the stories within this series, passed away before I could finish writing this book. I am grateful for the three short years I knew her. She will be sorely missed.

A very special thanks to Ian and Bridget Fraser (UK) for their friendship, hospitality, inspiration and belief in my writing. Their efforts to promote my series in the UK has been quite overwhelming. They are indeed special friends, and truly wonderful people.

Of course, to Sharon, my loving wife, thanks for putting up with the countless hours that I sit glued to my computer, wholly immersed in a world that vividly unfolded around me 120 years in the past.

As always, I thank you, my readers, for your support and encouragement. It has been truly humbling.

RESEARCH MATERIAL

Books and material consulted in the research the Langbourne Series:
(Listed by date of publication.)

Rhodesia Past and Present - SJ Du Toit (1897)
Three Years in Savage Africa - Lionel Decel (1898)
'96 Rebellions - BSAC Reports (1898)
On the South African Frontier - William Harvey Brown (1899)
Sketches in Mafeking and East Africa - RSS Baden-Powell (1907)
Jock of the Bushveld - P Fitzpatrick (1907)
Southern Rhodesia - Fergus W Ferguson (1909) (Rare Book)
Old Rhodesian Days - Hugh Marshal Hole (1928)
Commando - Deneys Reitz (1929)
The Monuments of Southern Rhodesia - RJ Fothergill (1953)
The Thirteenth Child - Vita P Ablett (c.1958)
The White Whirlwind - TV Bulpin (1961)
Encyclopaedia Rhodesia - The College Press (1973)
A Guide to the Rock Art of Rhodesia - CK Cooke (1974)
Rhodesia Before 1920 - National Gallery of Rhodesia &
National Historical Association of Rhodesia (c.1975)
The Boer War - *Thomas Pakenham* (1979)
Running the Gauntlet - *George Mossop* (1990) (1930)
It's Been a Wonderful Life - Marvin C Arthur (2005)
Girl in a Blue Bonnet - Dot Scott (2007)
Empire War and Cricket in South Africa - Dean Allen
(2015) Zebra Press

And

Records, journals, documents, letters, interviews and photos of the
descendants of the Landau Family

ABOUT THE AUTHOR

Alan Landau was born in Salisbury, Rhodesia (now Harare, Zimbabwe) in 1959. In 1978 he joined the British South Africa Police (formally the BSAC). At that time Rhodesia was entangled in a civil war that ended in 1980. After serving in the new Zimbabwe Republic Police for a short time, Alan retired to enter the commercial world.

Alan worked in Zimbabwe's widely known tobacco industry for five years before joining his father and ultimately taking over the family business when his father retired to the UK. Later on, Alan was involved in the travel, tourism, hotel, property, financial, and retail sectors. His service to his community took the form of Rotary International with a committed focus on the Rotary Youth Exchange Program.

Having migrated to Brisbane, Australia, in 2001, Alan bought a franchise in the retail sector, which he successfully ran with his late wife and two children. In 2012 he sold the business and went into semi-retirement. He now pursues his hobbies of writing, travelling, wildlife safaris and ornithology with his wife, Sharon.

More about the author can be found as follows:
Web: www.landaubooks.com
Twitter: @landaubooks
Facebook: www.facebook.com/landaubooks
Instagram: landaubooks

The Langbourne Series

Based on a true story, the Langbourne series follows the lives of four intrepid brothers who journey to Africa in 1891. Without parents, friends, or family, they disembark the ship at Port Elizabeth and set their minds to making enough money to support their destitute family in Ireland. But Mother Africa has ideas of her own.

A Landau Books Publication
www.landaubooks.com

"To Brave Men"

by

Alan P Landau

Based on the true story of the Shangani Patrol, delve into this enthralling narrative as the haunting tale of the ill-fated Shangani Patrol unfurls with gripping intensity.

Embark on a journey alongside the audacious Fred Burnham, whose adventurous spirit knows no bounds.

Meet Major Allan Wilson, a valiant officer navigating the harrowing perils of war with unwavering courage.

Discover King Lobengula, a complex figure embodying both ruthless tyranny and diplomatic finesse, leaving an indelible mark on his people.

Witness the loyalty of Mjaan, Lobengula's steadfast Induna, tested to his limits.

Set in 1893, against the backdrop of a war-torn southern African landscape, the remarkable bravery of these men echoes through time, reshaping the course of history. Immerse yourself in a world of bravery, sacrifice, and unbreakable human resolve in this captivating and unforgettable tale.

"Of Sand and Stars"
by
Brenda Kate

In the vast Australian outback, FBI agent Mandy Richardson and an enigmatic Australian astronomer kindle a forbidden romance while unravelling a sinister plot. Their combined knowledge uncovers a scheme for mass destruction, forcing them to navigate dangers and reconcile loyalties. Racing against time and torn between duty and desire, they must conquer ruthless adversaries and protect humanity. Prepare for a thrilling journey where love defies rules and survival hangs in the balance.

Another Landau Books Publication
www.landaubooks.com

www.ingramcontent.com/pod-product-compliance
Lightning Source LLC
Chambersburg PA
CBHW021422110726
47901CB00008B/2267